Her Irresistible Charmer

The Worthington Legacy
Book Four

Marie Higgins

ARE YOU SIGNED UP FOR DRAGONBLADE'S BLOG?

You'll get the latest news and information on exclusive giveaways, exclusive excerpts, coming releases, sales, free books, cover reveals and more.

Check out our complete list of authors, too!

No spam, no junk. That's a promise!

Sign Up Here

www.dragonbladepublishing.com

Dearest Reader;

Thank you for your support of a small press. At Dragonblade Publishing, we strive to bring you the highest quality Historical Romance from some of the best authors in the business. Without your support, there is no 'us', so we sincerely hope you adore these stories and find some new favorite authors along the way.

Happy Reading!

CEO, Dragonblade Publishing

Additional Dragonblade books by Author Marie Higgins

The Worthington Legacy
Her Perfect Scoundrel (Book 1)
Her Dreamy Deceiver (Book 2)
Her Adorable Cad (Book 3)
Her Irresistible Charmer (Book 4)

Love's Addiction Series
A Wallflower to Love (Book 1)
A Governess to Protect (Book 2)
A Maiden to Remember (Book 3)

Camilla Hardy needs money for her twin sister's burial, so she travels to meet her rotten brother-in-law to have him pay for his wife's medical bills. It surprises her that he isn't the monster her sister told her about. However, he still might be doing illegal business that will get him arrested, and she is determined to find fault. If only he wasn't so irresistibly charming, perhaps she wouldn't want to get to know him better. Perhaps pretending to be her twin sister isn't as bad as it seems...

Malcolm Worthington is determined to find the person stealing his drawings for his business, and he can't trust anyone—especially not his wife. But she is different since she returned from visiting her sick sister, and he doesn't know why he suddenly feels attracted to her when he hasn't felt that way since they were married. Dare he give in to temptation and reach for the love he has always wanted?

Prologue

HER TWIN SISTER had gone mad.

Camilla Hardy stood on the steps of Blackwood Asylum, unanswered questions pounding in her head. *Periodic dementia... unresolved melancholy,* the physician had written. It had to be a mistake.

Loathing the long wait for assistance, Camilla shivered. Her cloak offered paltry protection against the wind. The moon's pale light shone on the dull mahogany entryway. Shadows lurked all around and forced her to huddle closer to the scarred door. An owl's hoot echoed through the nearby forest. The disconcerting sound grated on her already frazzled nerves.

Camilla knocked on the door, not once, but three times. Still, no one answered. An abominable sting throbbed in her knuckles, and she rubbed the ache. She glared at the double doors' warped planks and rusted hinges. Craning her neck, she peered down the side of the building.

Perhaps there was another entrance. Obviously, nobody cared to receive visitors at this one. Before she could move off the step, the old door squeaked open. A stooped man peeked around the thick wood. He held up a lantern, and the mellow light illuminated the deep creases in his face.

"May I be of some assistance?" he asked in a scratchy voice.

She bundled her cloak around her throat and stepped closer.

"I am Lady Hardy. I received a letter from Dr. Smythe concerning my sister, Katherine Worthington. Is the good physician here?"

The elderly man squinted. "I am Smythe. I sent the letter."

She raised her brows. "Where is your caretaker, sir?"

"We have but a small staff, my lady. Everyone does what they can." He opened the door wider. "Please, follow me. I shall take you to your sister."

Camilla stepped into the dark corridor and lowered the hood of her cape. The stench of unwashed bodies and urine filled her nostrils, curdling her stomach. She fished through her wrist-purse and pulled out her handkerchief, quickly pressing the rose-scented cloth to her nose. In haste, she hurried her gait to catch up to the physician, and followed him down the shadowed hall.

Each room she passed had bars on the small windows of the doors. People stood behind them, watching her with wide, glassy eyes, as though they looked right through her. Chills trickled down her spine. Were these patients dangerous? And why, pray tell, was her sister here?

Answers. She needed them soon or she would be the one going insane.

"Excuse me, sir. How long has my sister been here?" she asked, lowering the handkerchief.

"For a fortnight."

"Then why was I not informed sooner?"

"Because it took her this long to start talking."

Worry clenched Camilla's heart. What on earth had happened to Kat?

The elderly man stopped in front of a door and withdrew a heavy set of iron keys fastened to his waist. He inserted the key and turned it with a loud click.

"Is a locked door necessary for my sister?" She spoke in soft tones, afraid her voice would carry through the halls.

The stern expression on the man's face never wavered. His white, bushy brows pulled together in concern. "Aye."

"May I ask why?"

"She is not well, Lady Hardy. Locking the door is for her safety."

Camilla's heart sank, and she frowned. Could her sister be ailing as their father had? *No, certainly not.* Kat had never been ill a day in her life. Signs would have shown if her twin suffered the same malady as their father. The physician must be speaking of a different person altogether.

He pushed the door open, wide enough for her to enter. Camilla straightened and took the lantern from his outstretched hand. With her chin held high, she proceeded into the room. Now was not the time to appear frightened, even if her heart hammered so fast, she feared it would bruise a rib or two.

Through the barred window, the quarter moon's silver light cast shadows about the room. The only piece of furniture was a bed with a threadbare mattress. One worn brown blanket covered the feet of the figure on the bed curled on her side, staring toward the door.

Camilla's heart wrenched at the sight of her sibling. It had been two years since Kat entered into a quick marriage to a man she had barely met. Camilla wanted to attend the marriage ceremony and meet her new brother-in-law, but she had been in Scotland visiting her in-laws during that time, sharing their grief after the death of her husband.

The person Camilla remembered while growing up looked nothing like the woman in this room. Matted light brown hair framed the woman's face in wild disarray, and the gray of the hospital gown erased all color from her complexion. Dull eyes, drooped to half-mast, slowly lifted and met Camilla's gaze.

"I will be right outside if you need me," the physician said before leaving.

The door slammed shut and Camilla jumped. Forcing a smile, she lifted a hand to her chest to calm herself. "Oh, Kat, I came as soon as I heard you were here."

Kat scooted on the bed, pulled her legs up, and rested her chin on her knees. "Thank you for coming. I didn't think Lord

Hardy would allow you to leave."

Camilla stepped into the room, closer to the bed. "Kat, Fredrick died a month before you married Mr. Worthington. Do you not remember?"

Kat's forehead creased as she stared at a spot on the bed. "Oh, yes. I remember now."

"Kat, what has happened to you?"

She tilted her head, and her gaze touched the wall behind Camilla as if she struggled to see. "I could not take any more torment, so I left."

"Torment? From whom?"

"From my cursed husband." She clenched both fists as if ready to strike something.

Camilla lowered the lantern to the floor and rushed to the bed, clasping her sister's hands. "Please tell me what he did to you."

Kat finally turned her stare onto Camilla. "All he wanted from me was a woman to do his bidding. He only wanted a mother to care for his children—not a wife to love and cherish. He treated me like a mere servant." A tear rolled down her cheek. "Camilla, he beat me when I didn't instantly do his bidding. He mocked me in front of his friends." More tears joined the others streaming down her face. "He didn't care if his children disobeyed me. I couldn't control them. He made them hate me."

Camilla's heart twisted and her mind scrambled for something encouraging to say. She realized she should have come straight home after her husband died instead of visiting his family in Scotland. If Camilla had returned home, perhaps she could have stopped her sister from marrying such an ungodly man.

Gently, she squeezed Kat's frail fingers. "Kat? Why did you come here to Preston? Why didn't you stay in Dorchester?"

Kat's lips curled up into a smile. "A minister who was on his way home to Preston helped me. He took pity on my plight and let me ride with him."

"Why did you come to this kind of institution instead of to

my home?"

"The minister insisted this would be the safest place, Milla."

"But Kat, why would a minister leave you in such a godforsaken place?"

"He says I have melancholy. Dr. Smythe agrees."

Tears filled Camilla's eyes, but she forced herself to take control of her emotions. Her sister didn't belong here, and Camilla would not allow her to stay. She straightened her shoulders. "What do you want me to do? How can I get you out?"

Kat shook her head until her chin limply fell on her chest. She rested her forehead back on her knees. "They will not let me out until I'm well."

"I shall help you any way I can." Camilla lifted her sister's chin and looked into her dazed eyes. "I want you well and away from this horrid place."

"I cannot leave. If I do, I will have to go back to Malcolm." Kat twisted a lock of matted hair around a finger. "Please, Milla, don't make me go back to him. If he discovers I have given him more bills to pay because of my illness, my torture will only worsen." She whined in a childish tone, "I would rather die here than endure the constant pain of being married to that monster."

Camilla touched her sister's hand, stopping her from knotting her hair any further. "I shall get you out of this place. Staying in this hellhole would cause any sane person to be melancholy. And I shall hire the best physician in Preston to care for you."

"Physicians cost money. I should know. The cost of staying here has depleted the small sum I pilfered from Malcolm." Kat's tone was bitter.

Camilla scrambled to think of a solution. She couldn't leave her sister, and yet she couldn't pay for her to stay. "I have a portion saved from when my husband died. I will give that to Dr. Smythe so he doesn't charge your husband."

Her sister pulled away. "Milla, it's not possible. I'm certain you barely have enough to live. I recall Lord Hardy gambled a lot of his money before he died."

Camilla nodded. "That he did, but he made money just as quickly."

"Being an agent for the Crown made him money?"

"Yes. Every time he turned in a spy, the Crown rewarded him greatly."

"So, will you have enough to pay for a good physician?"

"Just barely, but I'll do all I can to get you well. If I don't have enough, I shall obtain more." She lifted her voice in anger. "In fact, I will write your husband and ask—"

"No, Milla, don't bother. Malcolm will not give you anything. Why do you think I have been pilfering money from him? I know he will not give you his precious money. He is wealthy, but he does not enjoy sharing."

"If he does not share with me, I shall have him arrested for… for… something. I will think of a way." Camilla grumbled as resentment laced her words.

"Malcolm arrested? Doubtful that will ever happen. I have suspected he is doing something illegal in regard to his business partners, but I have not been able to prove it." Kat released a dejected sigh. "Saying he will be arrested shall only give me hope for a better life. A life I know I cannot have."

Camilla ran her hand across her twin sister's matted hair again. Anger burned deep inside her that Kat had been reduced to this. If only Fredrick hadn't died, she would have him investigate Malcolm Worthington. Then Kat's life might be better. "If I cannot get the funds from your husband, I will find the money elsewhere."

She waited for her sibling to speak, but Kat stared at the wall again. Camilla waited, wondering what her sister could be thinking, but she gazed into nothingness. Hesitantly, Camilla withdrew her touch. Soon, her twin rocked back and forth as she muttered incoherent words.

"Kat?" Camilla asked with a tight voice. When her sibling didn't answer, tears stung Camilla's eyes and a sob ready to come forth tightened her throat. "Kat, I'm here." She gingerly touched her sister's arm.

Kat jerked to a stop and swung her focus back to Camilla. "Do not worry about me, Milla. But promise me one thing?"

"Anything." Camilla choked on a small sob.

"After I am dead, seek my husband and punish him for making me suffer this existence." Kat lurched forward on the bed, grabbing Camilla's wrists. Dirty fingernails cut painfully into her skin. "Make him suffer as I have suffered in my marriage these past eighteen months."

"You are talking rubbish." Fear gripped Camilla's throat. "You are not going to die. You shall be just fine."

"Please, promise me, Milla."

Sadness shot through her heart, and she nodded, swallowing the lump in her throat. What had that man done to her once-vibrant sister? "I promise."

Kat fell back on the bed in a heap. Mental withdrawal clearly engulfed her, and her blank stare was riveted on the dreary wall. Camilla's chest constricted, making it hard to breathe. She couldn't take any more of this. If she didn't leave this place soon, she would be in a fit of tears herself.

As she stood, she studied her sister's sick form. Once again, anger welled within her chest. Kat hadn't deserved this fate. Camilla vowed she would make Malcolm Worthington pay. He had hurt her sister, which was unforgivable.

Camilla picked up the lantern, turned, and knocked on the cell door. It opened and Dr. Smythe peered inside. "Is everything all right, Lady Hardy?"

"I am ready to leave, if you please."

He closed the door behind her and locked it, then led her to the front of the building. The hall echoed with cries from other patients. She cringed, wanting to cover her ears and run far away. Instead, she remained strong, if only in her appearance.

"Pardon me, sir, but is there any hope for my sister's recovery?"

His lips pursed. "I have seen many in her condition. A few have survived, but most have not. Unfortunately, many take their own lives."

She covered her mouth as a sob escaped her throat.

"I'm not saying the same fate will befall your sister," he continued. "But I believe you should prepare for the worst."

Irritation swept through her again, and she lifted a defiant chin. "I most certainly will not prepare myself for the worst, Dr. Smythe. My sister does not deserve to be in this place. I want Kat moved immediately."

The older man shook his head. "That is impossible."

"Nothing is impossible. My husband had connections before he died, and if I have to find one of his associates, I will. Mark my words, within a fortnight, my sister will be moved to a more stable facility."

Marching past him and into the cool night air, she wrapped her heavy cloak around her, thwarting the chill, though her blood ran hot with volcanic anger. Straight ahead, her coach waited. The only servant left in her employ climbed down from the carriage and opened the door.

"'Ow is yer sister farin', m'lady?"

"She is not well, Timothy." A tear rolled down her already damp cheek, and she wiped away the moisture. "And that place is only making her condition worse."

Timothy sniffed and swiped his sleeve under his nose. "Is she like yer father?"

"No, God rest his soul. Kat is not quite as bad, yet. I shall not let it go to that extreme. If I have to, I shall contact everyone I know who might be of assistance." Determination guided her quick steps as she hastened into the coach. Timothy closed the door behind her.

One way or another, she would obtain the funds needed to move her—and to pay the medical bills. Her own deceased husband had gambled away all of his money before he met his maker, leaving her with very little to live on. She knew firsthand how a husband could torture his wife when not pleased, and she would make certain Mr. Worthington didn't know about this extra expense so he wouldn't punish Kat when she returned home.

Too bad someone couldn't arrest *that man* for his devious lifestyle and free Kat. If only Fredrick was still alive, investigating Malcolm would be his newest pursuit. He'd thrived on the chase.

Rolling her eyes, Camilla ushered the ridiculous thought from her head. She had only been married to Lord Hardy for a few short years, but when he died, there was no grieving on her part. No, her beast of a husband was better off six feet under, in the cold ground.

Unfortunately, with his death, the money stopped as well. If only she could do something to earn a living. If only she could be a good agent like Lord Hardy had been. If only…

Her thoughts skidded to a halt, and she straightened on the leather seat. *Why* can't *I be an agent?* Kat had let it slip about her traitorous husband doing something illegal in regard to his business partners. If Camilla could get enough information on the man to turn him in, surely they would see her value as an agent and enable her to pay for Kat's care.

A mischievous smile tugged at the corners of her mouth. She could do it. She had spied on her husband often enough, and he had never had an inkling of her activities. Confidence grew inside her.

There was only one problem she could foresee. It had never been in her nature to act bold and forward. Could she possibly get the information she needed and force the Crown to listen to her?

Assertiveness had always been a part of Kat's character. Now it was Camilla's turn to be aggressive—and it frightened her nearly to death.

Chapter One

Dorchester, two weeks later

CAMILLA HARDY STEPPED down from the stagecoach, breathing a heavy sigh. The trip had been too long and jostled her around so much that the coiled hair at the base of her neck fell in a disarray of curls. The constant sway of the coach made her feel like she had been on a ship at times, especially when she closed her eyes.

"Lady Hardy? Are ye all right?" Timothy trudged up behind her, pulling her trunk.

"Yes. I will be fine." She surveyed the busy street, pushing strands of hair out of her eyes. "So long as we can find lodging before I am jostled again."

Her servant, a man who was almost as old as her father, straightened and walked in front of her. "Although we've few shillin's left, I'll find a conveyance. Ye stay right 'ere with the trunk. It shouldn't take much time to locate transportation to yer brother-in-law's."

Sweeping the unruly mass of hair over her shoulder, she sat on the trunk and clutched her satchel. She must find lodgings soon. Funds were low, which placed a greater urgency on her plans.

Especially now.

Tears stung her eyes as she reached into the pocket of her cloak and pulled out the letter she had received from Dr. Smythe.

Lady Hardy, I regret to inform you that your sister, Katherine Worthington, died after you left the hospital. She found a knife and cut herself. When I found her, she'd lost so much blood, it was too late to save her. Accept my apologies and my deepest sympathy. I will send you the bill, since your sister didn't have the funds to cover it. Respectfully, Dr. Smythe.

Camilla swiped the tears from her eyes and placed the letter back in her cloak. There hadn't been time—or money—for a proper burial. When Camilla arrived at the hospital, the physician had already placed Katherine in the box and lowered her into the ground. All Camilla could do was utter a prayer and lay a red rose on top of the long wooden box. Not long after that, hatred had fueled her, and she couldn't wait to confront her brother-in-law.

When she imagined meeting Malcolm Worthington for the first time, her heart pounded fiercely, and fear caused her palms to moisten. She hadn't yet written to him to inform him of his wife's demise or about the added expenses of the hospital and burial. But that wasn't foremost on her mind any longer.

Staying in Dorchester, Camilla had planned to watch Mr. Worthington closely and gather as much information as she could in dealing with his traitorous actions toward his business partners. What words would convince him to treat her like family? She must figure out what she would say to him to get close enough to spy on him. If he were the demon Kat had accused him of being, he wasn't going to welcome Camilla into his home with open arms.

Off to the side, a street urchin standing near the apple cart drew her attention. The young lad's gaze darted around the street suspiciously. Dirt streaked his face and tattered clothes, and his hair appeared as if he hadn't combed it—or even washed it—for weeks. When the owner of the cart turned his back on the boy, the lad's hand snaked out, grabbing an apple.

That little thief! She stood as he ran past. Reaching, she tried to grab the imp, but only succeeded in stumbling forward. The owner of the cart swung around and faced her, and his eyes widened the longer he stared.

"Oh, it's you," he accused, pointing his finger.

Panic choked her throat. "No! I didn't take it. It was that little boy."

The man glanced up the street and cupped his hands around his mouth. "Constable, over here."

She shook her head, but the cart owner wouldn't listen. He continued calling for help, pushing aside patrons as he hurried toward her. She couldn't allow them to arrest her.

I must get out of here. Energy pumped into her legs, and she ran as fast as she could. Ahead of her stood a building with hedges planted in the back. If she could get there and hide...

She turned the corner and paused, resting against the wooden frame of the building. Deep breaths heaved from her chest, which burned from lack of air. Cautiously, she peeked to see if anyone had noticed her. They were still running after her, calling for her to stop.

Clutching her cumbersome skirt, she scurried toward the end of the building and ducked behind the far corner. Another street opened before her, and spectators gawked at the commotion she created. She continued until another alleyway loomed ahead.

As she glanced over her shoulder, she breathed a heavy sigh that the men following were farther behind. But within seconds, more had joined the chase.

She turned another corner and ran into a solid form. A scream tore from her throat as she grasped his arms to keep from falling. Two strong arms circled her waist. She looked up into the face of a soldier wearing a red coat.

"My, my." He grinned, tightening his arms around her. "What lovely package do I have here?"

Instead of being relieved to see a soldier, she worried he would think she stole the apple just as the others did. "Please, sir, release me at once." She squirmed, but to no avail.

"'Tis all right, my dear. I shall protect you." He winked. "Have I not always been your champion?"

His words confused her, but she didn't have time for his explanation. "Please, if you would be so kind. I must get away." The shouts of pursuing men grew louder. "You do not understand. I cannot be caught. I fear they will put me in jail for a crime I did not commit."

The soldier raised a dark eyebrow. "What stories are you telling now, Mrs. Worthington?"

She gasped and stared at the man holding her. *Mrs. Worthington?* He thought she was her sister? But of course he would. She and Kat were identical twins. And nobody knew Kat had died.

As she opened her mouth to deny his comment, heavy footsteps rounded the corner. Panic gripped her, and she couldn't breathe. They had come to take her away.

When she dared to peek over her shoulder, it surprised her to see the men's expressions showed no anger. Instead of scowls aimed at her, their brows were creased, mouths pursed tightly, as they glared at the soldier. Confusion filled her and she slowly shook her head, trying to understand what was happening.

"Release her at once, sir," the apple cart's owner said to the soldier.

Surprised, she blinked, switching her attention back and forth between the soldier and the other man. Why did they dare talk to this officer so disrespectfully?

A chuckle rumbled through the soldier's chest, but he didn't let her go.

The thundering hooves of a horse bore down upon them. Camilla switched her attention to the man on the steed. The small crowd parted, and the man atop the animal dismounted. The sight of the rider left her speechless and a bit weak in the knees.

His rugged appearance shocked her, and his strength was evident in his muscled arms and legs. Rather than the fancy clothes of an English nobleman, the beige shirt and brown leather vest of a farmer's attire stretched taut across his wide chest, and the dark brown material of his trousers molded to his legs and fit snugly into his dark brown knee-boots. But this man was no farmer. That much was apparent by the way he carried himself as he strode toward her, his step too confident, too graceful.

When he neared and she gazed upon his face, her breath caught in her throat. The sun had turned his skin a light brown, and the sureness of his jaw bespoke authority. Chestnut hair tousled by the wind framed his head, and she had a sudden urge to swipe the unruly locks off his forehead.

He was quite handsome, if she dared admit, and he literally made her lungs stop working. Never had that happened to her from just admiring a man. Looking into his fiery hazel eyes, she swallowed hard.

He stopped mere inches away, towering over both Camilla and the soldier like a dark cloud of doom. She leaned back to take in his height.

The handsome man met the soldier's stare. "Sir, will you kindly remove your hands from my wife?"

Her jaw dropped. *Wife?*

"Correct me, Mr. Worthington, but was your wife not running from you?" The soldier shook his head. "A few hours ago, I had heard that you reported your wife missing. Now here she is caught running. There must be a reason for that."

She sucked in her breath. *Mr. Worthington?* This handsome and very powerful man was her sister's husband.

The pulse in her temple grew stronger. She couldn't speak, and she couldn't think. Telling him about Kat's death was crucial, yet she didn't want to do that in front of all of these spectators.

If only her mind would cooperate with her tongue and voice, perhaps she wouldn't feel like a trapped animal. But more importantly, why did she find her brother-in-law dangerously attractive?

When the man in question settled his eyes on her, his expression softened, and a smile touched his mouth. "Yes, Mrs. Worthington. Please inform the captain and all these good people why you were running from me."

Silence stretched through the crowd as all eyes were aimed toward Camilla. Even the horses seemed remarkably quiet. Panic grew inside her chest like rising dough, suffocating her slowly. They all expected an explanation—one she couldn't give.

"My dear." Mr. Worthington took a step closer. "Will you please clarify why you were running from me?"

She needed to set the matter straight. Now. Although she assumed Mr. Worthington's change of attitude was all for show, her heart leapt at the tenderness he displayed. That could be the only reason her mind had gone into a momentary dither.

She opened her mouth to explain about Kat's death, but a thought struck her. She could portray her sister.

Obviously, these people didn't know she was Kat's twin. This mistake in identity might make the difference in pilfering the money she needed from Mr. Worthington and finding him guilty of the illegal actions against his business partners. After all, pretending to be his wife would be easier, since she would have free rein of the house—and more freedom to follow him or eavesdrop.

Yet what Kat had said about her husband caused a wave of nausea to roll through Camilla's middle. It would be as if she were married to Lord Hardy all over again.

The unspoken command to play along with Mr. Worthington loomed in the depths of his eyes. A warning buzzed through her head, commanding her to stop this insane idea of switching roles, but no other choice came to her. It had to be done.

Her tongue felt enlarged, and her mind had turned to mush. "I—I was not running from you. I thought the cart owner was after me." She switched her attention to the merchant. "A street urchin stole an apple, and I thought you were after me because of it."

She glanced at the soldier then pushed away from him.

"Thank you, kind sir, for breaking my fall, but I no longer need your assistance."

The soldier shook his head. "But why did your husband feel the need to report you as a missing wife this morning?"

She gulped, feeling like her throat had dried considerably within seconds. *Think, Camilla...* "I had been to Preston to visit my ill sister." She switched her gaze to Mr. Worthington. "Do you not recall my telling you?"

Worthington released a light laugh. "I do now." He aimed his attention toward the soldier. "I had a temporary loss of memory, but all is well now." Mr. Worthington's gaze softened as he held out his elbow. "Are you ready to return home, my dear?"

Could she be seeing right? He was acting like a gentleman instead of the monster her sister had described.

"Yes." She placed a shaky hand in the crook of his well-muscled arm, and he led her toward his horse. Another man followed and mounted a horse tethered nearby.

"Mr. Worthington." One of the townsmen in the group stepped forward. "Do you still want those chairs delivered to your residence on the morrow?"

"That will be fine, Mr. Perkins."

"Sir." Another man doffed his hat. "My Mary wanted me to ask the next time I saw you when you'd be needing more eggs?"

"I'll have my cook speak with her."

"As you wish, Mr. Worthington." The man nodded to Camilla. "A good day to you, Mrs. Worthington."

She smiled. "And a good day to you." Odd, but the townsfolk seemed to respect Kat's husband.

Without meeting her eyes, Mr. Worthington placed his large hands around her waist and lifted her onto his horse. Strange sensations flitted in her stomach and spread through her body until he released her. He mounted behind her, draping her legs over one of his. The intimate position had her shivering in a mixture of fear and awareness. Though this was the horrid man her sister had warned her about, a few moments ago she detected a softer side. His touch wasn't as rough as she expected, either.

She sneaked a glance over her shoulder to peer into his eyes. These were not the same pair she had seen a minute ago. Instead, they had turned incredibly cold. Had the monster she'd been warned about returned?

"Where have you been?" he said in a tone low enough that only she could hear. "I have been out of my mind with worry thinking you had been kidnapped... or worse."

Finally, Camilla was able to glimpse the atrocious man Kat had married. Apparently, he was only an angel of mercy in front of his acquaintances. The harshness in his voice caused Camilla's limbs to shake. What was he capable of doing in a fit of anger?

Before she had time to speak, his large arm tightened, holding her against him in a viselike grip. He wouldn't abuse her right out in the open, would he?

"You can explain after we get home." The sharp tone in his voice made her cringe. "I don't want to air our disagreement in public."

He reined his horse, turning in the opposite direction of her trunk—and poor Timothy, who probably thought she had been kidnapped or arrested.

"Wait." She touched Mr. Worthington's hand. "We have to go back and retrieve my trunk."

"Your trunk?"

"Yes. It is at the mercantile."

He growled but maneuvered the animal around. A man who'd been with Mr. Worthington earlier followed at a distance as they rode the few minutes in silence. Mr. Worthington's stiffness against her back conveyed his anger.

Ahead of them, Timothy stood by a wagon, loading her trunk. His skittish gaze roamed the street. The lines around his mouth gave evidence of his concern.

"Right there." She pointed in her servant's direction.

"Picking them older now?" Worthington sneered.

She glanced over her shoulder just in time to see his curt

expression. "Pardon me?"

"The man. Who is he?"

"My servant."

He arched an eyebrow and shrugged. "Well, nonetheless, he can ride with Broderick."

When they neared, Timothy lifted his gaze to hers, and his mouth hung open. His expression darkened as he switched his focus from her to Worthington. She tried communicating with her eyes to follow her lead.

Although under duress, she smiled. "Timothy, I have found Mr. Worthington, my husband I told you about. Can you bring the wagon and follow us home?"

Timothy's skeptical gaze moved from her to Malcolm. The servant's mouth opened and shut a few times, as if he wanted to speak but didn't have the words. Camilla's heart hammered against her ribs. Hopefully, Timothy wouldn't ask questions. She couldn't have her plan ruined so soon. She focused her pleading eyes upon her servant.

What seemed an eternity passed before he finally nodded. "As ye wish, madame."

The man named Broderick dismounted and tied his horse to the wagon. He helped Timothy with her trunk before climbing onto the seat with her servant.

Mr. Worthington urged the horse forward, and they traveled through the middle of town. People greeted him, and he answered in a kind, tender voice, but all were hesitant before addressing her, she noticed.

The busy section of town disappeared, and Mr. Worthington's warm breath was released on her neck in a heavy sigh. She gazed at his profile as he glanced over his shoulder at the fading town. The slight breeze made his intriguing scent drift to her nose—a mixture of cedar and leather. It roused her senses, and for some odd reason, she was eager to know more about him. Would pretending to be his wife bring back horrid memories of her marriage to Lord Hardy? So far, she'd caught glimpses of a totally different man underneath his hard mask of indifference.

Camilla shook away those thoughts. She couldn't think this way about her brother-in-law, even if her sister was dead and buried.

He turned away from the town and looked at her. His hardened expression made the lines across his forehead run together.

Camilla gulped. He was going to realize she wasn't Kat. Taking a deep breath, she prepared herself for his anger.

"Thank you for not making a spectacle back there." His voice was harsh, yet sincere.

She nodded, holding in the sigh of relief threatening to spill forward. Why had he said such a thing? After all, she'd been the one looking foolish not too long ago, not him.

"I am truly sorry for leaving. I hope I did not worry you." She spoke in soft tones, wishing to calm his anger.

His brows drew together. *"You* are sorry?"

Trembling, she took a deep breath. The time had come to play the bold woman she'd never been. "Yes. Before I left, I wrote you a missive, informing you of my plans. Do you really not remember, or were you just saying what you had to back there so as not to cause a scene?"

"Trust me, there was no such note."

She swallowed, moistening her parched throat. "My sister summoned me. She was deathly ill, and I needed to leave quickly."

His gaze snapped from her to the road. "We shall talk about this when we reach home."

"Why?" She glanced at the others riding well behind them. "They cannot hear."

"Because if we wait, I shall have time to cool my temper. I fear what I might say in my present state of mind."

"As you wish, but know I'm sorry for causing you any worry."

He looked down at her. Confusion still marred his dark expression. He shook his head as if he didn't understand. "Please, cease your prattle until we arrive home. You are confusing me."

He'd just shown clear evidence he was the ogre Kat had warned her about. The man seemed intent on a quarrel, refusing to accept her most heartfelt, if not completely honest, apology. Instead of prodding him with questions, she kept her mouth closed and stared at the road ahead.

After a moment of silence, he grumbled, "What ails you now?"

She glanced at him over her shoulder. "What do you mean?"

"Where is the argument?"

"Argument?"

"Cease playing the innocent victim, Mrs. Worthington. You know very well what I refer to." He sneered. "Your only form of communication is to argue, so why have you suddenly changed?"

She scolded herself for forgetting her role. Kat did possess the talent to argue. Camilla must try to remember this henceforth, but it would be difficult. Whereas Kat had a love for verbal sparring, Camilla avoided confrontation at all costs.

She arched a brow. "Perhaps I am also waiting until we get home."

She studied his face closely for a reaction, and it wasn't long in coming. The corners of his mouth lifted slightly and hinted at a smile. If not for the coldness in his gaze, she would have relaxed.

"Very well." He nodded.

After a short time, they rode into the drive of the most beautiful home she'd ever seen. A three-storied mansion with a massive chimney on each side loomed before her. Her breath caught in her throat. Two dormer windows accented the third floor, while the other windows were in the Palladian style. On the surface, her sister appeared to have been the most fortunate woman in the world, even more so than Camilla, who had married an earl. Yet it was this house, and the very man who lifted her off the horse, that had caused Kat's melancholy and eventually her death. Camilla wished Kat had told her how Mr. Worthington amassed his fortune.

Once the wagon stopped, Broderick jumped from the seat and walked toward the back. Timothy followed. In one fluid sweep, Broderick lifted her heavy trunk, resting it on his shoulder while Timothy carried her satchel.

"Timothy, please let me carry that." She stepped toward her servant, taking it from him.

Mr. Worthington's bark of laughter made her stop as she gave him a confounded stare.

Her sister's husband scratched his head. "Mrs. Worthington, you are full of surprises today. Broderick will take your luggage to your room."

Realization dawned, and she decided it best to comply with the man's instructions. After all, how else would she find her sister's bedroom? She gaped at the house's magnificent façade, once again amazed at the grand place where Kat had lived.

"What about Timothy?" she asked. "Where will he stay?"

"I will make certain he is assigned to work an area around the house that best suits his skills."

"Thank you." She gave her sister's husband a curt nod and followed behind Broderick. Although dressed in a similar style, Mr. Worthington's servant didn't fill out his clothes as well.

Quickly, she admonished herself. Although Malcolm Worthington had been blessed with the most favorable attributes—mesmerizing hazel eyes, smooth lips, hair a woman would love to run her fingers through—he was still an ogre on the inside. He only cared about his precious money.

Silence reigned until she reached the bedroom on the second floor. She followed Broderick as he walked in and set her trunk down, then turned to look at her with distrust darkening his brown eyes. The more he watched her, the more his expression sharpened, causing her heartbeat to hammer. He stood too close for a mere servant, almost threatening.

She stepped back. "Thank you for helping me, Broderick."

He took another step closer, and she retreated further.

"Do you need anything else, Mrs. Worthington?" he asked.

Folding her hands together, she held them firmly against her stomach, trying to stop them from shaking. "Thank you again, but that is not necessary. You may leave now."

The man stopped directly in front of her. Unease turned to fear, and her stomach wrenched. His glare was meant to frighten, but she would not cower.

"Good day, then," he said.

She hadn't realized she was holding her breath until he walked away, then she emptied her lungs in one big whoosh. What was that all about?

Stepping further into her sister's room, she scanned the area from top to bottom, tilting her head, admiring the pearly-white ceilings and walls. She moved to the green and yellow drapes on the window and pulled the cord to let the brightness from outside lighten the spacious room. A large marble fireplace ran alongside one wall. She walked to it, knelt, and peered inside, running her hand along the sandstone in awe.

On the other side of the room stood a hand-painted silk screen depicting delicate birds perched on thin vines with a waterfall in the background. She stood and rushed behind it. Shock washed over her. She gasped at the copper bathing tub with brass clawed feet. Even though Lord Hardy had had many expensive possessions while they were married, he had never owned a tub this size.

At the armoire, Camilla swung open the polished cherry-wood doors. The delicate scent of lavender swirled around her. Her hand fluttered to her mouth. This couldn't be correct. This wasn't the prison Kat had described.

She grasped the scarlet material nearest to her. Smoothing the velvet between her finger and thumb, she closed her eyes and smiled. She'd always loved the feel of velvet, always loved the way it caressed her skin when she wore it. She tugged down the fur-lined muff, noticing the matching cloak. There wasn't just one fur cloak, but several.

Kat had mentioned Malcolm wouldn't buy her anything, and

yet these clothes looked as though they belonged to royalty.

Concern washed over Camilla like hot molasses. Why had Kat lied?

Quickly, she pushed the negative thought out. Her sister hadn't been in her right mind before she died. Malcolm Worthington was at fault, and Camilla was determined, now more than ever, to get him arrested for whatever illegal activities he was doing.

Sighing, she plopped down on the enormous bed decorated with the most beautiful quilts and pillows she'd ever seen. Where did Malcolm get all of his money? And would his income have anything to do with his traitorous deals? There was only one way to find out, but unfortunately, she had to settle in her new place—and role—before she could spy on him. She couldn't have him suspecting her true identity.

Chapter Two

W*HY DID SHE return?*
Malcolm Worthington paced the green and gold carpet in the parlor, clenching his hands into fists. Where was that woman? What was taking her so long? Rather than cooling off, as he told her he would, his anger intensified.

Usually an understanding man, he couldn't forgive her this time for leaving without a word, amongst the other crimes she had committed since their wedding. For the past few months, his life had hung by a thread, and any more catastrophes could send him to his doom.

He wouldn't surrender without a fight. His wife held secrets—he just didn't know exactly how many. If he weren't so worried about it, he would have let her run away. But keeping a close eye on her was crucial at this point. Soon, he would go through Parliament and get the annulment they both wanted, no matter how it tarnished his name.

Grumbling, he raked his fingers through his hair. What had he been thinking, marrying a woman he had never met? His friend had told him of a man who had a daughter he was trying to settle with a good husband. Malcolm should have heard the warning bells when he realized how desperate Mr. Connelly was to have a quick wedding and hand his daughter over. Then again, he had been searching for a mother for his children, and was hoping that marriage would solve that issue, along with finding him a good wife.

Neither had happened.

Now two questions swam through his head—why had she returned, and what would he do with her now she was back?

The sound of swishing skirts close by caught his attention, and he turned. His wife entered, appearing as regal as the first day they had met at her father's house. Her light brown hair was upswept into a tight knot at the top of her head, with a few soft curls brushing near her ears. The dark gray dress had a high collar and long sleeves, and was snug enough to complement her slender figure. A cameo clasped at her throat was her only jewelry.

He pursed his mouth. Why had she dressed this way? She was neither a servant, nor in mourning. Seeing her attired thus reminded him why he had agreed to marry her in the first place, next to the constant echo of his dying first wife's wish rushing through his head at that time—*Find another wife who could be a mother to our children.* Kat had put on a façade of innocence, and he wanted to believe with all his heart such a woman existed.

Now something different glimmered from the depths of her green eyes. A steady, thoughtful regard had replaced the haughty glances.

Would she tell him where she had been all this time and why? No doubt whatever scheme she pursued had gone awry, and she had returned for the financial support of living as his wife. Despite her changes in dress and demeanor, Hell would turn to icicles before he ever trusted her again. It hadn't taken long after they were wed to discover what a fine performer she was.

"Have you misplaced all your other dresses, Mrs. Worthington?"

"I don't quite understand your question."

He rolled his eyes heavenward then strode to her. He gestured to her covered neck. "Planning to seduce a Puritan?"

She grabbed her modest neckline, her eyes wide. "I beg your pardon?"

"And well you should, but I fear your apologies come too late."

"You do not approve of my dress?"

"I prefer to see the package wrapped in something more fitting to your true self. In that manner, I would be well reminded of the true woman I married."

She gasped, and her cheeks blotched with red spots. "Are you insinuating that I—"

"Kat, cease playing innocent. It is unbefitting of your true character." He breathed a deep sigh. "Now, tell me where you have been, and what in heaven's name possessed you to come back?"

She clasped her hands against her stomach. "As I told you before, I went to care for my ill sister."

"Why did you return?"

Her brows drew together. "Because I'm your wife and this is where I belong."

He snorted as he walked in front of her. "When did you decide that?"

"Malcolm," she said, touching his sleeve, "I really had no intentions of worrying you."

He caught his breath and glared at her. "What did you call me?"

"Malcolm." Her face paled.

Hearing his name roll from her lips made his stomach churn. "What are you playing at now? You have never called me by my Christian name."

She clutched her hands together again, turning her knuckles white. "I don't know why I called you that." She shrugged. "I suppose I'm trying to show you I have changed."

He studied her forest-green eyes, trying to find the cold woman he knew her to be, but only saw a frightened rabbit. "Now I *know* something is wrong. Why would you want to change?"

She stood straight and lifted her chin. *Ah, now there's the wom-*

an I married.

"I'm well aware you have not been pleased with my actions of late, but I'm changing. If I'm going to live with you for the remainder of my life, I might as well make it as happy as I can."

A low chuckle escaped his throat, and he shook his head. "By your actions thus far in our marriage, I thought you were living only for yourself, gaining pleasure anyway you could. I thought marriage was a hindrance to your overall happiness." He shrugged off her wide-eyed stare. "What are your plans now?"

She licked her lips. "Um, I thought I would continue on with what I have been doing."

"I knew you would not change," he snapped, then marched out of the room, knowing if he stayed another moment, he would wring her lovely neck.

CAMILLA FURROWED HER brow. Why did that inconsiderate man question her attire? Studying her image in the fancy glass on the mirrored sidebar, she wiped her moist palms down her skirt. Nothing was wrong with her dress. It was certainly more proper than the gowns she had found hanging in her sister's armoires.

Her thoughts quickly came to a halt and her heart sank. Realization turned her blood cold. She was now her sister, and so must dress like her. Kat never once dressed modestly when she lived at home, so why would she change after marriage? Why hadn't Camilla thought of this before she decided to play her twin?

Her heart skipped in an erratic beat with the mere thought of having to wear something so improper. Why, it was absolutely scandalous. Her hand flew to her bosom. She had never shown that much skin, not even while wearing her nightgown.

The closing of the front door drew her attention to the corridor. She stepped to the doorway of the parlor and saw two small children tiptoe up the grand stairs. The lad, probably in his sixth year, looked exactly like Malcolm, with chestnut hair and an oval face, but the little girl looked entirely opposite. Her brilliant blonde hair curled in ringlets around her heart-shaped face. The adorable little angel, probably around four years old, held on to her brother's hand as she limped behind him.

"Good day," Camilla greeted them.

The children halted on the steps, and their heads snapped her way. The little girl's face lost all color, and the boy's jaw hardened.

The boy turned and moved in front of his sister. "Good day, Camilla. It pleases us to know you are home safe. We worried when Papa said you were lost."

She sucked in her breath. Two things worried her now. First, why did they act as if they cared when Kat said Malcolm's children hated her? And second, why were they using her real name? Malcolm called her Kat, yet the children had said the name Camilla. As much as she wanted to know, she couldn't ask without drawing suspicion.

Through her panic, she smiled. "Is something amiss?" She stared at the little girl. "Did you hurt your leg?"

The girl nodded, her curls bouncing all around her face, but she didn't speak.

Wearing a stern expression, the boy tried to block his sister from Camilla's gaze.

"I know you told us not to run, but we couldn't help it," he said. "The mean dog came after us again, and Lizzy couldn't run very fast." Big tears welled in the boy's eyes. "Please, don't be mad at her. I tried to stop the dog, but—" He paused, turning to show the rip on the backside of his breeches. "The dog got me, too."

Camilla's heart crumbled at the tender display, and she rushed to the children, kneeling on the step in front of them. She reached out to touch them, and they flinched.

"Let me examine your knee, Lizzy." Camilla gently lifted the soiled pink dress to the scraped, bloody skin underneath. "You are bleeding. We should clean that cut. It will make you feel better." She moved to pick up the girl, but she moved out of Camilla's grasp.

"I will do it," the boy said with authority.

Lightly chewing on her bottom lip, Camilla narrowed her gaze on the pair. She nodded. "If you do not mind, I would like to watch. Is that permissible?"

The boy's brow creased as he stared back at her. "Yes."

She followed the children up the wide staircase to the second floor. She found it very odd that they were so afraid of the woman who had married their father, but they certainly didn't behave in the manner Kat had described.

A nursemaid scurried from one of the rooms and swept Lizzy up in her arms. "Oh, Mrs. Worthington, don't you worry about these two. I will take care of them."

"Nonetheless, I would like to assist," Camilla said.

This time, all eyes widened. The maid finally nodded. "If you are certain, mistress?"

"I am." Camilla smiled.

While she helped the maid tend to Lizzy's knee, she listened to the boy talk about the incident with the dog. She discovered his name was James. Though she had no clue as to why the girl didn't speak. After Lizzy's knee had been bandaged, the maid pushed James off to his room to change his breeches.

"James," Camilla called after him. "If you want to bring your breeches back to me, I will mend the rip and they will be like new."

Once again, all three stopped and stared with wide eyes, but James appeared more confused than the other two with his creased forehead.

"It is all right," she assured them. "Make haste, and I will repair them."

James glanced at the older woman, who shrugged. He started to his room, but then turned back to Camilla.

"Thank you," he said.

She smiled. "For what?"

"For not scolding us." He grabbed his sister's hand, and they turned and ran to their rooms.

Her heart twisted. Could her sister have lied again? What had Kat been doing to Malcolm's children? Unless, of course, she had reprimanded them because of the way their father had instructed them to treat her. That must be it.

"And I thank you, Mrs. Worthington." The maid bobbed, then turned, but Camilla grabbed her arm and stopped her.

"Would you please explain something to me before you leave?"

"What might that be?"

"Why do the children call me Camilla?"

Confusion marred the maid's face, her forehead wrinkling her expression. Perhaps Camilla shouldn't have asked, but she really needed to know.

"Have you forgotten, Mrs. Worthington?"

"Apparently so." She massaged her temples. "I think my mind has been scrambled from my long and tedious journey."

"Well, you specifically instructed us not to use the name their father calls you. They see how upset you get when he uses that name, so they call you by your given name."

Camilla released an agitated sigh and trailed her fingers down to rub the back of her neck. So, that was the reason Malcolm called her Kat. It was meant to upset her. Yet why would her sister use *her* name? Malcolm and the children should be calling her Katherine.

Certainly another mystery to unravel.

"I'm sorry I have frightened those poor children. I shan't do it again. After you help them change, have them come to the parlor. I wish to speak to them."

The maid nodded and hurried into Lizzy's bedroom.

Camilla took slow steps down the stairs, her heart so low as to scrape the floor. She walked into the parlor and sank into the closest chair. Before condemning their father for doing illegal activities, she had so much work to do. First, she needed to repair the hearts of those two adorable children. She couldn't have them thinking she was a bad person. Indeed, she may be the only family they have, and if their father went to the gaol, Camilla might be the one left caring for them.

STARING AT HERSELF in the full-length mirror, Camilla groaned and twisted her mouth in distaste. The indecent rusty-red evening gown trimmed with dark brown lace looked horrid on her. Besides exposing much of her shoulders and bosom, the garment was too tight. The stays nearly squeezed the breath right out of her. Several times she struggled to lift the shoulders so they wouldn't drop down her arms, but they refused to go the way she wanted. She couldn't have people see her like this. She couldn't even look at herself without blushing.

"Beth? Could you choose another gown for me?" she called to the maid.

Beth scurried around the room picking up articles of clothes, and then stopped with her arms overloaded. "Why? It's the dress ye like to wear when ye entertain dinner guests."

Camilla frowned. She had only been here a day before Malcolm informed her of their upcoming dinner guests. She wanted to tell him how inappropriate that was, since she was fatigued from her journey, until she remembered her arrival had been a surprise to him. If Mr. Worthington was the monster her sister had described, he wouldn't cancel just because his wife was tired.

Beth dropped the clothes on the bed before coming to Camilla, stopping behind her. The maid ran her fingers over Camilla's hairstyle.

"Mrs. Worthington, I must say I do like yer 'air when it's wound up tight like this, so refined and sophisticated. It's different from 'ow ye used to wear it."

Camilla brushed the tip of her finger across one of the tendrils by her ear. "I want to look my very best for our company tonight." She bit her lip in hesitation, but just had to ask. "Remind me again who is in attendance this evening?"

Beth giggled. "I think yer mind is still jumpin' around from yer trip."

"Indeed, that is the reason."

"Well, I hope ye regain yer quick wit soon. I'd hate for Mr. Worthington to yell at ye again, although ye've handled his temper before. T'night, one of his business partners, Mr. Kennedy, and his wife are yer guests. Ye know how fidgety the master gets whenever Mr. Kennedy comes to dine."

Camilla assessed the maid. "I wonder why Mr. Worthington acts in such a manner?"

"I couldn't guess. Probably 'cause Mr. Kennedy owns most of the business and can drop Mr. Worthington like a boulder in the ocean if he doesn't approve of his work ethic."

Tilting her head, Camilla narrowed her eyes at the maid. "How do you know so much about Mr. Worthington and Mr. Kennedy?"

Another giggle. "Ye have left yer memory in Preston, to be sure. Do ye not remember teachin' me how to listen to their conversations without bein' seen?"

Shock vibrated through Camilla, and despite her effort to hide it, her jaw dropped. She closed her mouth and smiled. Apparently, Kat had had assistance in her search for answers about Malcolm. "And you are doing exceptionally well, Beth." She paused. "Is there any more you want to tell me?"

Beth's forehead crinkled, as if she were searching her mind for answers. "I don't think so." Then her eyes widened. "But Mr. Worthington kept attendin' those secret meetings after ye left. I know he promised ye he wouldn't go, but after ye left, I think he just didn't care."

Secret meetings? This was the very thing Camilla needed to know. She wanted to ask the maid but didn't want to look foolish, either. Watching Malcolm closely was the key to finding what she wanted. "I understand. I suppose I will have to talk to him about that."

"Just as I knew ye would." Beth took a step back and glanced over Camilla's attire again. "Ye look mighty fine, Mrs. Worthington. It will please Mr. Kennedy, that's for certain."

Camilla gasped, placing her hand on her neck. "Why should I want to please Mr. Kennedy?"

Beth's brows pulled together. "Because ye're the reason he made Mr. Worthington a partner, which, by the way, doubled yer husband's wealth. Do ye not remember? If not for yer influence, he would still be workin' his fingers to the bone at that small company he owned. Oh, for certain he made good money, but it was pure genius to have Mr. Kennedy bring on Mr. Worthington as a partner."

Camilla recovered, dropping her hand and squaring her shoulders. So that was why Malcolm was so wealthy. "Well, I only wanted what was best for my husband. What I meant to say was that I do not want Mr. Kennedy to think I dress this way to please him." She gave an uneasy laugh. "I would hate to distress Mrs. Kennedy."

Beth's sudden bark of laughter surprised Camilla yet again. She anxiously awaited the maid's response.

"Ye must be jestin'. Ye have seen how unattractive his wife is. I think Mr. Kennedy would be happy for yer attention, especially when we all know he can't stop from feastin' his eyes upon yer loveliness."

Camilla cleared her throat and turned toward the mirror. "Whomever I impress tonight, I better hurry so I do not miss the dinner party." She glanced down at her bosom again and frowned. "Beth? Can you locate a scarf that matches this dress?"

"Whatever for?"

"To hide the most daring décolletage I have ever seen."

Beth laughed again. "Ye're actin' strangely, Mrs. Worthington. Besides, I think Mr. Kennedy prefers ye in less, if'n ye knows what I mean."

Camilla's legs weakened, and she grasped the chair next to her to steady herself. Could she have heard wrong? Oh, please, say Katherine wasn't involved in a love tryst. She squeezed her eyes closed. *Somebody please tell me something good about my sister.*

Camilla composed herself and stood straight, meeting the maid's gaze. "Nonetheless, I would like something to place in my bodice to help me feel a little more covered. This sheer fichu tucked around the edges will not suffice."

Beth shrugged and moved into the next room to look through Katherine's accessories. Within minutes, she came back with a white lace handkerchief and gently stuffed it in the bodice.

"I think that is better, don't you?" Camilla studied her reflection in the mirror.

"Ye're just lovely, Mrs. Worthington."

Although the handkerchief hid a lot of her cleavage, it still didn't hide her bare shoulders. She shrugged. She couldn't have everything perfect. After all, tonight she was Kat.

She exhaled and gave the maid a nod. "I think I am presentable now."

Wringing her hands, Camilla made her way downstairs to Malcolm's guests. Her legs wobbled like a newborn calf's, but she forced herself to stay strong. Voices floated from the sitting room. She took a fortifying breath and entered. All eyes turned her way, and she feared her legs would collapse.

She must stay strong and make them believe she was Kat.

Chapter Three

THE OTHER MAN in the room gazed at Camilla in a leisurely fashion, making her stomach roll. She took a calming breath to keep from embarrassing herself and retching in front of Malcolm's guests.

Mr. Worthington's friend appeared older than Malcolm by at least ten years, but Mr. Kennedy was handsome, nonetheless. Streaks of silver highlighted his dark brown hair. He smiled at her as if they shared a delicious secret. Her stomach twisted again. Right now, she wanted to forget that her sister and this man might possibly have a past together.

She studied Mrs. Kennedy and realized Beth spoke the truth. Poor Mrs. Kennedy didn't have a single redeeming feature. Exceedingly plain, the skittish woman acted as if she were afraid of her own shadow.

Then Camilla rested her attention on Malcolm. Her heart must have stopped—either that or she forgot how to breathe. He looked so incredibly handsome in his evening attire. The bluish charcoal of his waistcoat matched his trousers, accenting his warm hazel eyes. His white ruffled shirt complemented his tanned skin. She had never seen anyone so handsome. Even the way his gaze slowly swept over her made her skin prickle with awareness.

Never in her life had she experienced these heady, disturbing feelings, even while married to her husband. Then again, theirs was an arranged marriage, and she had been utterly miserable.

Malcolm smiled and stepped forward, taking her hand in his. He bowed and placed a small kiss on her knuckles. Her heart raced out of control. His masculine scent of spice seeped into her senses and overwhelmed her, making her mind whirl and the room spin. She couldn't lose control. Not now, and certainly not in front of their guests.

Malcolm straightened. "My dear Mrs. Worthington, you look lovely tonight." His attention passed over her once again but lingered longer on her bosom.

"Thank you. And may I return the compliment? You are rather dashing tonight, my kind husband."

He arched an eyebrow, and she was relieved the two guests behind him couldn't see. Malcolm's wary grin widened, but he didn't comment. Instead, he took her hand and tucked it in the crook of his elbow, then turned toward his partner.

"Camilla, my dear, help me welcome our guests."

Surprised to hear Malcolm say her name and not Kat's, she hitched a breath. He'd only called her Kat in private to annoy her—or rather, her sister. But still, why did he use Camilla instead of Katherine?

Although a small pounding began in her forehead from all the confusion of the day, she did her best to converse with the Kennedys. During the evening, she remained conscious of how her sister might have performed. She exaggerated a flirtatious manner yet couldn't force herself to act as flamboyant as she suspected her sister to have done. As the men talked politics, she tossed in her own thoughts, even though this was something Kat would *not* do. But when it came to politics, Camilla had never been able to keep her mouth shut.

She kept close attention to the topics of conversation. Not once did she feel these men were discussing traitorous secrets. Other than talking about their business, both appeared to be on the up-and-up.

Mr. Kennedy's constant ogling irritated her, but she dared not show her displeasure. Although Mrs. Kennedy was polite and never commented on her husband's behavior, Camilla thought it very bold of him to carry on the way he did in front of her. It hurt that Malcolm accepted his business partner's conduct instead of stopping it. After all, she was supposed to be his wife.

Relief came when the evening ended, and she and Malcolm showed their guests to the front door. Malcolm acted the gentleman and placed a chaste kiss on Mrs. Kennedy's knuckles, but when Mr. Kennedy tried to do the same to Camilla, he didn't act polite at all. His lips lingered on her hand, disgust crawled inside her, and she quickly withdrew.

The arrogant man had the audacity to toss her a devilish grin. If Mrs. Kennedy were not present, Camilla would have slapped the rogue's face. Perhaps she would just wait until she was alone with Malcolm and shake some sense into him for not coming to her defense.

Once the door closed, Malcolm turned and strode past her. She waited for him to say something, but he hurried up the stairs to his bedroom without glancing her way. Anger washed over her, painfully wrenching her stomach. A million times tonight she had wanted to reprimand him. But now, when she had the chance, he left her standing alone, wallowing in her annoyance.

Camilla hurried to her room to change into her nightdress. The weary, stressful day had taken its toll, and she would relish sleep. Beth had placed her nightgown on the bed and poured water in the copper tub. The steamy bath beckoned, and she couldn't wait to relax.

She sat on the edge of her bed and slipped off her shoes. Stretching her feet in front of her, she wiggled her toes, enjoying the freedom from the shoes' restriction. As she stood, she reached for the buttons behind her gown, but couldn't quite touch them. A knock sounded at the door, and she was grateful to have Beth coming to help. "Come in."

Still fidgeting with the dress, she walked toward her bathing chamber. "Could you please help me with these buttons? I cannot seem to reach them."

"Are you certain you want my help?" a man's deep voice answered.

She gasped and swung around. Malcolm stood in the doorway, minus his evening coat and waistcoat. His missing cravat and unbuttoned shirt allowed her a glimpse of his muscular neck and chest. Her heart accelerated. He looked so casual, so relaxed, and so irritatingly handsome.

Was he here for a little entertainment only his wife could give? She could not... She *would* not. The mere thought terrified her, yet excitement danced over her skin at the same time. Breathing deeper, she reminded herself he wouldn't want to share his wife's bed if he loathed her very presence.

She cleared her tight throat. "Forgive me, but I thought you were my maid."

"Obviously." He stepped toward her. "But since I am here, I might as well assist you."

"Don't worry yourself." She swallowed hard. "I can get it."

"Nonsense. Accepting my help is perfectly proper."

As he moved behind her, her hands trembled. One by one, he slid the buttons loose and cool air touched her back, accompanied by his warm breath. The combination of this with his soft fingers grazing her skin sent chills over her. Although her body was melting faster than a heated candle on a scorching day, she fought for control.

"I want to thank you for your little performance tonight," he whispered huskily near her ear.

She shivered. Clutching her bodice tighter, she prayed it wouldn't fall away from her. "What performance?"

He laughed lightly. "You seem to forget I have seen you and Brandon Kennedy together. Since when have you cared for his wife's delicate feelings and snubbed Brandon's flirtation?"

With the last button undone, she turned and faced him, still holding her bodice to her chest. "Since I have seen how much it bothers his wife." She arched a brow. "And while we are on the subject, why did you not put a stop to his flirtations? You have eyes and could see it bothered Mrs. Kennedy."

He folded his arms across his wide chest, drawing her attention to that specific part of his body that would now be forever branded in her memory. She lifted her gaze, and his eyes were just as earth-shatteringly effective.

"Why should I put a stop to it?" He shrugged. "Mrs. Kennedy knows about her husband's liaisons. She is not a dimwit."

Inwardly, Camilla groaned. Malcolm had confirmed her worst fear. But even though he knew, he apparently didn't care. That explained why he had treated Kat so horribly.

"Believe it or not, I have changed," she said, trying to sound convincing. "I will not be an embarrassment to you or your family any longer."

His eyes widened and he laughed. "Oh, this is too much, Kat. First you dress differently..." He stepped closer, and her heart nearly leapt right out of her body. His gaze dipped to her bosom as he tugged at the lace handkerchief between her fingers until he'd pulled it completely out. "I do not think I have ever seen you hide yourself before." He touched a tendril by her ear. "And now you are wearing your hair like a regal lady and acting the part in front of guests." His finger trailed down her neck. "What strange form has moved into your body and taken over? Up until now, you have never bothered to help my children, yet this afternoon I hear you sewed a rip in James's breeches." He shook his head. "If I didn't know any better, I would think you were an imposter."

Her chest constricted. "What an absurd thing to say, Mr. Worthington. Who else could I be?"

"Who indeed?" The corners of his mouth lifted. "But I didn't come to discuss your scheming heart. I came to thank you for a pleasant evening." He nodded and turned to leave, but before reaching the door, he peered at her over his shoulder. "Have a good rest, Mrs. Worthington."

She smiled, though her knees quaked so badly they threatened to topple her. "And the same to you."

After he left, her breathing evened out, but she doubted rest would come easily this night.

A NEW DAWN crept through the partially opened drapes of Malcolm's room, touching and stirring him from the depths of a dream he didn't want to remember. Last night's events had kept his mind awake into the wee hours of the morning. Despite his sluggish body, he pulled himself from his exhausted state and climbed out of bed. The refreshingly cool air stroked his skin, awakening him even more. With half-closed eyes he slid into his robe, before ringing for his manservant.

His servant carried up buckets of water and filled the copper tub. Once he was relaxed in the liquid comfort, Malcolm's foggy memory of the previous evening claimed thoughts. His wife had been stunning, and her charming personality made a better impression than normal on his guests, yet nothing about her was normal.

Why had she acted so different last night?

Although she still paraded around in clothes unbefitting the mold he'd wanted for his wife, something strange had happened in the way she carried herself. Her words were polite, respectful, and she spoke in quieter tones. Kat hadn't even wanted to stand by Kennedy, let alone flirt with him. It also surprised Malcolm to discover she had an intelligent mind. Since they had married, he thought of her as a brainless henwit, but last night she'd present-ed herself in a new light. Not only did she have a head for business, but her political views had also changed.

Her actions confirmed his suspicions, and he needed to maintain his guard. He couldn't allow himself to soften toward her. With one little snap of her fingers, she could have him in front of the firing squad or a hangman's noose. He had to do what she wanted, if just for a few months longer.

After his bath, he dressed his best for the important meeting this morning. Colonel Burwell had scheduled an appointment to consider the sketches Malcolm had drawn for the new vessels the prince regent's navy were interested in purchasing. And, if all went according to plan, Malcolm would find himself a guest at the colonel's weekend party in a couple of weeks.

Exactly what he wanted in order to spy on the man.

He studied his reflection in the mirror as he tied his cravat and grinned. One way or another, he'd find not only the person responsible for stealing the drawings Malcolm had been working on for the prince's navy, but he would find the person responsible for trying to ruin his life. He knew they were two separate people, and he had to keep searching for more clues.

However, he had to do this alone. Mr. Kennedy and the other partner, Mr. Joseph Crowley, couldn't suspect what Malcolm was trying to accomplish—just in case they were involved, too. Under no circumstances would he allow someone to ruin his good name... even if it meant doing things that may not be legal in order to make justice prevail.

For the past twelve months, he'd secretly been soliciting himself and his drawings to the neighboring towns and farther out. He absolutely hated working with Brandon Kennedy, and he wanted to be on his own once more. But in order to make the money he was accustomed to, he must sneak around without anyone knowing. Especially Kat. If his wife knew, she'd run to Kennedy, and the man would drop Malcolm as a partner. Until he had enough clients on his own, he had to stay with Kennedy and Crawley.

Sadly, he suspected Kat was behind the stolen drawings, but he couldn't figure out how or why.

His upcoming meeting with the highly decorated prince regent's soldier was very important, and he couldn't let Kat sabotage this deal. But could the colonel have reasons for contacting Malcolm other than to draw plans for the vessels?

Malcolm shook his head, trying to force the questions to leave. He couldn't think of that. Right now, Kat's return would be of the utmost importance. Her strange behavior made him more prudent.

Slipping on his waistcoat, he strode out of the room. Halfway down the stairs, voices of his wife and one of the servants lifted, echoing in the corridor. He stopped, wondering why Kat was awake at this hour. And why were she and the cook discussing the shopping list? Kat had never once acted the part of his wife, especially when it came to household duties.

Quiet as possible, he stepped softly into the corridor. Kat's back faced him, and the schoolmarm's knot of hair on her head made him pause. What happened to the wild, untamed mass of curls she always wore? And why was she wearing a conservative dress? The straight lines of the high-waisted yellow and dark brown gown flattened over her back yet accentuated her slender neck. She looked very regal, and very fitting as his wife. Finally.

If only she was the woman he'd always wanted, instead of one that didn't keep to her marriage vows.

Clearing his throat, he forced his thoughts in a different direction. When she turned and he caught the full effect of the modest dress, his interest in her grew. Why did she look prettier than he'd ever seen her? Anger boiled inside him, and he clenched his fists. That was something he should *not* think about her.

He narrowed his eyes. "Good morning, Mrs. Worthington. You are up early this morning."

She smiled, and for the first time he could remember, it looked genuine. She stepped toward him as Horace moved into the kitchen.

"I could not sleep a moment longer. The sun practically pushed me out of bed." Camilla's voice lifted with enthusiasm.

An ache pounded in his forehead, and he rubbed it with his fingers. Something wasn't right. She usually slept late because of her nocturnal interests. "What are your plans for the day, may I ask?"

"I'm collecting a shopping list and will venture into the marketplace. I thought about taking James and Lizzy."

Anger grew inside his chest like a boiling volcano. What was she thinking? He could never trust her with his children again. Shaking her back to reality seemed like a logical choice, but instead, he stuffed his hands into his pockets. "Why would you want to take my children with you, may I ask?"

Her smile faded. "I... I just thought they might enjoy an outing."

"Why, so you can leave them frightened and alone again?"

She frowned, but blinked with surprise. Clearly, she was appalled by his words.

"I wouldn't do that," she said.

He rolled his eyes. "Of course not," he mocked. "Except for those occasions you were tempted by another man and felt the urge to be alone with him, instead of watching my children."

She sucked in a quick breath but kept her chin up. "I assure you, the children will be at my side at all times."

"Do you expect me to believe you?" He folded his arms across his chest. "I don't think so. I will feel more at ease if you take along one of the servants."

"As you wish."

What he *wished* was to understand her. Since she returned, her actions had left him very confused. Frustration built inside him as he wondered what schemes were brewing in that devious mind of hers. He knew how to handle her shrewish ways, but not her complacency.

He stepped closer, and the skirt of her dress brushed against his leg. Her rose scent surrounded him, and he breathed in the heavenly fragrance. He wondered why she wasn't wearing the overpowering perfume that could stun small animals helpless for several minutes like she'd always worn.

Hard to admit, but he liked the changes in her. At the same time, he couldn't control the doubts burning inside his head. She'd mentioned before she wanted to change, but he just couldn't grasp the notion that she would. And even if she *wanted* to change, it didn't matter. He had no room in his heart for women like her.

"Kat, I know not of your game, but mark my words, you will not succeed in toying with my mind any longer. You will not win, especially when it comes to my children."

Her throat jumped. She blinked several times as excess moisture built in her eyes. Through her obvious emotional state, she kept her chin high and back straight. When she touched the sleeve of his arm, her hand shook, and once again he questioned her motives.

"Malcolm, please believe I will not harm your children. While I was away tending to my ailing sister, I realized the error of my behavior, and I vowed I would do everything possible to change myself." She licked her trembling lips. "I will not hurt James and Lizzy ever again."

A small throb built inside his head and confusion overwhelmed him. She was a good performer, but he wouldn't fall victim to her schemes, and he'd make certain his children didn't either.

"Mrs. Worthington, I will never again trust you with my children. If you want them to come with you then take a servant." She withdrew her hand, but he grabbed her wrist. "And if I find out you have hurt them, I swear to God—"

"Malcolm, I'll not hurt them. I assure you."

He detected a spark of fear in her wide eyes, and a hint of sadness, too. He quickly ushered out the idea of her being sorry for her actions. Kat cared naught for anyone but herself. This was just part of her plan to destroy him.

He dropped her wrist like a hot coal and stepped back. "Make certain Jane goes with you. Have a pleasant afternoon, Mrs. Worthington."

Tears filled her eyes. He couldn't stand to look at her any longer—for fear her tears would make him sorry for his words—so he turned and stormed out of the house. Indeed, she was a great performer, but he would stay one step ahead of her.

Chapter Four

C AMILLA PLACED A shaky hand over the erratic beat of her heart. Once the door slammed, announcing Malcolm's departure, she breathed a sigh of relief. Thankfully, she hadn't humiliated herself in front of him by crying.

He thinks I'm Kat, she tried to reason, but her trembling body would not listen to that rationale. Changing his mind was most important. If he couldn't trust her, he wouldn't allow her into his life so she could spy on him.

A nudge of guilt lodged in her heart for the deception, yet when she remembered the way Kat had pleaded, *begged* for Camilla to make Malcolm pay for ruining her twin's life, she hardened her heart once more. Kat had been a loving woman at one time until Malcolm altered her.

Dabbing a fingertip at the moisture gathering in her eyes, Camilla proceeded into the kitchen, where the large, cheerful woman awaited her.

"Is everything all right, Mrs. Worthington?"

Camilla smiled. "Splendid, Horace."

"Here's the list."

Camilla took the paper from Horace. "Do you know if my husband left money for me to go shopping?"

The servant's brow creased. "Why no, Mrs. Worthington, of course not. He has an account in all the stores."

"Oh, I know," Camilla said, recovering quickly, "but I just thought about purchasing something nice for James and Lizzy."

The older woman arched a suspicious eyebrow. "You can charge it to Mr. Worthington's account."

Camilla tried to keep the smile pasted on her lips, although she wanted to scream with frustration. Perhaps she was being too obvious. She needed to gain Malcolm's trust, therefore she must act like a good wife and loving mother. Convincing him of that would be a challenge, though.

"Yes, of course." Camilla folded the paper and slipped it inside her small wrist-purse.

"Have a pleasant outing, Mrs. Worthington."

"Thank you. I plan on having a wonderful time."

She left the kitchen and moved toward the stairs to collect the children, hoping the maid, Jane, had them ready. The children descended the stairs with dreary expressions that tugged at her heart. She wanted to be the one to remove their frowns and, more importantly, their fear.

In their morning together, she hoped to prove Kat wasn't the bad stepmother Malcolm had convinced them she was. When the truth finally came out, she wanted James and Lizzy to look upon her as the caring aunt—someone they could depend on to care for their welfare when their father was arrested for his crimes.

As the children neared, she gave a reassuring smile. "I'm so delighted you will be joining me. We shall have an exciting day."

James shrugged, and Lizzy's gaze stayed on her shiny brown shoes. Camilla sighed. The morning would be difficult, but well worth the effort. She took James's hand and tried to take Lizzy's, but the little girl scurried to the other side of her brother and clasped his hand. She led the two outside to the awaiting buggy.

Malcolm's servant, Broderick, stood by the vehicle waiting to assist. She tried to ignore his wry stare as he helped the children climb aboard, but when she made an attempt to step up into the back, he tugged on her arm.

"Mrs. Worthington," he said. "Where are you going? You

always sit up here with me."

"Not today, Broderick. I will sit in the back with James and Lizzy. Jane can sit up front with you."

She pulled her arm from his grasp and climbed in back. James locked his stare with hers, his eyes wide.

"Is that all right with you?" she asked the boy.

He nodded, a small grin tugging at his mouth. Her heart melted.

The morning turned out better than she expected. Although Lizzy still didn't speak, James enlightened her about some of his adventures. She listened and laughed at his stories. She even dared tell a few stories of her own childhood. The boy's countenance changed. She was headed in the right direction in her quest to win his heart.

James held her hand as they wandered through the market, Lizzy and Jane following not far behind. Every so often, she turned and looked at the adorable four-year-old and smiled, asking if she were all right. It was Jane, not Lizzy, who gave a positive response each time.

Although Camilla tried not to act as if this were her first time in Dorchester, she couldn't help but fall in love with the town. Finally, a place she could walk down the streets and feel free. No restrictions from her deceased husband's gambling debts. And if she dared admit, no restraints from her twin sister's overpowering hold.

Yet Kat still controlled her now, even in death. Thankfully, it wasn't the same.

The group hurried into the next shop, and Camilla's smile stretched wider. Just what she had wanted to find.

"James." She crouched to his level. "Would you and Lizzy like to get a gift for your father?"

"Oh, yes." He nodded fiercely. "May we?"

"Of course. Let's see." She scanned the room that held only a few patrons. "What do you think your father would like?"

Jerking on her arm, James pulled her to a table of elegant and expensive slippers. She gasped at the price. These merchants were nothing but thieves.

James and Lizzy moved to the next table, and Camilla took Jane aside. "Do you think my husband would mind us purchasing some items at this shop?"

"Why would he mind?" Jane shrugged. "This is where he buys most of his clothing."

Camilla sighed. "Splendid. Then I shall not worry."

Jane joined the children as they wandered through the store, but Camilla's attention shot to a full case full of beautifully crafted sabers and daggers. Hopefully, Malcolm wouldn't think it too personal if she bought him a gift too. After all, she was his wife.

The store attendant came to her side. "Good afternoon, Mrs. Worthington. Are you finding everything you need?"

She smiled at the silver-haired gentleman. "Yes. You have such a remarkable selection I wouldn't know which one to choose."

"You are purchasing something for your husband?"

"I am." She looked back at the shelf. "What do you think he would like?"

"Oh, madame, I can help with that." He reached inside the glass case and pulled out a jeweled dagger. "Your husband has been eyeing this for weeks. This particular dagger came from a German trader. As you can see, the handle is littered with sparkling emerald and rubies, which was the very thing that caught Mr. Worthington's eye."

She nibbled on her lip, hesitating. The dagger was indeed the finest she'd ever seen.

"May I say, Mrs. Worthington, many men have come into the store and gazed upon this particular dagger in envy. Any man would love to be the owner of this elegant gift."

Malcolm would certainly think her forward for purchasing this for him. She barely knew him. Then again, from what she'd observed so far, Kat hadn't known him well either. And Camilla wanted to gain his trust any way she could.

However, she would eventually sell it and use the money to pay for Kat's medical bills. The end result would be worth it.

"Shall I put it on your account, Mrs. Worthington?"

"Yes, put it on my account," she said before changing her mind.

"Fine choice, Mrs. Worthington. Knowing your husband as I do, I believe he would appreciate a gift like this."

While the man wrapped it, she clamped her mouth closed, trying not to withdraw her decision. She didn't necessarily have to *give* it to him. Although she hated to lie, she would tell Malcolm some excuse of how she bought it for him but lost it.

Guilt for what she was doing gnawed at her stomach. But when she remembered what her sister's frail body in the unkempt room had looked like, Camilla hardened her heart. Not only that, but the box Kat had been buried in wasn't fit for an animal.

Her sister's memory came first, as it should be.

As COLONEL BURWELL flipped through the drawings, Malcolm held his breath, waiting for him to make a decision. He could ill afford another problem at this point, and he prayed the colonel would be impressed with his work. The man turned the last page, and his eyes narrowed as if he were studying the final outline.

"Worthington?" He stood as a smile finally touched his mouth. "These sketches are fascinating. How soon can your company build these vessels?"

Relief poured through Malcolm and his heart hammered with anticipation. He wanted to shout with happiness, but kept focused on remaining serious in front of the man. "That particular matter we will have to take up with Mr. Kennedy and Mr. Crowley. Building the vessels is their part of the business. I only draw."

Burwell laughed and slapped him on the back. "I like you,

Worthington. You have a good head on your shoulders, and it's refreshing to know a man who is not afraid to use his intellect."

"Thank you. That is quite a compliment, colonel."

"Since I'm already acquainted with Mr. Kennedy, I have no qualms about hiring your team to build new ships for the navy—if the sketches don't get lost as they did the time before. We cannot wait for you to draw up new ones, you know."

Inwardly, Malcolm grumbled. He would find the person responsible no matter what. "Of course, colonel. I shall make it my duty to guard them with my life."

The colonel nodded. "I'm certain you will, Worthington." He grabbed his hat and turned toward the door. "Have Mr. Kennedy pay me a visit and we shall discuss payment."

Malcolm held his breath again, praying for the invitation he had been hoping would come for a couple of days now, but the arrogant Colonel Burwell just plopped his hat on his head and walked out of the office without another word.

Malcolm gnashed his teeth and stormed to his desk. The deal he made with Colonel Burwell would make him a very rich man, but if he didn't find those responsible for stealing his drawings, Malcolm would be out of work permanently. Rumors alone could ruin him.

Sighing, he sank into his hard wooden chair and turned his gaze to the office window and the busy main street below. Although grateful for his partnership with Brandon Kennedy and Joseph Crowley, he longed for the freedom during the day to do whatever he wished. Before he married Kat, he'd had that kind of life. In fact, he could have made a decent life for his new wife and children, but Kat had to have more. She had to have a wealthier husband. Well, now she had one, yet she was still drawn to other men and thrived on their compliments—amongst other things.

The brilliant scarlet coat of Colonel Burwell drew his attention as the man stopped in front of a shop and talked with a woman. Malcolm wouldn't have bothered with his curiosity, but two small children stood by the woman's side.

Kat!

Malcolm jumped up and moved to the window. Although the colonel had his back toward him, Kat smiled as she chatted with the soldier. Even from Malcolm's vantage point, he realized the way she spoke with the other man was far different than before. Kat always had to touch the man, bat her eyes, and use her perfectly shaped lips to pout. But she was doing none of that now. Why?

After a few minutes, the colonel walked away, and Kat and the children moved on to the next shop. Malcolm had threatened her this morning to take special care of his children, and it surprised him she had actually listened. Even the maid walked behind holding Lizzy's hand.

He raked his fingers through his hair and exhaled deeply. His mind hadn't been focused since Kat had returned from her secret little holiday, and he didn't like the confusion swimming in his head. It was as if she were a completely different person.

The chiming from the bell on the door pulled Malcolm's attention to the front office. His friend stepped into view and pulled off his hat.

Malcolm smiled. "Broderick? What are you doing here?"

The younger man walked to the desk and sat on the corner, swinging his leg. "I followed your wife as you had requested, but I must say, there is something very different about her."

"What have you seen?" Malcolm sat behind his desk again, linking his fingers and resting his elbows on the top.

"To begin with, she wouldn't sit in the front of the buggy with me but insisted on being in the back with your children. Not once throughout the morning has she flirted with any men. When she walked past the soldiers outside the tavern, she just nodded and proceeded on her way." Broderick shook his head. "I tell you, Malcolm, her strange behavior has me worried."

"I think she knows we are watching her, so she is on guard." Malcolm scrubbed his hand over his chin. "She is a great performer, but she will slip up one of these days, and I will be right there when she does."

"What are you watching for?"

"I don't believe she went to visit her sister. I'm more inclined to think she spent time with some soldier. It could have been Colonel Burwell, for that matter. I think she knows a vital piece of information that might help me find the true thief, but I'm going to catch her before she acts on her knowledge. For some reason—which I cannot fathom—I think she wants to bring me down. She wants me to fail and lose my reputation. Yet I don't know why she would want that, since my wealth affects her as well."

Broderick nodded. "I'll be alert for any peculiar activity."

Malcolm stretched his legs beneath the solid oak desk. Two things were certain: someone was trying to ruin him by stealing his drawings and selling them, and his wife was up to something that was not good. His gut told him the two were related in some way. Already the people on his suspects list were Brandon Kennedy, Captain Wilkes, and Colonel Burwell. And Malcolm also suspected his competitor, Mr. Clarkston. That man had always been sneaky. He couldn't help but wonder if Kat was the ringleader in this conspiracy.

Inwardly, he groaned. Thinking of that woman caused him more worries than normal. He hesitated in asking his friend one particular question, only because the subject made him irritable, but he had to know. "Broderick? Has she snuck away from the house to meet secretly with a man since she has been back?"

"No, not at all. And I have kept constant watch on her." Broderick moved to the window and peered out.

Malcolm shook his head. "Something isn't right, and it's maddening."

Broderick turned and looked at him. "I shall keep following her. I'll not let you down."

Malcolm smiled, but it wasn't fully. "I know. Keep a sharp eye. She is a sneaky one."

Broderick left the building, and Malcolm was thankful his

friend was so loyal. Broderick had discovered Kat sneaking out of the house one week after she and Malcolm were married. She enjoyed charming almost every man she came in contact with—except her own husband. Sometimes Malcolm wondered why he repulsed her so.

Kat was very much like his first wife, Victoria, in that respect.

He groaned and slunk lower in his chair. Victoria, the sweet, caring, and tender mother of his children. The perfect wife... until it came to performing the wifely duties she abhorred. He tried to convince her making love wasn't a chore, but a pleasurable, natural experience between husband and wife. Victoria didn't see it that way.

At times during their marriage, he had felt less than a man, but he always stayed true to their vows. On her deathbed, she urged him to find another wife, a mother to raise their children. When he first met Kat—through her father—Malcolm thought she was the one. Just like Victoria, Kat had been innocent and shy, so he didn't rush her. Within a week, he discovered from Broderick that Kat had been unfaithful. Even with Malcolm's business partner, Brandon Kennedy, for goodness' sake! After that, Malcolm hadn't wanted to touch his wife.

He picked up his quill and concentrated on his sketches, but from outside, a woman's sweet laughter rose above the hustle from the busy street. He lifted his gaze out the window. Kat skipped with his children down the street. For the first time since Victoria died, a smile highlighted his son's face as he held on to Kat's hand and looked up into her eyes.

The mismatched pair hurried across the street toward his office, and Malcolm's heart melted. Quick as lightning, he cursed the feeling, reminding himself this was only an act. Kat wasn't the loving and charming woman she portrayed, but a she-devil in disguise. He couldn't allow himself to trust her.

Not now.

Not ever.

Chapter Five

MORNING WOULD SOON be here, yet Malcolm hadn't slept. He moved to the window and parted the curtain. He couldn't understand his wife and her actions of late, which had his mind whirling with speculation.

A sheath of dark brown cloaked the land, and lightning flashed in the distance, followed by a low rumble of thunder. Storms had always soothed him, and he was content to sit and watch.

Yesterday, Malcolm had anticipated a visit by the little group at his office, but instead Kat took his children home. When he returned to the house after work, his eager little boy described in great detail their morning, and both James and Lizzy presented him with gifts—a silver clothing brush and brown slippers.

The joyous moments with his children felt like Christmas all over again. It softened Malcolm's heart to know Kat had indeed treated them well, yet that worried him even more. He couldn't trust her, no matter what.

Malcolm dressed for the day. Both Kennedy and Crowley would be back in the office, and Malcolm awaited the news of their new contract with the Royal Navy. He especially hoped to hear more about Colonel Burwell's activities, since he still sought an invitation to the colonel's weekend party.

Malcolm suspected there was something secretive going on

between the colonel and Kennedy, especially regarding Malcolm's partnership. Brandon had never really wanted Malcolm to become a partner, but Kat convinced Brandon to bring him on.

He left the bedroom and walked down the stairs to the dining room. The scent of scones and strong coffee filtered through the air, making his stomach grumble. He sat at the table, where his morning newspaper awaited him.

"Good morning, Horace," he greeted the cook.

"It sure is a happy morning, Mr. Worthington."

He flipped open the paper. "Did my children tell you about their eventful morning yesterday?"

"Aye, they did." She laughed, and the extra flesh on her chin and neck shook in rhythm. "James is still talking about it this morning."

Malcolm lowered the paper and stared at her. "This morning? James is already awake?"

"Why, yes. Him and Mrs. Worthington went outside to watch Levi and Hiram exercise the horses."

"What?" Malcolm jumped out of his chair, hurried to the window, and looked toward the stables just down the hill.

His son stood beside Kat, his eyes wide as his head swung back and forth between her and the horse. Then his son laughed for the second time since his mother had died. Kat reached down and stroked James's cheek, her face lit with merriment.

A throb in the base of Malcolm's skull began, pounding harder the more his anger climbed. He fisted his hands before slamming them on the windowpane. What was her intent this time?

Putting aside his morning meal, he marched outside toward the stables, ready to verbally shred his wife. He neared, and the joyous peals of laughter from his son filled the quiet morning air, decreasing his anger. Crisp morning wind whipped around his son's head and teased the baby curls dampened against his moist forehead. James glanced Malcolm's way, broke away from the fence, and ran toward him.

"Papa, do you know what? We're watching the horses get exercised, and in a few minutes Milla will let me ride with her."

Malcolm knelt in front of James and brushed his hand across his son's red cheeks. Kat met his gaze over James's head. She smiled, and tightness gripped his chest.

"Good morning, Malcolm," she acknowledged him, her voice filled with sweetness.

He wished she wouldn't say his name in such a soft tone. The sound compared to heavenly harps as they played in his lonely ears, making him long for a relationship that would never happen. More importantly, it made him wish for the wife she would never be.

"Good morning, Kat. What is this I hear about your going for a morning ride with my son?" He stood and stepped toward her.

"Yesterday James mentioned he had not been riding, and I thought—"

"You should not think without consulting with me first." His voice boomed through the air.

Kat's smile faded and the light in her green eyes dimmed. The urge to apologize hung strong on Malcolm's tongue. He shouldn't have spoken so roughly. But he remained stern in his decision. That woman could *not* be trusted.

"As you wish. I will do so now." She lifted her chin. "Will you allow James to go on a short ride with me this morning?"

Before he could answer, his son yanked on Malcolm's sleeve. "Please, Papa? I really wanna go with Milla."

Malcolm arched his brow at his wife. "Milla? When did he start addressing you by that name?"

"When I gave him permission to use my nickname."

"I thought your nickname was Kat."

"No. You are the only person who has ever called me that name, which I still don't understand, since it's not my name."

"I call you Kat because of the wild streak in you. You are a wild cat."

"I believe you call me that to irritate me."

"Aye. The name fits the reputation of the woman I married quite well."

"Papa?" James tugged on his sleeve again. "Please don't be mad."

Malcolm glanced down into the pleading eyes of his son and smiled, knowing he couldn't deny him anything. "I'm not angry, James, but I would like to talk to Camilla for a few minutes. Will you go to the house and help Horace in the kitchen?"

James frowned. "No. You're gonna yell at Milla again, and I wanna go riding."

"James," Malcolm said in a sharp tone. "Do as I say."

"James, honey?" The mysterious woman crouched to the boy's level. She smiled, her eyes softening. "If your father doesn't wish you to go riding with me, we must obey. Perhaps he thinks you are still too young. I should have asked before inviting you."

Malcolm's heart softened. Frowning, he gritted his teeth and wished he wouldn't react in such a way when she displayed such kindness. Obviously, it was just an act.

"But..." James mumbled, and then looked back at him. "Papa? It's all right, you know. I'm a big boy now. I think I can ride a horse as long as Milla helps me." He moved away from her and over to Malcolm's leg. "'Sides, I like her now. She isn't mean anymore." His grin widened. "Even Lizzy is starting to like her."

Anger welled inside Malcolm, threatening to suffocate him. He swallowed and forced a smile. "Fine. You can go riding, but not today. You and Kat can go another time. Right now, I need to speak with her."

His son pouted and hung his head. "Oh, all right." James turned to Kat. "We shall have to go riding another time."

She stood. "That is fine."

With wilted shoulders, James moved back toward the house, dragging his feet with every step and kicking the damp soil.

Once the boy was out of sight, Malcolm turned his attention back on Kat and glared. "What is going on?"

He stepped closer, and the fragrance of her rose-scented soap eased his anger slightly. He closed his eyes and breathed deeper. Realizing what he was doing, he jerked them open and clamped his teeth.

Not knowing what was happening to him, he vowed he wouldn't let the deceiving woman get to him. Yet when he gazed over every inch of her face, his heart leapt to his throat, ignoring the anger he wanted to hold on to. Her beautiful forest-green eyes had a hint of liquid as if she struggled with her emotions. Her heart-shaped lips parted, and a scent of mint blew across his face.

Without being able to control his actions, he touched his finger to her chin, stroking it across her delicate, smooth skin and down her neck until it rested on the high collar of her jacket. Her beauty and the softness of her creamy skin turned his mind to mush. He was helpless to stop the burning sensations ripping through him. He waited for her to swat his hand like she'd done before whenever he touched her in a personal way. She didn't, and his heart picked up rhythm.

He arched his brow. "Kat, why are you doing this?"

"Doing what?"

"Why are you trying to act like somebody you are not? Your words are very confusing."

The corners of her lips lifted. "I assure you, I'm not trying to be."

He slid his finger from her chin upward to touch her delicate earlobe. "Stop playing this game with me."

"But Malcolm, I have changed."

"Nobody can make such a drastic change."

"I have." She touched the lapel of his coat. "I'm not the same woman you first met." Her shy smile widened. "And I have come to care for the children."

A powerful jolt shot through him as if he'd been scorched. Between the heat from her hand touching him and her unbelievable words, his confusion grew by leaps and bounds.

He dropped his hand and stepped back. "I don't want you to

care for them, Kat."

"Malcolm, will you not give me another chance?"

Aha, her game was out now. She wanted to charm him like she did other men. Well, he wasn't like other men, and he wouldn't let her succeed.

She stretched her hand out to touch him again, but he grasped on to it.

"Stop, Kat. I'm warning you, your charm will not work with me."

"Malcolm, please—"

"And stop calling me Malcolm."

"Why?"

"Because I don't like the way it sounds when it comes from your deceiving mouth." He dropped his focus to her enticing, delicate raspberry lips, imagining what her kiss would taste like. Honeysuckle? Whatever the taste, he was quite certain it would be heavenly. But he couldn't think this way. Ever!

"What do you want me to call you then?" she said hesitantly. "Mr. Worthington is too formal. I'm your wife and should address you with some kind of endearment."

"You are my wife in name only, and I plan on keeping it that way."

She swallowed, and his gaze dropped further to the slender column of her throat. The urge to press his lips to that location overwhelmed him. His grip loosened, but she didn't pull her hand away. In fact, she moved closer.

"Malcolm." Her voice softened. "I will not give up. I deserve a second chance."

Between her intoxicating scent and her alluring mouth, he was a drowning man. How could he resist? But he had to. He tried to remember how she had deceived him since they were first married, hoping it would cool his ardor, but her sweet charm made him weaker.

Confused by mixed emotions, he growled in anger, and then stepped away. "You are wrong, Kat. Women like you deserve no second chances."

He turned and stalked back to the house, resisting the urge to look at her. He couldn't risk a glance. He didn't want to think that he could have taken her in his arms and kissed her. Being attracted to her was dangerous—especially when he had never been before.

CAMILLA RODE THE horse hard, disappointed in how the morning had gone so far. The cool breeze from last night's storm stung her cheeks, dried her lips, and unraveled the ringlets in her hair. She didn't care, because riding this way usually healed her. Yet today, it hadn't. She still couldn't believe she had allowed Malcolm's nearness to affect her. And his touch nearly had her melting to the ground.

Today's outing was to ride to the neighboring towns and sell the dagger she had bought, but sadly, none of the shops would offer the price needed to pay Kat's medical bills. If only Camilla could trust Malcolm enough to ask him.

When she pictured his wounded face from this morning, guilt gnawed at her conscience. It seemed he had been the person truly wronged by her sister's actions. But he wasn't the one who had gone mad and died, either. She must remember her sister above all else.

Was Malcolm the real reason for her sister's melancholy? Camilla had begun to think differently. Now that she knew him a little better, she didn't think he was at fault. From what she had observed and heard about her twin, Kat had done some despicable things to his children. Because of this, Camilla was drawn to his family. She wanted to show James and Lizzy a caring side, and to do anything she could to gain Malcolm's trust.

Although she really shouldn't feel attracted to Malcolm. Eventually she would discover those illegal things her sister had hinted about, and at that time, she would have him arrested. As soon as she accomplished this, she would take his adorable children and raise them as her own.

But the more Camilla thought of this plan, the more her heart crumbled. For some odd reason, she didn't *want* to discover he was doing something unlawful. The fluttering emotions in her belly and the tingling in her bosom—caused by Malcolm—were new and powerful. Against her own principles, she had enjoyed the way he looked at her with his smoldering gaze.

She glanced behind her to see Timothy crouched over his horse, eager to catch up. She slowed her horse until her servant rode beside her. She had already informed him about why she played her twin sister's role. Eager to help, Timothy had told her she could count on his assistance.

"Mistress?" he asked, out of breath. "Where are we going now?"

"There is one last town we can try, but I fear, because we have had no luck thus far, that our trip has been for naught. We will travel home after I visit a few more shops."

"I promise to do all I can to help you, but I fear being on the horse this long has bruised my backside."

Guilt tightened her chest. She should have thought of poor Timothy's frail body and perhaps taken the carriage. But horses were faster than a carriage, and she didn't want to be gone all day.

"Forgive me for torturing you this way, but when we return home, I'll let you rest the remainder of the day."

"Bless you, mistress."

As they came into town, she ran her hand over the package inside the saddlebag. After she had purchased the jewel-encrusted dagger, she changed her mind about selling it, and instead wanted to give it to Malcolm, hoping she would gain his trust quicker. But after the jolt of pleasure she had received from his soft touch and heated gaze this morning, she'd quickly changed her mind again.

The last thing Camilla needed right now was for the doctor to inform Malcolm his wife had died and debts needed to be paid. At least giving the doctor some money would keep him quiet for a little while longer.

Another hour later, and after being turned away from yet another store, tears stung her eyes. Panic edged its way into her mind. Would she ever get the money to pay Kat's bills? Needless to say, she would have to collect money in a different way. Now she must pick up the small amount of pride she still had and return to Malcolm's house.

As she moved toward her horse and servant, a man's red uniform captured her attention. She gaped at the tall soldier coming toward her. He was the same man she'd run into upon her arrival that first day. By his sly grin and arched brow, it appeared he wished to further their acquaintance.

He stopped in front of her and bowed. She curtsied, even if she didn't want to.

"Good afternoon, Mrs. Worthington." He tipped his hat.

She quickly studied his uniform to determine his status. "Good afternoon, captain."

"Soon to be colonel, remember?" He took her hand and placed a small kiss on her knuckle.

"Of course I remember." She wanted to withdraw, but his kiss wasn't completely improper... yet.

He glanced up and down the street, and when his eyes met hers again, a mischievous grin touched his mouth. His grip tightened as his fingers softly caressed the skin.

"Have you any more information for me, my dear Mrs. Worthington?"

She moaned inwardly. *Oh, no, not him, too.* What had Kat done this time? Camilla shook her head. "None whatsoever."

"And why not?" His brow creased. "Have your husband and his associates suddenly fallen off the face of the earth? I'm certain you have stumbled across some little tidbit about your husband's dealings."

Silently, she studied him. Could he be after what she was

after—information that would prove Malcolm a criminal? Although he was a royal soldier, she hesitated to trust him.

She pulled her hand away. "If you have not heard by now, captain, I have recently returned from Preston. What sort of information could I have gathered being gone?"

The corner of his mouth twitched into a half smirk. Again, he took her hand and brought it to his lips, brushing a soft kiss across her knuckles. She shuddered and yanked her hand away.

His eyes widened in surprise. "Are you toying with me again, Kat? Or are you waiting for a kiss before you give me what I want?"

Her stomach lurched. Instinct told her she had to act like Kat, but she couldn't bring herself to play this part. "No, captain. I am not waiting for any sort of kiss. As I told you before, I have no information. Now, if you will let me by?"

When she attempted to pass, he gripped her elbow, stopping her. Pain shot up her arm and she whimpered. Fear tried to make her succumb, but after everything that had happened today, anger took over.

"Madame Worthington, I warn you—"

"You warn *me*? I think not, sir. In fact, I'm warning you." She yanked her arm out of his grasp, hopefully for the last time. "I would appreciate it if you would cease jostling me in public. Moreover, you had better display your patience more accurately, my dear captain, or you will receive nothing further from me. Information or... other gifts." She marched back to her horse and quickly mounted. Timothy glared at the inane soldier as any protector would.

Before riding away, she witnessed the captain's shocked expression. She said a silent prayer of thanks for being able to control the conversation. From what she had gathered being in Kat's role, her sister had easily fallen for men's charms. But these men would soon learn this particular Mrs. Worthington comported herself with restraint.

Confusion clouded Camilla's mind, and she wanted the

pounding in her head to disappear. She must discover what secrets Malcolm hid, and soon. If Malcolm were a criminal, she would turn him in. If he wasn't, she prayed she would have the strength not to give him her heart.

Chapter Six

C AMILLA HESITATED TO leave her bath of luxury that evening, but the cold water threatened to turn her skin to prunes. As she towel-dried herself, the rose-scented soap assailed her senses, reminding her of home—a place she could not revisit in her mind without missing her father and sister.

She changed into a red evening dress. The selection of garments in her sister's closet didn't leave many suitable options. This particular dress had short, puffy sleeves, with white trim around the square bodice that was cut lower than she wanted. If only she could find that handkerchief she used the other evening.

Beth's absence, tonight of all nights, had Camilla sighing in frustration as she sat at the dressing table trying to style her own hair. She coiled her hair in a loose knot, leaving a few tendrils around her ears, then found some white earbobs.

Satisfied with her appearance, she made her way down the stairs toward the parlor, where the playful voices of Malcolm and his children resounded through the corridor. Although she had yet to hear Lizzy speak, the little girl's laughter lifted with merriment through the air.

The threesome didn't see her when she stepped into the room. What a heartwarming scene with Lizzy and James perched on Malcolm's lap as he read them a nursery story. Camilla had memorized the story when she was young, but it amazed her to hear Malcolm tell it. He added excitement, made the characters come to life, entertaining his children—and her—beyond belief. Warmth in her heart spread toward the man who might be committing unlawful acts. His ability to love his children unconditionally made her question whether he was truly as dishonest as Kat had led her to believe.

Malcolm's gaze finally lifted from the book and fell upon her, his expression softened, and a smile touched his mouth. The sentence he had been reading stopped as he scanned her from head to toe.

Fluttering sensations swept through her, and the new emotion turned her mouth dry, but the palms of her hands moistened. Her numb mind wouldn't allow her to think of a single word to say in greeting.

He closed the book, lifted his son and daughter off his lap, and stood. Like a panther stalking its prey, he slowly came toward her. The beating of her heart slammed against her ribs, but she remained still. A cheerful greeting came from James, but she couldn't take her eyes off the incredibly handsome man in front of her. His light gray coat blended with his fawn trousers, the color enhancing his eyes, making them sparkle brighter.

He stopped and lifted her hand to his lips, brushing a soft kiss on her knuckles. His eyes held hers. Scents of spice drifted around her, and although she wished otherwise, they stirred to life emotions hidden deep inside.

"Good evening, Camilla. It pleases me that you would join us."

Her heart soared. *He said my name!* The tender sound coming from his lips was like fingers plucking heavenly music from a harp.

"Of course, Malcolm. Why would I not want to be a part of such an entertaining group?" She bestowed upon him her best smile. "I don't think I have ever heard a more interesting story than what you were telling James and Lizzy."

James tugged on her skirt, his smile stretched from ear to ear.

"Milla? Do you wanna have Papa read to you, too?"

She nibbled on her lower lip and hesitated before nodding.

"Papa?" James continued. "Milla wants to read with us."

Malcolm chuckled. "But James, with you and your sister on my lap, I don't think I'll be able to fit Camilla there as well."

Her gaze snapped up to meet his smoldering eyes. Just the idea of sitting so close to him, and in that fashion, made her cheeks burn. She cleared her throat. "That is just as well. I'll be more comfortable on the sofa."

Malcolm took her hand and wrapped it around his elbow. "Why do we not all sit on the sofa?"

She was certain she appeared like a love-struck girl while dreamily staring into his eyes as she walked with him to the furniture. Yet she couldn't tear away from him. His charm intoxicated her, and she wanted to lose herself in it.

James and Lizzy climbed back onto their father's lap, and Camilla sat by his side. Every once in a while, his elbow brushed against her arm, and she forced herself not to sigh aloud from the warm pleasure rippling through her. Strange how one subtle movement could create such heated explosions.

Malcolm's deep voice hypnotized her. Laying her head on the back of the sofa and turning slightly, she stared at his profile and absorbed his words. After three more stories, he had complete control over her, whether he wanted to or not.

When the servant announced the children's bedtime, Camilla jumped to a sitting position and blinked the daze from her eyes. James gave her a kiss on the cheek, then a hug. Lizzy wouldn't kiss her, but Camilla received a small hug from the little girl.

Her heart tugged from their sweet gestures. Lizzy and James placed kisses on their father's cheek before leaving the room with Jane. Although Camilla had never conceived a child with her husband, perhaps someday she would find a man to have children with that would shower such affection on her.

Malcolm closed the book and placed it on the table in front of them. He stretched his arms over his head. It fascinated her, the way the fabric of his clothes pulled tight across his muscles. As he relaxed, he laid an arm across the back and turned and looked at her. His hand rested dangerously close to her shoulder, and she wanted to cuddle against it, but resisted with every fiber of her being.

A smile touched his lips. "Thank you for spending time with the children. They really enjoyed your presence this evening."

She returned a smile. "It was my pleasure." She glanced over at the parlor door, then back to him. "But why did they leave before supper?"

"They have already eaten."

"Why can they not share the meal with us?"

He opened his mouth to answer, but hesitated as his brows drew together. "I have never thought of that." He shrugged. "I suppose they may join us, if that is what you wish."

"I think it would be wonderful to have us all eat together."

"Why would you find that wonderful?" He turned his body her way. "In fact, why are you here right now?"

She sighed heavily. *Oh, not again.* "I haven't done so lately, and I wished to get to know you and your children better." She paused. "Does that make me a criminal?"

"No, just different from the Kat I know."

She tried to swallow the lump caught in her throat. She didn't dare encourage him, but she must. "Then forget the woman you once knew and look more closely at the Camilla sitting next to you now. I assure you, they are two different people."

His gaze touched every inch of her face before resting on her lips. Her skin warmed, and she enjoyed the feeling. She waited for him to unleash his anger, but he remained calm and relaxed. Envious of his ability to stay composed, she worried her whole body would come apart at any moment.

"At times you almost have me fooled, Mrs. Worthington. Deep down I want to believe you are different, but I have lived with you long enough to know otherwise."

His fingers moved to her cheek and stroked her skin. Tingles danced down her spine.

"Outwardly," he continued, "you are the beautiful woman I thought I married, but..." His finger trailed down her neck to her collarbone.

She held her breath. Why did she ache for his tender caress, and especially his kind words?

"Inside this beautiful woman lurks evil, darker and more sinister than I could have imagined. You have plans swimming around in your lovely head that are meant to hurt and destroy people's lives."

Inwardly, she cringed. What exactly had her sister done to make him believe such things? She wanted to confess her true identity, simply to hear soft, gentle words leave his mouth.

"Malcolm," she whispered, her breaths coming in short gasps. "You shouldn't be so unkind. You don't know what happened to me when I went to be with my sister."

"Shh," he said in a husky tone.

She wanted to continue, but his knuckles continued to stroke her neck. Holding her breath, she waited for his next move.

"Say no more." He leaned closer as his other arm dropped from the back of the sofa and circled her shoulders. His mouth was mere inches above hers. "I don't care what happened. But just for tonight, I want to imagine you are somebody else and not the selfish woman I married."

"I *am* somebody else," she whispered.

Gently, he touched his lips to hers. Heated sparks multiplied through her body, and she released a sigh. His lips nipped at hers and then caressed back and forth, urging her to relax. She mirrored his movements, hoping nothing would break the spell. He pulled her closer, and she laid her hand on his chest. Beneath her palm, the wild beating of his heart vibrated. Her heartbeat matched his rhythm perfectly.

He cupped the side of her face. The tenderness of his touch melted her even more, and a small groan tore from her throat. Within that moment, he slid his tongue into her mouth. Shock vibrated through her, but so did pleasure, overriding any emotion she had. The hot, velvety texture of his tongue stroking awareness into her mouth was her undoing. This time when she sighed, her chest rattled.

She had never felt anything so exhilarating in her life. Her husband had been too demanding, and she liked the gentleness Malcolm displayed much more. She itched to caress him, to run her fingers through his hair just like she had imagined that first day when they met. But before she could summon the courage, the dinner bell rang.

He jerked away, peering at her with smoldering eyes. His gaze jumped between her mouth and her eyes before his brows drew together in confusion.

She caught her breath, hoping he didn't doubt his own actions. She hadn't. She wanted more. "Malcolm." She reached for him, but he jumped from the sofa as if he had been burned.

"Mrs. Worthington." His tone had turned cold once again. "I hope you have a nice meal tonight, because I have suddenly lost my appetite."

He rushed out of the parlor. The slamming of the front door confirmed his departure.

ANGRY VOICES WOKE Camilla from a most pleasurable dream. As her mind slowly became alert, she still experienced the tingling of Malcolm's lips on hers, and his fingers across her neck. In her dream their kiss hadn't been interrupted, and he had caressed her neck, her shoulders, and down her bosom. In her dream, his lips had followed the trail of his hands.

Now awake, she scolded herself for becoming so infatuated with her sister's husband.

Camilla's mind argued, reminding her Kat was dead. But she countered that Kat would be turning in her grave if she knew what thoughts swam in Camilla's mind right now.

The volume from below increased, bringing her fully awake. Whoever had intruded upon the Worthington home hadn't stopped to think of the early hour.

She slipped out of bed and wrapped the silk robe around her nightgown before going to the bedroom door and opening it. She listened to the voices rising from the entry hall. Broderick's voice boomed loudly, commanding the rude visitors to leave, but judging by the grumbles and protests, his demands fell on deaf ears.

Camilla stepped to the railing and peered down toward the front door. Four soldiers stood just inside, scowls etched on their faces as they clutched their rifles, looking ready for battle. When she recognized the captain who had accosted her the night before, her heart sank.

The captain puffed out his chest and moved directly in front of Broderick. "We wish to speak to Mr. Worthington. Sir, this is not a request, but an order."

Broderick blocked their entrance with his body, keeping his arms straight as he braced the doorframe. "And I told you, Mr. Worthington is sleeping. No decent person with any scruples would call at this hour. Please return at a later time."

The captain pushed a finger in Broderick's chest. "Listen, you rude slip of a man, I'm on important business and I have matters to take up with Worthington himself, so if you will kindly move aside?"

Defiantly, Broderick shook his head. By the soldiers' scowls and creased brows, they weren't going to turn and retreat either. Any moment now the soldiers would override Broderick's tactics, Camilla realized.

"What is your business, Captain Wilkes?" Broderick demanded.

"Late last night, a mob of men broke into Mr. Clarkston's office and stole some important files. We were told Mr. Worthington and Mr. Clarkston have had grievances with each other in the past."

Broderick nodded. "They have, but only because Mr. Clarkston has the same career as Mr. Worthington. So, what of it?"

"A witness to the incident thought he recognized Worthington."

"Impossible." Broderick snickered. "Mr. Worthington was home all evening. Last night he played with his children and had dinner with his wife. After dinner, they retired for the night, and Mr. Worthington has been in his room ever since."

Camilla gasped, then quickly covered her mouth. *He lied!*

"Well then," Captain Wilkes snapped, finally pushing past Broderick and entering the house, "Mr. Worthington should not be too upset if we ask him a few questions."

Camilla's heart hammered. Malcolm had left last night, and although she didn't know what time he'd returned, she prayed he hadn't done what the captain accused him of doing. Giving him an alibi would not only help him but help her. She didn't want Malcolm to be arrested by the soldiers... yet. She needed more time to discover the truth. Perhaps doing this for Malcolm would also allow him to trust her.

Without another thought, she rushed down the hall and into his bedroom. The drapes were pulled closed, and very little light helped her find his bed. After stubbing her toe on the corner of a chair, and then again on the end of the bed, she reached the side. She threw off her robe before crawling on the mattress next to him.

"Malcolm, wake up." In desperation, she shook him. Moaning, he turned toward her, and his muscular arm pinned her down. Just like last night when he had touched her, tingles spread throughout her body. She put aside the glorious feeling for now.

"Malcolm, please wake up." Her heart hammered. "The soldiers will be here at any moment."

She blinked, adjusting her eyes to the darkness until Malcolm's face came into focus. He raised his head and looked at her with confusion on his face.

"Malcolm, it is I, Camilla. Now wake up."

Quick as lightning, he bolted up straight and cursed. He grasped his head as if it were going to explode.

"Malcolm, be silent and listen. There are soldiers downstairs trying to force their way into the house. Broderick is keeping them away for now, but he cannot overpower them. I heard the captain say you were with a group of men last night who broke into Mr. Clarkston's office and stole some files." His forehead creased, but she continued. "I want to believe you were not part of that, but because you left last night, I cannot be certain."

He scowled, pursing his lips.

"Malcolm, I can make them believe you were here all night, but you have to promise you were not part of that group."

"I wasn't part of that group," he rasped.

She breathed a sigh of relief. "Good, but now I need to know where you were. If I lie and say I was with you, I have to know those soldiers will never discover the truth. If they find out, my very life would be at risk."

"I am aware of that."

Out in the corridor, pounding feet running up the stairs echoed. She gasped. "So, will you tell me?"

He looked away, but a small growl came from his throat. "I was at a tavern." His eyes darted back to hers. "But it is not the way you are thinking." He grumbled again and shook his head. "I don't know why I'm telling you. You don't care, anyway."

A wrenching pain speared her heart, making it hard to breathe. How could he leave her arms right after sharing a heated kiss and go get sloshed in a tavern? She wanted to yell at him and give him a sermon on the effects of consuming such vile drinks, but there was no time to act upon her turbulent emotions.

Forcing aside the hurt feelings, she laid her hand on his arm. "I will help you." Angry voices and hurried footsteps grew louder. "Quickly, lie back and pretend you are sleeping," she commanded, cuddling beside him.

He wrapped his arm around her shoulders, pulling her up

against him. She rested her cheek against his bare chest, inhaling his wonderful, musky scent. His legs touched hers, and she automatically entwined them with his. Against her cheek, his chest hair tickled her skin.

I am in bed with a naked man who is not my husband.

Taking a deep breath, she forced herself to calm down, and prayed the Lord wouldn't punish her for trying to help Malcolm. The soldiers were right outside the door. Now wasn't the time to analyze these stirring emotions fluttering through her belly.

Squeezing her eyes, she snuggled closer, clinging to him for protection. Within seconds, the soldiers kicked open the door.

"Captain Wilkes, I must protest," Broderick shouted.

Playing in character, she stirred and rubbed her eyes. Next to her, Malcolm bolted upright then cursed.

"What in all that is holy—" He stopped and grabbed his head again.

Broderick rushed forward. "Mr. Worthington, I tried to stop them, but Captain Wilkes was most insistent."

One of the other soldiers stormed to the window and yanked open the drapes.

Camilla squinted and clutched the bed covers to her chin. The men stared at her with wide eyes and mouths agape, especially Broderick. She prayed they would believe her.

Chapter Seven

THE GLARE FROM the sun hitting the window stung Malcolm's eyes as he peeled them open. He scowled at the men occupying his bedchambers, but mainly at Captain Wilkes. "What is the meaning of this?" he demanded.

The soldiers aimed their wide-eyed gazes at Camilla, seemingly perplexed and at a loss for words. Malcolm glanced over his shoulder at his wife. He sucked in a breath. In the light, she created an alluring silhouette. Although her face was scarlet, she looked absolutely breathtaking. Her light brown hair wildly framed her head. Her modest white nightgown made her appear as pure as newly fallen snow. How could she look that way when she was exactly the opposite?

But at the moment, it didn't matter. He was stunned. He forced away the inappropriate thoughts creeping into his head and concentrated on the uninvited men in his room. "Excuse me, sirs, but have you no decency? Bursting into a man's private chambers while he and his wife are still under the covers is very ill-mannered."

"Umm, well..." Captain Wilkes's cheeks flushed red. "You see, Mr. Worthington, we came to ask you a few questions about last night."

"And this couldn't wait until I was out of bed and dressed?" Scowling, he leaned over and pulled the quilt up, bundling it around Camilla, who, thankfully, had the decorum to look embarrassed. He was almost proud of her acting ability.

Broderick stepped forward. "Mr. Worthington, the captain thought it imperative to speak to you right away. Trouble occurred at Mr. Clarkston's office last night, and a witness thought they saw you as part of the group of men."

Malcolm inhaled sharply. "I fear you are mistaken, Captain Wilkes. I was home last night, reading stories to my children and enjoying the, er... company of my wife."

Broderick cleared his throat as his gaze moved to Camilla. A blush crept up his neck. "I have already told them as much, Mr. Worthington."

Malcolm turned his attention back to Captain Wilkes. "Explain to me, captain, why the royal soldiers are involved with this matter anyway? Shouldn't this be something for the constable to investigate?"

Captain Wilkes arched an eyebrow. "Have you forgotten that one of Mr. Clarkston's sons is a soldier?" He puffed out his chest. "We take care of our own."

Malcolm rolled his eyes. "Well, captain? As you can see, I wasn't part of that group. What have you to say now when the proof is right before you?" He nodded toward Camilla.

The captain stepped forward and removed his hat then clutched it against his chest. He looked directly at Camilla. "Mrs. Worthington? Can you confirm your husband has been here in the house with you all night?"

She snuggled closer to Malcolm, and he wrapped his arm around her. He still couldn't understand why she had offered to help, but at the moment he was grateful she had. Yet could this be a trap? Awaiting her answer, he held his breath.

"Yes, captain. My husband was with me the entire night."

Malcolm exhaled a deep sigh.

"My deepest apologies, Mr. and Mrs. Worthington." The captain nodded, then stepped away, as did the other soldiers. A few moments later, the thudding of their boots on the stairs echoed their descent.

Broderick winked and nodded at Camilla. "I shall leave you two alone now." Then he closed the door behind him.

Silence ensued for a few awkward minutes. Malcolm prolonged the moment, savoring the feel of her soft body nestled against him. But then reality struck, and he pulled away and tried to think of something intelligent to say. Her kindness of late—mixed with her beauty—had created an unexplained numbness in his brain. When he glanced at her, a timid smile touched her heart-shaped mouth.

"I suppose I can say a pleasant morning to you now," she said.

He sat up fully, keeping the covers protectively around his lower half as he pulled up his knees and rested his arms across them. "Well, considering the way I was awakened, I don't think it has been very pleasant so far." He cocked a brow and ran his focus over her tousled figure. "Of course, I must amend that. The way I was awakened was quite pleasurable, but once I awoke, reality intruded. Tell me, how was your night? Did you sleep well?"

A blush tinted her cheeks, and she looked adorable. "Yes."

He chuckled. "I want to thank you for what you did, but—" He blew out a gust of air and ran his fingers through his hair. "Why did you crawl into bed with me, knowing the soldiers were on their way up?"

Her eyes avoided his. She appeared to study his back, and then her gaze slowly wandered over his chest. That simple look caused the inner demon of desire to ignite his body, and he finally admitted he enjoyed the way she studied him, as if she had never seen anything so pleasing in her life. That was something she had never done before.

Her cheeks darkened and she cleared her throat, then pulled herself into a sitting position beside him. "Considering I haven't led an exemplary life since I married you, I realized the soldiers wouldn't believe my story unless they saw me in your bed. I didn't want you accused of a crime you didn't commit, and this was the only way for me to prove them wrong."

Could he believe her sincerity? She appeared so innocent, so honest. Yet her past made him cautious. He wasn't about to tell her the real reason he and Broderick were at the tavern last night. She would run to her precious Captain Wilkes and give the information to him.

Malcolm nodded. "Thank you for your quick thinking, then."

She turned to slide out of bed, but he reached out and placed his hand on her leg, stopping her. Her brilliant eyes stared at him, bringing back feelings he didn't want to have, but this time he rather enjoyed the way his body burned. "I don't know why you did it, but I thank you. You saved my backside."

Her gaze dipped to his buttocks. A blush flamed her cheeks. "And such a perfect backside to save." She smiled before climbing out of bed and slipping the robe around her.

He watched her leave his room, growing more uncomfortable by the second, mainly because he didn't know if this was a trick or not. Letting out another big sigh, he lay back in bed. It was getting harder and harder to resist her. Strange, because he'd been so immune before she'd left to go help her sister. What could be different now? Was it possible she really had changed?

THE FOLLOWING WEEK, Camilla stayed home and played games with the children. She and James formed an attachment, but Lizzy proved more difficult. The adorable little child played with them, but still refused to speak.

Stepping into the role of woman of the house, Camilla enjoyed planning the daily meals and organizing the staff, just as she had done when she was married to Fredrick. Doing something productive took her mind off her worries.

At first most of the servants seemed afraid of her, but as the days flew by, they warmed up just as James had. Camilla dared to ask them questions about Malcolm, hoping they wouldn't suspect she was prying for information to see if he was the criminal Kat had mentioned, but the staff only knew Malcolm as a kind, understanding, and hardworking man.

Learning more from Malcolm proved extremely difficult, though. After the little incident with the soldiers in the bedroom, he'd hardly spoken to her. Every day he worked late at the office, blaming it on the new line of ships they planned to build for the navy. In the back of Camilla's mind, she doubted his story, especially when her maid mentioned Malcolm didn't build ships—he just drew the plans.

Another evening came with Malcolm staying late at work, so she put the children to bed. James kissed her cheek and gave her a hug. Lizzy only hugged her.

As she left and walked downstairs, the house was too quiet, so she wandered into the library. Not really knowing what she was in the mood to read right now, she walked around the room, touching Malcolm's belongings, hoping by doing this, she would feel closer to him.

She shouldn't be so emotional, but she couldn't help feeling like a love-struck child. The man's piercing gaze forced her to experience new feelings, things she had no right to enjoy. Since the day they met, his unkind words had struck like a knife to her chest, even though they were aimed at Kat. His treatment of her should have frightened her and hardened her heart against the rogue, but it only made her want to show him how different she was. She wasn't anything like her twin.

A strong knock pounded on the front door, and she jumped. Who could be here at this time of night?

After settling her nerves, she walked into the entry hall and opened the heavy oak door. When she recognized the man standing before her, her heart plummeted to the floor. What was Brandon Kennedy doing here? Wasn't he at the office working late with Malcolm?

He leaned against the door and gave her a sly grin. "Good evening, Mrs. Worthington. I hope I have not caught you at a bad time."

He stepped into the house without an invitation and closed the door behind him. Irritation filled her, but she would remain polite. "No, Mr. Kennedy, you have not caught me at a bad time. In fact, I have just put the children to bed."

The rude man glanced around the corridor, then up the stairs. "Is your husband about? I need a moment with him."

She hesitated to tell him her husband was working late, because Mr. Kennedy would certainly know if Malcolm was at the office.

"I believe he and Broderick stepped out for a little while." She paused, hoping she could get rid of him quickly. "Is there a way I might assist you?"

Brandon gave her a mischievous smile, confirming her suspicions. He hadn't come to see Malcolm at all.

He motioned to the parlor. "May we speak in private?"

"We have privacy now, Mr. Kennedy. I don't see anybody around." She primly clasped her hands to stop them from trembling.

He tilted his head to the side and raised his dark eyebrows. "I think you know what I mean." Without waiting for an invitation, he walked into the parlor. "You have kept to yourself lately, and I came to inquire about your welfare."

She took a quick inspection of the corridor and upstairs, hoping someone would be around so she wouldn't have to face this man on her own. She pressed her linked hands against her stomach to cease the sudden churning inside. "Thank you for your concern, but I am well."

His bold gaze raked over her, and her stomach lurched. Thankfully, she had chosen to wear one of her own gowns instead of her sister's.

"Actually, Camilla, I have noticed a change in you, and I don't think you are well at all." He walked toward her. She remained still until he stood in front of her. He rested his hand on her shoulder, lightly caressing his thumb over her sleeve. "Didn't you think I would notice when my lover shuts me out of her life?"

She knocked his hand away. "Mr. Kennedy, I don't think it's my place to hear about what happens between you and your wife."

He laughed, and then stepped closer, slipping his arms around her waist and pulling her against him. She lifted her hand to block the contact, and struck his hard chest. "Mr. Kennedy, I must protest."

"Oh, my dear Camilla, you can be so coy when you want to be."

"Well, right now, I choose to be uncooperative."

She pushed harder, and when that didn't faze him, she stomped on his foot. Releasing a small yelp, he let her go. She hurried out of the room and to the library. The rude man followed with a slight limp. She moved around one of the sofas, keeping it between them.

"Mr. Kennedy, I don't welcome your attentions," she said, out of breath. "I have a good relationship with my husband, and I would like to keep it that way."

Anger lines creased his forehead and around his pursed lips. A spark of fire lit his eyes.

"You thought you would use me to get what you wanted then discard me like some wealthy man's leftovers?" He shook his head. "I think not, Camilla. We had a bargain, one you were quite eager to see through, may I remind you." He folded his arms. "I took your husband on as my partner just as you wanted, and now you refuse my attentions?"

"I have decided it was a mistake, and I wish to withdraw." Anger swept through her, making her breathe faster. How long could she hold out before screaming for assistance?

"Too late, my sweet." He chuckled. "If you withdraw, I'll have to release your husband as my partner. Now, that would not be very ethical, would it?"

Taking slower breaths, she calmed her panic, which gave her strength. She wasn't about to give in to his threats, but then, she didn't want to see Malcolm without a job.

She lifted her chin in defiance. "By joining your business with Malcolm's, I have made you a rich man. If you let him go now, I can assure you your business will flounder. If you remember correctly, you cannot build vessels unless you have a drawing first."

His dark brows drew together, and he sneered. "You little hussy."

"But I think you knew that when you decided to make a deal with me, am I correct?"

He stomped toward her, fire dancing in his eyes. She skirted away, keeping large objects between them.

"Your husband wants something badly, and I'm the only one who can get it for him. Are you willing to risk that lovely neck for him once again?"

"I'm certain I don't know what you mean."

"He wants an invitation to Colonel Burwell's country estate party this weekend, and I'm the only person who can get him in."

She straightened. "If you think I'll lower myself to do your bidding just so my husband can go to some party, you are sadly mistaken." She pointed to the door. "Now, Mr. Kennedy, I do believe you have overstayed your welcome. Next time, may I suggest waiting for an invitation before dropping by?"

"I'm not finished with you."

"Oh, but you are. If you don't leave in the next minute, I will call for one of my servants and have you physically removed from this house."

He scowled and stormed out of the room toward the front door.

"Have a good evening, Mr. Kennedy, and give your wife my regards."

After the door slammed shut, Camilla exhaled, releasing all her anger. Her hands trembled, as did her knees. Could what Mr.

Kennedy have said about Malcolm wanting to be invited to the colonel's party be correct? But why? Malcolm didn't look like a man who attended such functions.

When her legs could no longer hold her up, she wobbled toward the sofa. Just before she reached it, her toe caught on the rug, and she tripped. Her hand bumped the family Bible placed on the side table, making it fall on the floor. She righted herself then slumped on the cushions.

As she picked up the papers that fell out of the Bible, one caught her eye—a marriage certificate.

She traced her fingers across Malcolm's name and a woman by the name of Victoria. James had never spoken of his mother, and of course Malcolm wasn't going to offer any information, but the niggle of curiosity had her wanting to know about the woman who had been Malcolm's first love. Had he truly been in love with Victoria, or had he married her like he'd married Kat—quick and without proper time to get acquainted?

She glanced at the other sheet of paper—another marriage certificate. In big, bold letters, her very own maiden name jumped out at her: *Camilla Emily Connelly*. She gasped, her hand flying to cover her mouth. I'm *married to Malcolm?* Ridiculous. Why had her sister forged her name on her own marriage certificate? At least that explained why they called her Camilla.

Her heartbeat quickened. A knot formed in her throat. From this certificate, it appeared as if Malcolm had married her instead of Kat. This couldn't possibly be legal. She must find out these answers without raising suspicions.

Is Malcolm my husband... or Kat's?

Chapter Eight

M ALCOLM STARED AT the plate of eggs, sausage and honey scones his servant placed in front of him. Not in the mood to eat, he couldn't stop thinking about his wife's actions with Brandon Kennedy last night. Broderick had overheard the conversation between Kennedy and Camilla and had spied on them from another room to see how she handled him.

Malcolm shook his head in confusion. What was his wife up to now? For heaven's sake, she'd *lied* to his business partner. That in itself was out of the ordinary. Malcolm's wife would never snub Brandon, even in front of her husband, yet lately she had done it twice.

Leaning his elbows on the table, Malcolm cradled his head in his hands. Kat had actually told Brandon she had a good relationship with her husband—another lie. Why?

Then there was the incident the other morning when soldiers came into his room. It had shocked him when she climbed into his bed and acted innocent in front of their uninvited guests, but what perplexed Malcolm more was her motivation. Once again, she was willing to lie for him.

Not only were her actions misplaced, but he couldn't decipher why his body reacted so violently to her beauty and charm. It had never spun out of control before, so why now?

He pushed himself away from the table and stood. His appetite had disappeared. Rest was even a stranger to him. Perhaps it was time to find out what happened when his wife went to Preston and why she returned a different person.

From out in the corridor, a rustle of skirts and the clicking of a woman's shoes echoed through the front of the house. He swung toward the door. When he rested his lonely eyes upon Camilla's beauty, his heart leapt. This morning she'd adorned herself with a rose-colored dress. The deep bodice had been altered, and a small amount of lace had been sewn in the material to hide her bosom. Her lovely hair was upswept into the same fashionable arrangement she had worn since returning from Preston.

Her outward changes stirred softer emotions in his heart. She appeared more reserved, more regal. More fitting as his wife—the kind of wife he had always wanted.

Cursing, he buried his weakening sentiments. He could never think of her as his wife. "Good morning, Mrs. Worthington."

She smiled. "Good morning, Malcolm."

From her sweet tone and the soft smile with which she greeted him, his heart sprang to life. He had repeatedly told her not to use his first name, but the stubborn woman wouldn't listen.

He grinned. "I must say you look fetching this morning. Have you plans for the day?"

"I thought about going into town. Lizzy's birthday is just a few days away, and I would like to buy her a gift."

Shock spread over him. *She remembered?* "Yes, of course. Are you going to take the children?"

"Indeed, as long as you agree. Their nursemaid won't be able to accompany us today, though. Will you let me take them alone? I promise to keep them in my sight at all times."

Her eyes pleaded that he wouldn't object, and it gripped his heart. His breath caught in his throat. Just a simple look, a softly spoken request from her, had the ability to weaken his resolve.

He cleared his throat. "I'm certain the children will love to go. They had an enjoyable outing with you the last time."

Her smile widened. "As did I."

She stepped nearer to him, her rose fragrance knocking his senses off balance.

"Is there anything you would like me to purchase for you?" Her warm breath caressed his face.

"No." His heart hammered as he fought for control. He swallowed hard. "Is there something special you need?"

Her gaze focused on his lips. He balled his hands into fists to keep himself from taking her in his arms and kissing her. The other night was still very fresh in his mind, making him want to give in to temptation again.

"No, Malcolm. You have given me too much already."

She remained close to him, and the longer she stayed so near, the more uneven his breathing became. "Have a pleasant outing, then," he said in a strained voice.

"Thank you, Malcolm. And thank you for allowing me to take the children." She raised and touched her lips to his cheek, kissing him briefly before stepping back. His heart beat out of control, and he didn't have the slightest urge to stop it.

"What was that for?" he asked breathlessly.

"For being so kind and for trusting me with your children."

"You deserve it." His answer was whispered, and he couldn't understand why he had said that. Did she really deserve it?

She slid her hands over his, and automatically he clamped on to her, wanting to keep her from leaving his side. The urge to take her in his arms and devour her mouth with his became overpowering.

"You have no idea how long I have waited to hear you say that." Her eyes sparkled. "I won't disappoint you, Malcolm, I assure you."

She leaned up to kiss his cheek again, but he turned his face and met her kiss with his mouth. The kiss was soft, as were her lips. He hungered for more, but just as he released her hands to hold her, she broke the kiss and stepped away. A pink tint highlighted her cheeks, making her eyes sparkle.

He waited to see what she wanted to do next, hoping she would decide to fall into his arms, but she took another step back toward the door.

"Thank you again, Malcolm." Her voice was sedate. "Have a good day at work, and I shall see you tonight."

His emotions tied into knots, and he let her walk out of the room. The wild beat of his heart knocked against his ribs and his lips tingled from the memory of her sweet kiss. But it was still too soon. As much as his body starved for passion's touch, he didn't trust her with his life or, more importantly, his heart.

THE LOVELY MORNING passed too quickly for Camilla, and the time she had spent with James and Lizzy would soon come to an end. Within an hour they would be going back home, and she didn't want the pleasure to stop. When each child clasped her hand, her heart soared. She was bursting with happiness.

The morning had started out perfect, first with the tender conversation with Malcolm, followed by the brief but earth-shattering kiss that had left her body weak and shaking. Then to have Malcolm's children come to accept her kindness and love… Definitely, the day could not be better.

Camilla traveled through town, purchasing a few items for the kitchen that Cook had requested, but her main purpose was to find a shop that would buy Kat's dresses. The other day she had gone through her sister's closets and pulled out the gowns that could be altered. Many of the dresses Camilla simply couldn't modify. She wanted to find somebody to buy them.

Several dressmakers agreed to purchase the slightly used garments at a fraction of their original cost. Camilla couldn't refuse the offers, and made arrangements with them for a delivery date. The money earned would go to pay her sister's medical debt.

After making the final arrangements with the last shop own-er, she and the children walked outside. Breathing in the fresh air, she pondered what they could do next. From up the street, the *bong* of the church bells rang through the town. She hadn't been to church for so long, and she missed it greatly.

The wide doors opened at the cathedral-style building and several people walked down the few steps onto the road. At last, a priest exited the church, but stood at the top of the steps, waving to his congregation.

Although she hadn't been to church in a while, there was one problem weighing heavily on her mind that she would like to discuss with the priest. Marriage to Malcolm. According to the marriage certificate, she was legally Mrs. Worthington. Yet how could she be married to this man if she never attended the actual ceremony?

"Children," Camilla said. "Would you like to come with me to the church?"

Both James and Lizzy nodded, so Camilla hastened toward the man of God. Since she had stumbled across the certificate, she had been trying to convince herself this wasn't possible—that a vital piece of information was missing. Things didn't add up, and Camilla didn't know how to go about finding answers. Now with the priest not far away, she would take a moment and see if he could shed some light on her worries.

The priest rested his gaze on the children and smiled, but when he turned his eyes to Camilla, his expression appeared forced. Inwardly, she groaned. *He knows about Kat as well.*

"Good day," she said sweetly.

"It is a very good day," he answered stiffly.

"Might you have a moment to spare to answer a question for me?"

"Only a moment, my child."

"That is all I need." She took a deep breath. "My question will seem a little strange, but I assure you I have a good reason for asking."

"What is it, my child?"

"I want to know if proxy marriages are legal."

The older man's eyes widened and his bushy gray eyebrows lifted. "Proxy marriage, you say?"

"Yes. Can you tell me about it, please? I beg you, I desperately need to know."

"I shall answer you to the best of my knowledge." He folded his arms. "It was common for European monarchs and nobility to marry by proxy. Were you aware that Marie de' Medici, the second wife of King Henry IV, was married by proxy?"

Camilla gasped. "No, I wasn't aware. So, if she was married by proxy, then it is indeed legal to have another person stand in for an absent person who cannot attend their own wedding. Correct?"

"Yes, my child."

Peace settled over her confused mind. *I am married to Malcolm!* Her heart flipped with excitement, yet at the same time, confusion filled her. Did she *want* to be married to him? Little by little, she realized Malcolm was not the monster Kat had created in her mind, but she still needed to discover if he was doing something illegal behind her back. How could Camilla possibly want to be a criminal's wife?

"Thank you, Father. We will leave you now and let you attend other matters of God."

Now that she knew she was Malcolm's wife, would she still want to find evidence against him? Could she possibly turn him in and see him hanged?

Camilla took a deep breath and released it slowly. First things first—she must obtain his trust. Maybe then he would open up to her and tell her the truth about his life. Then, and only then, would she decide what needed to be done.

With the decision in mind, she smiled and continued on her way with the children. Just then, a wonderful scent drifted around her and tickled her senses. Freshly baked sticky buns permeated the air with their wonderful cinnamon aroma. Her belly growled in response to the irresistible smell.

She stopped and crouched to the children's level. "Lizzy? James? Are you hungry for a sticky bun?"

Happy, energetic eyes widened, and the children giggled. She laughed, joining in their mirth. She raced with the two into the next shop to buy the treats. Within minutes, the three left with rolls and icing-caked fingers and lips.

She found a small patch of grass, and they sat under a tree to eat their treats. The gentle breeze blew a lock of hair across her warm cheeks, and the shade from the tree prevented the sun's rays from making them too uncomfortable.

"Oh, Milla," James said in a voice filled with joy, "this is the best day in the whole world."

"I think it is a wonderful day as well. Don't you think so, Lizzy?"

The girl's head bobbed, making her blonde ringlets bounce in rhythm, but still she said nothing.

Milla frowned. "James? Why doesn't your sister speak?"

He shrugged, and then took another bite of his roll. "She talked a little before you and Papa got married, but I don't know why she stopped."

"Is she still frightened of me?"

"Don't think so."

Camilla stroked Lizzy's cheek with her knuckles. The girl didn't flinch, which was a good sign. "Lizzy?" The little girl's eyes met hers. "Will you say something for me?" Lizzy shook her head and concentrated on eating her roll, but Camilla continued. "Can you say Papa?"

Without looking up, Lizzy nodded as she licked her fingers, but she remained quiet.

"Lizzy?" The girl looked up. "You don't have to say a word now, but will you talk to me one day? I would really like to play dolls with you." The girl's eyes widened, and light danced inside the huge orbs. In excitement, Camilla's heart picked up a faster rhythm. "Would you like that?"

Lizzy nodded faster.

"I would, too, but I cannot play with you unless you talk to me."

Lizzy lowered her eyes as she gobbled down the remainder of her roll.

Once again, Camilla's heart ached. With a deep sigh, she admitted defeat for now. She wouldn't give up on the poor girl, just like she hadn't given up on Malcolm.

She opened her reticule and pulled out an embroidered handkerchief. She dabbed the end to her tongue to moisten the cloth, then wiped Lizzy's messy face and hands, then gave the same treatment to the boy. Before putting the cloth away, she wiped her own hands and face.

"I think we should head back home now." She stood and helped the children up, but just as she turned, the ferocious bark of a dog made her jump. The beast bounded toward them from across the street.

James and Lizzy screamed and ducked behind Camilla, hiding in the folds of her skirt. This must be the dog that had attacked them before.

Camilla scanned the area, looking for an object to use as a weapon. She spied a rock, grabbed it, and aimed for the oncoming animal. He bared his teeth and growled.

"Shoo," she shouted, but the animal didn't stop.

When he reached them, he slowed. His growl moved deep in his chest as he padded around them, his intent gaze never leaving their faces. His hackles rose.

Lizzy and James cried, burying their faces further into her dress. The dog continued to taunt them. Then the animal lunged. Camilla threw the rock, hitting the beast between the eyes. The dog gave a sharp yelp before tucking its tail and running away.

Camilla released a gust of pent-up air. She turned, gathered the two frightened children in her arms, and held them tight. "It is all right now. Don't fret. The dog is gone."

James wiped his runny nose on the sleeve of his jacket and

looked up at her with wet eyes. "You made the doggie go away and you wasn't afraid."

"I was afraid, but I was more afraid of him hurting you or Lizzy, and I wouldn't let that happen." She gave him a reassuring smile.

Cupping Lizzy's chin in her hands, she lifted the little girl's face and met her teary eyes. "Are you all right?"

Lizzy nodded, then swallowed. She cleared her throat and opened her mouth to speak, but snapped it closed.

Excitement pounded in Camilla's heart. Lizzy again struggled for words, and Camilla waited.

With the back of her hand, Lizzy wiped her wet eyes then looked back at Camilla. "Tank you," she mumbled in a barely audible voice.

A small cry escaped Camilla's throat, and she hugged the child against her bosom. "No, thank you, my darling Lizzy."

From behind, a woman called out. Camilla turned just as the woman stopped before them.

"Excuse me, madame," the woman said breathlessly.

Camilla eyed the well-dressed woman, perhaps in her late forties. The older lady looked to be very wealthy. Camilla wouldn't doubt she was prominent in town as well.

The woman placed her hand over her heart and sighed. "Oh, good heavens, child. Are you all right?"

"Yes. We are just still a little shaken from the ordeal, but we are fine."

"My husband's dog got away from my servants, again, the horrible animal. I wish he would get rid of the beast, but my husband loves Rottweilers." She sighed. "I'm impressed with how brave you were when you stood against him."

"I couldn't let the dog attack us."

The woman shook her head, a light of admiration gleaming in her eyes. "Well, I must say how happy I am to see that the animal finally lost a battle. He breaks away from my servants much too often, and I hear about all the children he attacks."

"Well, I hope the dog will think twice before coming my way again."

The woman laughed. "Can I put a name to such a brave young lady?"

"I'm Camilla Worthington. My husband is Malcolm Worthington, and these are his children."

The lady held out her right hand in greeting. "And I'm Lady Burwell. Colonel George Burwell is my husband."

Camilla's eyes widened. Could this woman be the wife of the same man whom Malcolm sought an invitation from? "It is a pleasure to finally meet you. My husband speaks highly of the colonel."

Lady Burwell's forehead creased. "Your husband knows my George?"

"Yes. Colonel Burwell asked my husband to draw plans for the navy's new ships, and Mr. Kennedy is going to build them for him."

A light of awareness shone on the woman's face, and she laughed. "Oh, yes, I know who your husband is now. Quite charming, he is, and very handsome, if I might add."

"Thank you. I think so, as well."

"If you are friends of Mr. Kennedy, then my husband has invited you to come to my party this weekend, has he not?"

"I'm sorry to say no. I don't believe we have received an invitation, Lady Burwell."

"You must be jesting." The woman gasped. "Why, Mr. Kennedy and Mr. Crowley are coming, so it is only proper you and your husband also attend. In fact, although it is late notice, I'll send over an invitation this afternoon."

Camilla's heart leapt to renewed life. She couldn't wait to see Malcolm's reaction. What would he say? Would he reward her with a kiss? Just the thought made a different kind of thrill course through her body, moistening the palms of her hands.

As soon as she realized how excited the thought made her, she squashed the idea. She could *not* be feeling this way, even if she was legally his wife.

"It will be a pleasure to get to know you and your dear husband," Lady Burwell said. "I cannot wait to tell my guests what a brave lady you are. They will love to hear how you wounded that horrible dog."

"Don't make me out to be more than I am." Camilla laughed. "The reason I reacted that way was to protect my children." She reached down and drew them against her side.

Lady Burwell crouched to the children's level and smiled. "You two are very lucky to have such a loving mother." She patted their heads before standing. "I will see you this weekend, then?"

"Yes. And thank you for the generous invitation."

After the woman left, Camilla held in the bubble of joyous laughter threatening to escape her throat. She grabbed James and Lizzy's hands and hurried toward their coach. The day had been more productive than she could have ever imagined, and now she couldn't wait to see Malcolm.

Chapter Nine

M ALCOLM CLIMBED INTO his coach and tapped on the roof, then braced himself when the vehicle lurched into motion. Today had been as bad as yesterday—worse, in fact, because he couldn't stop thinking about this morning's kiss. Undoubtedly, his wife's charms had bewitched him, because she was certainly an enchantress. How else could he explain the sudden yearnings he experienced whenever she was around?

Exhaling a deep sigh, he relaxed in the seat and stared out the window. The sun descended over the horizon, pink and red shades highlighting the sky. Another day was almost gone without an invitation to Colonel Burwell's weekend party. His plans to secretly search the man's house were slowly fading from his grasp, and he feared he would never be able to find out if the colonel was behind the unfortunate things that had been happening to Malcolm of late. He still felt the colonel had something to do with them.

Why hadn't the insufferable colonel invited him? Did the man suspect what Malcolm was secretly searching for? Had Kat told him? Why else would he invite Brandon and not Malcolm? Indeed, this was probably part of the plan to ruin Malcolm's good name. What else could it mean?

The coach stopped, and he climbed out, storming into the house. After closing the door, he detected a change in the atmosphere. Servants chatted happily amongst themselves, and his butler and groomsman whistled. Certainly out of the ordinary.

When Camilla's personal maid scurried past him toward the next room, he stopped her. "Excuse me, Beth."

She turned his way. "Aye, Mr. Worthington?"

"Have you seen my wife and children?"

"Oh, yes. They are upstairs in the nursery."

"Splendid, but... where is my wife?"

"In the nursery with them."

A confused throb caused a dull ache in his skull, and he rubbed his forehead. He bolted up the stairs and hurried into the nursery to see what Camilla was doing this time. Just before he reached the door, laughter echoed through the room. Not only James and Camilla's voices, but a little girl's, too.

He stopped inches from the door. Camilla and James sang a silly song as they clapped their hands together while Lizzy laughed. He leaned forward and peeked around the corner. His daughter's face lit up as bright as sunshine. When the song stopped, she giggled and clapped her tiny hands.

"More, more," she cheered.

Malcolm choked on a gasp, and his heart jumped to his throat. She spoke? When had this happened? He hurried into the room, and their laughter stopped.

"Papa," James shouted, and ran to him. Lizzy lifted herself off the floor and grinned.

Malcolm gave James a quick hug and turned to his daughter. "Lizzy? Did I hear you speak?"

She nodded, her full head of curls bouncing together. "Uh-huh."

His throat tightened, and tears of joy sprang to his eyes. He swept his daughter into his arms and hugged her to his chest.

"Papa." James pulled on his pant leg. "Milla saved us from that mean dog."

Malcolm glanced down at Camilla, who remained sitting on

the floor, her smile relaxed and her eyes twinkling like emeralds.

"What is James talking about?" he asked her.

"While we were in town this afternoon, a dog broke away from his owner and charged us, giving the children a terrible fright. I couldn't think of any way to keep him from attacking us, so I picked up a rock and hit him in the head."

Another jolt of surprise pierced Malcolm's body.

"And Papa," James continued, "it was so wonderful, 'cause the doggie yelped and ran home with his tail 'tween his legs." He laughed. "You should've saw'd him, Papa."

"Milla scared him, Papa." Lizzy laughed.

Malcolm's heart melted the longer he gazed at his wife, and like the forbidden fruit, she tempted him to sample her kiss one more time. He moved by her side, knelt, and reached to caress her cheek. Her skin grew warm beneath his fingers.

"Is this true?" he asked. "Did you save my children?"

"I… I didn't want the dog to harm them."

Lizzy jumped out of his arms and ran to Camilla. His daughter threw her arms around Camilla's neck. "Papa? Milla loves us."

His legs weakened, and he sat on the floor beside his wife. He touched her cheek again, and she snuggled her face against his hand. "How can I thank you?"

She smiled. "You don't need to thank me. I did what any good mother would do."

His heart twisted in confused pain again. He wanted to take her in his arms and smother her with his appreciation, yet doubt stopped any form of action. It wasn't like Kat to be kind toward another. *A good mother?* That didn't fit the Kat he knew.

Her eyes glittered as if sprinkled with diamonds, and the gentle beckoning of her delicate lips pulled him closer. He pushed all negative thoughts, wanting to feel her mouth against his again. He didn't even care that the children were present.

He leaned forward, and she sucked in her breath but didn't pull away. His heart sang. Emotions he wanted kept hidden had surfaced, convincing him she'd finally changed into the woman he had always dreamed about.

She tilted toward him, and he pressed his lips to hers. Energy ignited inside him, and he longed for more. He moved to wrap his arms around her, but his laughing children jumped on them both, knocking them to the floor. Keeping the children in his arms, he pulled Camilla against him. Her wide smile and glowing eyes held tender emotion as she looked at him, and he realized he loved seeing her like this.

"Milla," James said, "were you going to give Papa his gift now?"

"What?" Malcolm sat up.

Nodding, Camilla stood. "Yes, James, if you think your father is ready for it."

"Papa," Lizzy said, tugging on Malcolm's waistcoat. "You ready?"

Malcolm laughed. "Of course."

Camilla went to the bookshelf and lifted the wrapped package on top. She brought it to him, her eyes never leaving his.

She knelt beside him and smiled. "I have waited for the right moment to give this to you, and I suppose now is a perfect time."

He took the package, not believing any of this. His daughter talking, his son laughing with his stepmother, and Kat... Kat wasn't herself and hadn't been for a while. In fact, the name *Kat* didn't fit her. Camilla did.

"Open it, Papa," James encouraged him.

Malcolm ripped at the package while his children giggled and helped him remove the wrapping. A long, dark brown steel case sat in his hands, and when he opened the lid, he couldn't believe his eyes. He had been eyeing the jeweled dagger for a few weeks, wondering if he should purchase it.

He brought his gaze up to Camilla. How did she know? "I don't understand," he said. "Why are you giving this to me?"

She touched his hand tenderly. "Because I wanted to thank you for everything you have done lately. You are an extremely kind and forgiving man. You have made me very happy here," she ended in a whisper.

His heart burst for the second time today. He dropped the cased dagger in his lap and pulled Camilla in his arms. She met his kiss halfway, and he didn't hold back on showing her how he felt. A deep sigh escaped her throat as she clung to him. But before he could enjoy the moment, heavy footsteps sounded in the corridor and Broderick called Malcolm's name.

He cursed and withdrew. His wife's cheeks flamed an adorable pink. Couldn't he kiss his own wife for longer than two minutes?

"Malcolm, wonderful news," Broderick yelled. He entered the nursery then came to a dead stop.

"What is it?" Malcolm stood and joined his friend, keeping the cased dagger in his hand.

"Umm... well," Broderick stammered as his gaze shifted from Malcolm to Camilla and the children. "I'm sorry to disrupt your, er... pleasant moment, but I have wonderful news." He showed Malcolm the highly decorated card.

Malcolm snatched it away, reading over every word. "When did this arrive?"

"Just a few moments ago by messenger," Broderick replied.

"But why?"

"What is it, Malcolm?" Camilla lifted herself off the floor and moved to his side.

"An invitation to Colonel Burwell's weekend estate party. I have waited for two weeks for this." He shook his head. "I just don't understand why it arrived two days before the big event. One usually doesn't send invitations out so late."

His wife's hand touched his arm, and he met her amazing eyes, still glistening with warmth. "Lady Burwell apologized and explained there must have been some kind of mix-up. She promised she would send the invitation over right away."

Doubt crept into his mind, and happiness drained from him slowly like a leaky bucket. "When did you talk to Lady Burwell?"

"This afternoon. It was Colonial Burwell's dog that attacked us, and she came to see if we were all right. We talked, and I mentioned—"

"You told her I had not been invited?" He raised his voice. "Do you know how that makes me appear?"

She frowned. "No, Malcolm, it wasn't like that at all. In fact, she assumed you *were* invited. When I explained you were not, she apologized and promised to send over an invitation."

"What exactly did you tell her?" He folded his arms across his chest.

"I told her we would love to come."

"We?"

"Yes, of course." Her perfectly shaped eyebrows rose in challenge. "She wanted both of us to come."

He cursed under his breath for his bad fortune and glanced at Broderick. Apparently, the past few moments of splendor had been a dream, and now reality reminded him he could *not* trust his wife. Kat only did nice things for *her* selfish purposes.

"Lady Burwell," Kat continued in a shaky tone, "led me to believe this weekend gathering was for husbands and wives."

Malcolm growled, bunching his hands into fists. "It is."

"Then why should I feel discouraged in going? Do you not want me there?" Pain diminished the sweetness highlighting her eyes.

His chest constricted, and he attempted to crush the guilt that filled him. "Of course I want you there. Don't be ridiculous," he snapped.

"Then why—"

"Camilla," he cut her off, "please ask your maid to pack your trunks sufficiently. I shall have my servant load my belongings posthaste." He turned and walked with Broderick out the door, calling over his shoulder, "I'll be late for supper tonight, so don't wait."

Malcolm strode down the stairs, anger burning within him like a raging storm. Why did his deceiving little wife want to come along? What was she up to? Had the missing puzzle piece to her new behavior just fallen into place? Did she want to come to the party in order to spy on him?

"HERE WE ARE."

Ignoring Malcolm's grumble as he stared out the carriage window, Camilla sat forward in her seat and admired the enormous estate. Full trees, the land, and green, rolling hills made it a splendid sight.

The Burwells' three-story manor had at least three wings added to the structure circling around the backyard. She caught a glimpse of the rose garden that seemed to last forever. At the edge of the yard, a cluster of trees led into a small forest.

"Amazing," she gasped.

"Yes, quite a sight, is it not?"

"Unbelievable."

"And can you believe I drew up the plans?"

She swung her head around so hard it unbalanced her bonnet. She stared at him as she adjusted it back on her head. "You did?"

"The people who first bought the estate moved away two years ago when the taxes became so high, they couldn't afford to live here." He smoothed his waistcoat into place. "Not too long afterward, the colonel and his wife moved in." He shook his head. "Now it makes me wonder if the Burwells pushed the people away on purpose."

His tone of voice became guarded when he spoke of the taxes. Then again, in these hard times, everyone was upset about the high taxes.

"I think you are extremely talented." She smiled. "This is a lovely manor."

"Thank you." His acknowledgment held no emotion.

The coach pulled to a stop, but before the footman came to open the door, Malcolm touched her arm. "Please remember your act. Continue to play the sweet, innocent woman you have been trying to fool me into believing you are."

His words cut through her like a sharp knife—quick and painful. She wished she could make him think differently. "I assure you, I shall be on my best behavior." She leaned toward him and placed her hand on his knee. His muscles tightened beneath her fingers. "If you like," she continued, "I will show these people I have changed and the only man in my life is my husband."

His expression remained solemn, and her heart sank further. Not even a twitch touched his lips. What had happened to the man who had been so loving and sweet with her the other day in the nursery while she played with the children? Once she had explained to him how she was able to obtain the invitation to the party, he'd clammed up and turned back into the monster she met that first day.

He nodded, still wearing a blank expression. "If you think you can convince these guests that you have changed, I'm all for that."

She gritted her teeth and bunched her hands into fists. Sometimes—like now—she wanted to slap some sense into him.

Malcolm stepped out of the coach first before lifting her down. His grip wasn't gentle, and when her feet touched the ground, he withdrew his hands and moved away as if touching her offended him.

She took a deep breath, trying to gain more courage. She would show him what kind of woman she really was. Hopefully, he would come to have tender feelings for her. Eventually the truth would come out about their marriage, and she didn't want him loathing her when that happened.

Hooking her arm around his elbow, she let him escort her into the manor, where servants waited to take their hats and cloaks. Colonel Burwell and his wife stepped away from their other guests to greet them. Once again, Lady Burwell, dressed to perfection, wore clothing that appeared very expensive, befitting a queen.

"I'm so happy you could make it," Lady Burwell greeted them. "I must apologize again for my husband's memory." She elbowed him gently. "He really thought he had given Mr. Kennedy an invitation for you."

Malcolm shook his head. "It is I who should apologize for any inconvenience my wife and I have put you through."

Lady Burwell laughed. "Nonsense."

Malcolm took Lady Burwell's hand and placed a proper kiss on her knuckles. "Lady Burwell, may I say you look very fetching, making the sunshine envious of you for taking away its brightness."

The woman giggled like a girl, and Camilla held back a laugh. Malcolm certainly knew how to captivate a lady.

"Oh, you are a charmer, Mr. Worthington," the older woman cooed.

Camilla had to agree. That man was irresistibly charming.

Malcolm turned to the colonel and bowed slightly. "Thank you, for the generous invitation. I commend you for the remarkable additions you have made to this property since the last occupants owned it."

George Burwell chuckled. "Yes, it was a mere shack until we made the proper accommodations. But I heard you were the one who designed the manor. Is that correct?"

"Indeed, sir."

Lady Burwell gasped. "Are you jesting?"

Malcolm shook his head. "I would not jest about matters so important, my lady."

"Well, then I shall have to hire you to build me more."

"You wish to add on another wing, perhaps?"

"Oh, no." She laughed. "This manor suits my needs for the moment, but I wish to have a different stable. The one we have is too small."

"I shall be more than happy to draw up the plans for you."

Camilla kept silent as her husband conversed with the couple.

There was an underlying tone to his answers, almost as if he lied through his teeth. Outwardly, his expression held a pleasant look, but she could read him well. His behavior wasn't quite right, and the nerve on his cheek twitched. This had happened before when he tried to hold his anger.

When more guests arrived, the Burwells excused themselves. Malcolm hooked her hand around his elbow again and walked away. She tried not to ponder the doubts creeping into her mind and instead concentrated on the furnishings.

"I think this manor is immaculately decorated," she said.

"Take a good look, my dear," Malcolm whispered, and leaned closer. "This is funded by the hardworking people of Dorchester. Their taxes pay for Lady Burwell's furnishings."

She gasped, turning her head to meet his narrowed gaze. "You cannot be serious."

"Can't I?" His eyebrow rose. "Where do you think the money goes, but to the soldiers and their families? Have you not noticed that all the higher-ranking soldiers live almost as wealthily as the royals?"

Different doubts filled her now. The more she thought about this, the more she realized Malcolm was correct.

"These are difficult times, thanks to Napoleon trying to take over Britain," he told her. "However, I don't believe the prince regent is handling things correctly."

She nodded. "You are probably right."

"I know I am," he answered with sadness in his voice.

A servant joined them, interrupting her errant thoughts on the political matter.

"Excuse me, Mr. and Mrs. Worthington," the younger woman began. "Lady Burwell has asked me to show you to your room. I'm certain you'll want to freshen up before the garden luncheon."

Camilla smiled. "Oh, yes. That would be wonderful, thank you."

She and Malcolm followed the maid up the grand staircase.

When they stepped into the room, Camilla inhaled sharply. Hers and Malcolm's trunks sat side by side. Her heart jumped to her throat with the mere thought of their sharing a bed.

"Excuse me," Malcolm said. "Why are my trunks in my wife's room?"

The maid's cheeks bloomed with color, and she glanced down at the floor. "Lady Burwell hadn't enough rooms when you responded to her invitation, and she offers her apologies for you having to share one." She peeked up from beneath lowered lashes at Malcolm. "And she hopes you will understand and not be too inconvenienced."

Camilla's uneven heartbeat accelerated, but she must calm the maid's fears, although she was having a hard time with her own. Displaying her practiced smile, she nodded. "No reason to fret. This is acceptable. Tell Lady Burwell we are most happy with our accommodations."

The young girl bobbed once and then left the room, closing the door behind her.

The room seemed larger than the one she occupied at Malcolm's home. Her gaze flew to the large bed decorated in a blue and yellow patchwork with matching pillows, and her throat turned dry.

"Things can't get worse, can they?" Malcolm grumbled behind her.

His rotten attitude gnawed on her nerves, and she whipped around, planting her hands on her hips. "You wanted to come here, so what are you harping about? Although we have to share a bed, you will not even notice me in it. The bed is big enough that we can each have a side to ourselves and not worry about bumping into each other during the night."

After a few awkward moments in silence, his mouth twitched into a grin. "My, aren't we edgy this morning?"

"I'm having a hard time understanding you, Malcolm." She rolled her eyes. "Are you never satisfied?"

He folded his arms across his wide chest and lost his smirk.

"Lately, I haven't been satisfied at all. Have you forgotten the reasons you gave for not wanting me as a husband—in all senses of the word—right after we married?" He walked over and stood mere inches in front of her. Fire shot out of his eyes.

She swallowed the lump of fear quickly rising to her throat. "I must have forgotten."

"Let me remind you, then," he continued. "According to your standards, I wasn't a fitting bed partner because I couldn't understand your disloyalty. You accused me of complaining about everything, and you didn't like the way I lived my life."

She gulped at the crudeness of her sister's words. The apology gathered on the tip of her tongue, but she dared not voice it. She needed to let him speak to understand his feelings. "I'm certain I spoke without thinking," she whispered.

He grasped her wrist. "You knew exactly what you were saying, my dear. You didn't like the way I touched you, the way I kissed you, and especially the way I treated you."

Defiantly, she took hold of her fear and straightened her shoulders. "Well, if you were as gentle then as you are now, it's no wonder I didn't like the way you touched me." Anger quickly replaced her fear. She nodded toward his fingers around her wrist. "Most women like a strong man with a gentle, loving hand. Not a forceful beast that will take whatever he wants, whenever he wants. That is barbaric." A memory flashed through her head of the way her own husband treated her right after they married, and her stomach rolled.

He released her as if he had been burned and stepped away. "How odd you would say that, because you informed me immediately that you enjoyed a rough man in bed." His brows drew together, and anger lines remained around his mouth. "When you finally realize what you want, please let me know. I'm not going to take any action, mind you, but I would like to keep it straight in my head what you want and don't want, so I can warn your next conquest." He turned away and marched out the door, slamming it hard behind him.

Her heart shattered, and she wished he didn't affect her so. The main purpose of being here was to keep him alive, and to make him come to accept his *new* wife. She had to make him see she was not the same woman he'd stood beside on their wedding day.

Anger rose within her, and she stamped her foot. Looking heavenward, she growled. "A fine mess you made of *my* life, isn't it, sister dear?"

Why had Kat married Malcolm using her twin's name? Nothing made sense.

Camilla's chest ached, and she knew everything about Malcolm's marriage had been a lie brought on by her own twin sister. But now Camilla must make things right. She was falling in love with Malcolm, and she was unable to stop it.

Chapter Ten

MALCOLM COULDN'T WAIT to leave the men who had gathered in the library. Not only was their topic of conversation boring, but Brandon Kennedy watched him closely. Malcolm knew his business partner suspected him of something, and it was his duty to prove the irritating man wrong.

When he found the right moment, he slipped out of the side door and walked outside. He didn't know what his wife was doing, but knowing Kat, she had probably found one of her lovers and met with them in private. He really wished he could get that confounded woman out of his thoughts. He especially hoped his body would stop reacting to her tender touch.

As he walked up the slope in the yard, he noticed women had gathered on the back lawn under a canopy. They all sat with straight backs, sipping tea like it was the most important function in the world.

Then a woman with light brown hair and a curvy figure caught his gaze. Strange that her appearance would distract his attention from the other women. Camilla looked so pretty in the sunlight, and the lavender dress complemented her creamy skin. This afternoon she wore another of her altered dresses, hiding the deep-cut bodice with some fancy stitching and lace. She was probably the youngest woman here, and definitely the loveliest.

He sauntered toward them. At first none had noticed him,

and when he came close enough to hear their conversation, he realized why. They talked about politics. He didn't think most of these women here had intelligence enough for that. They also chatted about the events going on in Dorchester.

Lady Burwell spoke about the other night when Mr. Clarkston's office had been ransacked, and he froze. Someone had done this to make him look like the culprit. He backed behind a bush and listened as he spied on them.

"I heard it was nothing but a bunch of drunken fools," another lady mentioned.

Lady Burwell nodded. "Yes, but there had to be a mastermind behind the break-in. Such lowlife miscreants wouldn't be able to have an intelligent thought without having a leader."

Malcolm held his breath for the next comment.

"I heard they didn't catch the person responsible," another woman said. "Is this so?"

Lady Burwell set her teacup down. "I'm not certain they even have a suspect." She puffed out her chest. "But if there is a leader, I assure you, my husband will find him."

A gust of air escaped Malcolm's lungs as murmurs of agreements bounced throughout the small group of women, but Camilla didn't speak. Once again, his suspicions were aroused. The night Brandon and his wife had been to dinner, Camilla had voiced her opinion about nearly every topic, but now she merely glanced around the circle of guests. She sucked in her bottom lip, nibbling it. Her brows drew together as if she were confused. Then she cleared her throat, receiving their attention.

"Lady Burwell?" Camilla asked, frowning. "Exactly what was damaged in the man's office?"

Lady Burwell smiled politely and met her gaze. "I don't know. However, I was told a few files were missing. Mr. Clarkston's son is one of our fine soldiers, and good people such as the Clarkstons should be treated with more respect."

"Forgive me," Camilla continued, "but can you tell me what qualifies someone as *good people* in Society's eyes? Is it those who are wealthy? Is it those who have solid reputations? Because I, for one, have known lower-class people who are just as good, and yet they are not treated with respect."

The wealthy woman sitting next to her snickered as she toyed with her pearls. "Perhaps it's their actions that merit other's disapproval. I have noticed the lower class are without manners."

Ringleted heads bobbed in agreement, but Camilla's brows still pulled together. She was obviously not pleased with the answer.

"Pardon me for saying," she continued in harsher tones, "but I was raised as a lower-class woman. My father raised his daughters well. We had manners. I don't believe it's right to judge someone by their upbringing. How do we know who broke into Mr. Clarkston's office wasn't one of the other officers, or even someone in good standing with the community?"

A few women gasped. Malcolm bit back his surprised response, too. It was a little strange to hear her speak this way. Although he hadn't broken into Mr. Clarkston's office and stolen files, Malcolm *would* have done it to save his own neck. However, he understood why she was so derisive about the way the higher-class women degraded those of the lower class.

He wanted to hear more of what his wife thought. So far, he approved, as evidenced by the quickening of his heart.

"Mrs. Worthington, you are indeed an amazing woman, since you came from so little and now you have so much," Lady Burwell said before clapping her hands twice. "Ladies, let us cease this serious conversation and join our husbands." She nodded behind Camilla. "I see the men are finished with their brandy and cigars."

Malcolm glanced toward the manor. He cursed under his breath, noticing that men were walking out on the lawns now.

He moved around the bush and toward his wife. When Camilla's gaze landed on him, her eyes widened, and she smiled. His heart leapt, and he cursed himself again for responding like a fool.

He stopped by her side. "Good afternoon, my lovely wife.

Are you in the mood for a walk?" He held out his arm. All around them, glares from the other ladies were aimed their way, but Camilla seemed not to notice as she stood and took hold of his arm.

She nodded. "I have been hoping to see Lady Burwell's lovely garden."

Malcolm looked at the other ladies. "Please excuse us."

They all smiled and nodded. Having Camilla walk beside him made him feel like the luckiest man, and he wished he didn't feel this way. But the conversation he had overheard made him proud. Not only had she voiced her questions amongst a den of wolves, but she had also entered this party knowing full well most of these women thought poorly of her.

Once they were far enough away from the others, he chuck-led.

She cocked her head to look at him. "What do you find so humorous?"

"You."

"Why?"

"Because you are determined to make those ladies hate you." He met her questioning stare. "Half of them know you have a close relationship with their husbands, and now I'm certain the other half wonder if you know who broke into Mr. Clarkston's office."

She huffed. "If they do, they are imbeciles. I only asked those questions because I was curious." She paused, and her brow furrowed. "How much did you overhear?"

"Enough." He stopped and moved in front of her, keeping his smile only because he couldn't control it. "But why did you say what you did?"

Shrugging, she glanced down at her hands as she twisted them against her stomach. "I recall you telling me how uppity these women were and how our taxes are paying for their luxuries, and, well... when I could tell they were being judgmental, I couldn't stop my thoughts."

He took her hands in his, stopping her nervousness. The heat from her body blended with his. Once again, the incredible feeling of desire crept into his system. He stroked her cheek with his finger then lifted her chin until she met his eyes. "Camilla?"

"Yes?"

He smiled wider, his heart beating much faster than before. Excitement welled inside his chest, softening his feelings toward her. This time he didn't fight it. "I'm very happy to see you have a heart, and it's not as selfish as I thought."

"It's as I told you several times already, I have changed. I'm no longer the woman you married."

"I'm beginning to see that," he said softly.

She grew silent as her gaze roamed over his face. He enjoyed the way she studied his eyes before letting her attention move to his lips. The erratic thud in his heart increased. What kind of power did she have over him? More importantly, why did he let it affect him?

"Camilla, you shouldn't look at me that way unless you want to be kissed good and hard."

"Please forgive me. I suppose it's not proper for you to kiss me in public."

His heart flipped, nearly knocking him over with surprise. "Are you saying you *want* me to kiss you?"

Her mouth turned up in an impish smile. "If you don't know the answer to that, then I haven't made my desires known very well, have I?"

"My dear wife, it's dangerous to tempt me like that." He wrapped his arm around her waist while he cupped the back of her head, pulling her close. "I'm a normal man, no matter how much of an ogre you wish me to be."

He waited, expecting her to curl her lip as she often did. Instead her face softened and tenderness gleamed in her green eyes. Where had the witch gone, the one who had made him regret his decision to marry? This enchanting woman was certainly not that creature.

Her gaze warmed with invitation as she shook her head. "I never thought you an ogre."

"Oh? That's not the impression you gave me a while ago."

"Malcolm, please forget about back then." She swept back a lock of hair that had fallen over his brow. "I don't even want you to remember that woman."

How he wished he wished he could just erase the past two years. But he couldn't.

"I'm sorry, Camilla." He dropped his hands and stepped away. "But you are asking too much of me."

Her gaze lowered to the ground, and she gave a forlorn nod.

"But come." He took her hand and placed it on his elbow. "I promised to show you Lady Burwell's flower garden, and I'm not leaving your side until you see it."

She gave his arm a slight squeeze, and he looked down into her serious expression. "You know, Mr. Worthington, I think you like me more than you realize."

He laughed, cursing under his breath for being so obvious. "Just like you, Mrs. Worthington, I'm a good performer."

THE EVENING'S MEAL and dancing afterward was a huge success for Lady Burwell. But Camilla thought the bigger success belonged to Malcolm. He played the part of an adoring husband well. If only she could find that glimmer she had seen in his eyes when he kissed her, then her day would be complete.

When other men asked her to dance, she grudgingly accepted, but the distrust in Malcolm's eyes tugged at her heart. More than anything, she wanted to tell him the truth. She was Kat's twin—and nothing like her sister.

Finally, the moment she both dreaded, yet anticipated, arrived. She postponed retiring for the night as long as possible, but once the gazes of her host and hostess fell upon her, she realized they too had heard the rumors and wondered about the Worthington marriage. Camilla had to give the impression all was well.

Inhaling a deep breath for courage, she walked to Malcolm, who conversed with Brandon Kennedy and another man she wasn't acquainted with. She tapped her husband on the shoulder to get his attention. When he looked at her, she smiled.

She glanced at the group. "Gentlemen, forgive the interruption." Then she turned to Malcolm. "I just wanted you to know I'm retiring for the evening." Heat gathered in her cheeks from her announcement.

"I'm ready to retire, also. I shall come with you."

"Malcolm," the other man interceded. "Don't forget about the fox hunt tomorrow at dawn."

"Yes, Mr. Crowley, I plan on attending. Now, gentlemen, if you will please excuse us, we shall see you in the morning."

Apparently, this was the third partner in the business. Short, plump, and balding. He didn't look much older than Malcolm, but then, the way the man carried himself and waddled as though his legs ached, he was probably much older than she suspected.

Camilla slipped her arm around Malcolm's elbow as they walked side by side up the grand staircase toward the bedroom. Her heart pounded with every step, and she hoped he couldn't feel her shaking.

He opened the door to their room and followed her inside. When the door closed and locked, her heart leapt to her throat. Squeezing her eyes closed, she tried to control her mind from wandering toward the bed.

"So," he began.

She jumped and turned his way. He leaned back against the door with his arms folded over his broad chest. The corner of his mouth lifted in a grin, and merriment twinkled in his eyes. Why did he have to look so sensual?

"Yes?"

"Are you ready to share the bed with your husband?"

"Of course, Malcolm." She forced a laugh. "I don't want you sleeping on the floor."

"Good, because I wasn't going to sleep on the floor. I have a big day tomorrow, and I need my rest."

"Yes, I heard mention of a fox hunt."

He nodded.

"Have you ever been on one?" she asked.

"It has been a while, but I still remember."

She waited for him to say more, but he didn't. It irritated her the way he looked so casual and unaffected, especially as the nerves inside her body played leapfrog. Then again, she was his wife. There was no reason she should be nervous, except for the fact she wanted him to know she was Camilla and not Kat.

"I suppose I shall get ready for bed now." She glanced toward the massive four-poster, the sheets already invitingly turned down. She walked to the armoire where the maid had placed her possessions, then caught sight of a nightgown already lying at the foot of the bed. "Who put this here?"

"Burwell's servant, of course."

She glanced over her shoulder. "I didn't instruct her to do this."

"I did." He shrugged. "It's her job."

A tremble ran through her body, but she smiled. "Thank you."

"I shall step outside for a few minutes while you change," he said.

"I appreciate that."

When he closed the door, she sighed. But the worst wasn't over. She still had to lie next to him throughout the entire night. It was a good thing the mattress was so large.

She undressed without hesitation then quickly threw on her flimsy pink nightdress. How could she spend the night in the same bed with him? What if he tried to kiss her? She would certainly melt into his arms. Under no circumstances could she let that happen until she told him the truth.

And that wouldn't happen anytime soon. Not until she knew he had feelings for her—and that he wasn't a criminal.

She blew out a few of the candles, hoping to hide herself as much as possible. She rushed to the vanity and yanked out the pins holding her hairstyle together, then pulled a brush through her hair, not worrying how it tortured her scalp. Before she had brushed the mandatory one hundred strokes and had time to braid her hair, heavy footsteps sounded outside the door. *Malcolm.* She dropped the brush on the vanity and darted to the bed. Just as she crawled under the blankets and pulled them to her chin, the door opened.

Chapter Eleven

MALCOLM GLANCED INSIDE. In the poorly lit room, a flash of pink flew by and then disappeared under a flurry of blankets. He chuckled softly. His dear little wife was acting shy again. That was so unlike her.

She had extinguished the candles, leaving only the moonlight that poured through the sheer curtains. Yes, she certainly had been behaving strangely, but he forced aside his confusion and proceeded as if she weren't even here.

He closed and locked the door. After he shrugged out of his overcoat and waistcoat, he draped them over the nearby chair, where he sat to remove his boots. Out of the corner of his eye, her face drew his attention. She peeked over the tops of her protective blankets like a woman afraid of her own shadow.

He focused back on his boots. "Is anything amiss, my dear?"

"What do you mean?" Her voice squeaked slightly.

"I mean," he said, pulling one boot off and starting on the other, "is this the way you are going to behave all night?" He removed the other boot. "Do I have to guard myself from accidentally bumping into you? I would hate for you to scream and have the whole household running to our door."

She lowered the blankets to just below her chin and gave a forced laugh. "You have an overactive imagination. I wouldn't do that."

"Your actions make me wonder, my dear. I can see the signs proving my own wife is repulsed by my body."

Her wide eyes softened and her tight mouth relaxed. "I may have told you that back then, but now… it is very different."

"Nothing is different."

"Malcolm, why won't you believe me?" She leaned forward, keeping the sheet up around her neck. "What do I have to do to make you believe?"

"Not one thing." He stood, turned his back to her, and unfastened his shirt. Silence hung in the air while he removed the garment and placed it over the back of a chair. He reached for the latches on his trousers, stopped, and glanced over his shoulder.

Her gaze roamed over him with a look of interest. As she studied him, the lines around the corners of her eyes softened and her lips lifted in a grin. Perhaps she wasn't repulsed.

"I'm going to remove my trousers, so you might want to hide your innocent eyes," he teased.

Her face flamed like a bonfire, and her lips curled in a cringe before she squeezed her eyes shut.

His anticipation shattered. Obviously, his judgment had been wrong. He frowned and turned his back to her again, proceeding to undress. The sheets rustled. She must have buried herself further under the covers.

"Malcolm? Do you have your nightshirt?"

"Yes. Why do you ask?" He reached for the garment and shrugged it over his head.

"The other morning when I crawled into your bed to help convince the soldiers, you weren't wearing a nightshirt."

He wanted to laugh but didn't. "You remember well, my dear."

"I… I had hoped you would wear one tonight. If not, I shall not be able to get a moment's rest."

Anger and pain sliced through his heart. Apparently, she still thought of him as a monster. "That is not my problem," he spat before climbing into bed.

His terrified wife hugged the side of the bed as if she were going to flee at any moment, so he stayed close to his side and made himself comfortable. Lying on his back, he stretched his arm over his head, staring at the ceiling.

What was so wrong with him that made her recoil every time she saw a hint of his skin? What was it about him that made her think he was a lowlife miscreant? He scolded his thoughts. It shouldn't matter what his wife thought of him, but for some reason, lately it *had* mattered. For once in his life, he wanted a wife who looked at him as if he were the most perfect man on earth.

"Malcolm?" Her soft voice broke the silence.

"Yes."

"Are you enjoying your stay at the Burwells' thus far?"

He rolled his head toward her. She lay on her side with her back to him, her brown hair flowing across the white pillowcase.

"So far, my stay has been quite pleasant." He paused. "How about you? Are you enjoying yourself?"

Keeping the blankets clutched in her hands, she turned toward him, but stayed as close to her side of the bed as possible. "I really don't know many women here, but they aren't allowing me into their circle of friends."

"If you remember, I warned you."

"Yes, but I thought I could act as if it didn't bother me. Truth be told, I do care what they think of me, and I especially care about what they think of you."

"Well, if it's any consolation, you are fooling most of them. They actually believe you have given up your former life and are concentrating on your own husband. I commend you for accomplishing that feat."

She smiled, and his anger sapped away. Strange how her smile could do that to him so quickly.

"And, Malcolm, I want to thank you for helping me. You didn't have to do it, you know."

"And do what, pray tell? Leave you to the wolves? What kind

of man would that make me?" He chuckled. "You know, I do it for purely selfish reasons. I don't want them thinking that I'm inconsiderate."

"No, they would never think that of you. You are a well-respected man in Dorchester. Everywhere I go, people tell me so."

"Indeed?" He turned to his side, leaning on his elbow. "Who tells you such lies?"

Her gentle laughter softened his heart even more.

"People around town tell me, and they don't lie. You really are a wonderful man. Who else would have put up with the kind of life my sis—" She suddenly broke off, and her face turned ashen.

"What?" His stomach clenched with uncertainty.

She swallowed hard. A pasty smile touched her mouth but didn't reach her eyes. "What I meant to say was that people are impressed with the way you publicly handled my past transgressions."

That wasn't what she'd intended to say, yet he had no idea what had been on her mind just then. There for a moment, he thought she was going to say *sister*. If so, why would she say that?

He relaxed on his elbow. "Thank you."

"Well, we better get some sleep." She snuggled into the covers and lay on her back. "You have to get up early tomorrow and win the fox hunt."

"I don't believe there are winners or losers in this particular sport, my dear. Except for the fox, of course." He chuckled again. "Have you never been to a fox hunt?"

She met his gaze. "No. I stayed home most of the time taking care of my ill father."

Confusion washed over him. "I thought you told me your sister took care of him."

Once again, color drained from her face. "Actually, both of us took care of him."

"Oh, well... Then I feel sorry for your lack of knowledge on the fox hunt. Just don't let the other women know tomorrow, and you will be just fine."

"I appreciate the advice."

He rolled on his back, making himself comfortable again, hopefully for the last time. But his mind swam with questions. Of course, it had been happening quite a bit lately, but tonight he'd received the impression she were purposely trying to hide something from him.

"Camilla?"

"Yes?"

"I have been meaning to ask since you returned from visiting your sister, but never had the chance."

"Ask what?"

"How is she faring? Is she well?"

Silence followed, and he turned his head to see why she hesitated. She chewed on her bottom lip, making her appear much younger. Something pressed on her mind, that was certain, and he hoped she would share that with him.

She licked her lips and met his stare. "To be honest, she isn't doing well at all."

"What ails her?"

"Do you recall how my father died?"

"I think you mentioned he slowly lost his mind, and then his body ceased to function."

"That is correct. Now my sister is showing the same signs. I'm extremely worried about her. I fear she may die, but her stay in the hospital is necessary and certainly creating bills."

He turned to his side to face her again. "Was she like that during her marriage to the earl?"

"I don't believe so."

"How bad is she?"

"She is in an institution for those who have gone mad."

He widened his eyes. "It's that serious?"

"Yes."

He reached out and caressed her cheek. "I'm sorry."

Her breath hitched, and then a small sigh escaped her throat. His heart picked up its rhythm again, and he wanted more.

With a sinking heart, he knew that would never happen.

"Thank you," she whispered.

"Are her needs being met?"

It was her turn to widen her eyes. She opened her mouth to speak, but then quickly bit her lip again.

"Camilla? What is on your mind? What are you avoiding telling me?"

She gave an uneasy laugh. "It is really not my place to ask what I have to ask, and I don't want my request to upset you."

He took a lock of her silky hair and rubbed it between his finger and thumb. "You will not upset me, I promise."

She took a deep breath. "I would like to get better care for my sister, but—" She paused. "But she doesn't have the funds to pay for a professional physician. I was just wondering, if... if..." She bit her lip again.

He smiled and cupped her face. "You were wondering if I could pay for a physician."

She nodded. "Mainly the hospital stay."

"And you couldn't ask me this before now?"

"I was too frightened."

"Frightened of what?"

"That you would say no."

If she had asked him for money the day she came back from Preston, he would have definitely refused. But now... Well, now their situation was different. Was it because they were in the same bed together and he experienced those heated feelings awakening inside him again? And there was a definite change about her since she'd returned. Dare he hope she was reforming?

"How much do you need?"

Her lips stretched into a wide grin, and her eyes twinkled like midnight stars. She grasped his hand, unaware she had dropped the blanket, which pulled his attention to her lovely bosom, and especially the thin pink nightdress she wore. Why had she worn such an enticing gown?

"Oh, Malcolm, thank you. You are such a wonderful brother-in-law." As soon as the words left her mouth, she stopped. Her jaw dropped.

"Brother-in-law?" he asked, momentarily forgetting about her nightgown.

Her laugh was strained. "I mean my sister has such a wonderful brother-in-law. You don't know how relieved I am at your willingness to help. Indeed, you are a gracious man."

She would quickly change her mind if she could read his thoughts right now. The longer the fullness of her breasts pressed so seductively against the flimsy nightdress—giving him wonderful images of what possibly lay underneath—the more he wanted to take her in his arms and kiss her. And yes, he wanted to make love to her.

Maneuvering himself, he leaned over her. She withdrew into the bed, and her eyes widened. "You better watch what sweet words you say to me, my dear." He ran his finger over her lips. "I might get the impression you like me."

Her pretty features broke out into a genuine smile again. "But I do like you."

Inwardly he groaned, fighting for control. Those weren't the words he wanted to hear right now. It was hard enough not to act upon his lonely, manly urges. "You have a strange way of showing it when you are sweeter to other men than your own husband."

Her other hand slid out from under the covers and touched his cheek, caressing his skin so very tenderly. "That was a different woman, Malcolm. I have changed. You will not see me behaving that way ever again."

His breathing became ragged. "Just for humor's sake, let us say I believe you. Tell me, if you plan on living a proper life, will you allow me in your bed?"

Her chest rose and fell quickly. "I um... Well, I don't think I'm ready," she answered slowly. "Although in time—"

"That is what I thought." The stab of rejection dug directly into his heart. He yanked his hand away. Rolling on his side, he turned away from her. "I don't wish to hear any more tales tonight. Good night, Kat."

He cursed his wandering thoughts. When was he going to learn not to be so gullible?

MORNING LIGHT PEEKED through half-closed curtains, warming Camilla's face. She stirred to awareness, and the silky sheets rubbed against her arms. Her mind cleared a little more. Last night had come to a terrible close. When she recalled the defeating way the conversation had ended with Malcolm, her heart withered in agony.

Yet other memories came sneaking through, those which happened to her during her sleepless night. Every time her leg bumped into Malcolm's, she awakened and scooted to the side of the bed. At one point she found herself curled against his muscular arm, and the memory still made her sigh with pleasure. Once during the night, she'd awakened to his arm wrapped around her waist, but when she shifted, he turned, facing the opposite direction. Why hadn't she stayed on her side of the bed like she had planned?

Still half-asleep, she rolled onto her side and reached for him, but the space next to her was empty. She came fully awake and glanced around the room. Malcolm stood by the window peering through the slits of the drapes out into the yard, and she sighed with relief.

He looked so handsome in his beige shirt and coffee-colored riding pants. She would give anything to know what was on his mind. The hollow, faraway look in his eyes revealed his inner turmoil.

She lifted herself on her elbow and swiped the long hair from her face. The small movement caught his eye, and his soft gaze jumped to her. At this moment, she wanted the unobtainable. She wanted him as her husband in all senses of the word. She didn't know whom to blame—her half-insane father for sending the wrong sister to Dorchester to marry Mr. Worthington, or her twin for the role she played in this game of deceit.

Camilla's love for Malcolm hadn't developed out of revenge for her sister's actions. The deep swell in her chest revealed an inner emotion for the incredibly kind man. A permanent love. Her mouth turned dry, and her heart hammered out of control. She had always wanted a man like Malcolm, and now she had one but couldn't do anything about it.

"Good morning, Malcolm." Although interest still touched his face, his jaw hardened.

"Good morning, Camilla," he answered in a tight voice. "Did you have a pleasant rest?"

"When I finally fell asleep, I slept fine."

He pulled away from the window and slowly came toward her. "Why couldn't you sleep?"

"I think the different bed kept me awake." She twisted the sheet between shaking fingers.

He sat on the mattress beside her. "Or was it the company you shared the bed with?"

"No, it wasn't the company."

"Are you certain? I know I didn't sleep very well because of who lay next to me." He touched her cheek then trailed his fingers down her neck in a tender caress.

Her heart hammered. His touch made it difficult to breathe. Another knot formed in her throat, harder to force down this time. "Did I toss and turn and keep you awake?"

The corner of his mouth lifted in a teasing grin. "Oh, yes, my dear, and it kept me alert for most of the night."

"Forgive me."

He chuckled. "I believe you have misunderstood. Every time you turned, you cuddled against me." His gaze dropped to his hand as it swept over her shoulder. "All night you were lying next to me, and I nearly couldn't contain my pleasure."

Her face burned from embarrassment. "Once again, I'm sorry."

"Don't be. It is a feeling I haven't known for quite some time." His voice grew husky. "You are very beautiful while you are asleep. You are especially beautiful now."

"Malcolm..."

He pushed her back on the bed. Winding a lock of her hair through his fingers, he continued to stare into her eyes. "I must be insane," he muttered, looming over her, "because right now I haven't a care how much you are repulsed by my presence."

"You are incorrect, Malcolm. I'm not repulsed in the least."

"Then why do you always pull away?"

"Because... I'm frightened."

His hands stilled. "Frightened? Of what?"

"Of the way you make me feel... the way my heart dances when you look at me as you're doing now," she finally admitted.

A soft groan tore from his throat. "Oh, Camilla, if only you meant it." He shook his head. "I wish I knew what was wrong with me. I have never wanted you this much before. I don't understand my own feelings."

She combed her fingers through his silky hair, holding his face close to her. "I think it's because you know I have changed. I'm not the woman you thought you married."

"If only that were true."

"It is." Making the first move, she leaned up and kissed him.

He tightened his embrace and kissed her passionately. His lips stroked hers tenderly, almost reverently. His hands splayed across her back as he held her body tight—so tight that she felt the beat of his heart as it knocked in the same rhythm as hers. Happiness burst inside her, but she held back the tears of joy.

Opening her mouth wider, she allowed the kiss to deepen until his hot tongue stroked hers. A small groan tore from his throat, matching hers. His body upon hers was comforting, much more than she realized, and she writhed beneath him, yearning for more. He broke the kiss, moving his mouth down her neck. She ached for his touch, for his mouth upon her, but it was still too soon. Her heart soared with the knowledge that he desired her just as much as she desired him, but nothing could happen between them. Not yet.

"Malcolm." She sighed his name as she toyed with his wavy hair. His lips traveled lower on her chest, getting very near the point where she wouldn't be able to stop him. Not ever. Although she wanted this badly, the timing was not right. "I fear if I don't let you go, you will be late for the fox hunt."

He lifted his head enough to gaze into her eyes. His mouth stretched into a wide smile, and it warmed her heart even more.

"Why should I care about a fox hunt when I'm enjoying myself with you?" He kissed her lips again before withdrawing once more. "Would you rather I attend the fox hunt instead of holding and kissing you until we are both mindless with passion?"

Just that thought made her sigh again. No, she didn't want him to leave, but perhaps it was better this way. He couldn't discover her identity yet. "Although that sounds completely wonderful, I would rather be at home than here. I want to be isolated in the privacy of our own bedchamber instead of having people I don't even know nearby and able to hear us. So perhaps we can do this when we return home?" She stroked the side of his face lovingly. "Besides, what would Lady Burwell's guests think if we didn't come down for most of the day?"

"They would think me a very fortunate man."

She arched an eyebrow. "Or that I'm a very fortunate woman."

Bending, he covered her mouth with his again. Heat spread through her quickly, and just as she began to enjoy it, he moved off the bed. "You are right, my dear. I would rather be at home doing this with you. Thanks for making me think clearly."

She laughed. "Your kisses were clouding my mind quickly."

"I'm happy to know that. You can rest assured that we will

continue this the minute we get back home." He winked before moving back to the chair as he finished dressing.

A sigh of relief escaped as she relaxed on the mattress. She had to find a way to tell him the truth soon. She couldn't fulfill the dream of truly being his wife otherwise.

Chapter Twelve

TWO HOURS LATER, Camilla stared at herself in the full-length mirror as she adjusted the sash on her dress. The woman staring back at her had sparks of excitement in her eyes and a rosy hue to her cheeks. Even her lips looked fuller, if that were possible. She giggled. How could she not feel so elated after what she and Malcolm shared this morning?

She wasn't anxious to meet the other ladies downstairs because she worried her expression would give away this morning's enjoyment. Yet if she dallied in her room any longer, they would think her lazy.

As she made her way down the grand staircase, the manor seemed unnaturally quiet. She supposed most of the guests either watched or participated in the hunt. When she strode onto the patio outside, a wild commotion caught her attention. People ran into the group of trees where the fox hunt was in progress, their voices raised in panic.

Curious, she quickened her step and followed, hearing bits and pieces of conversations carrying through the air.

"…someone has been hurt."

"…fell from his horse."

"…he is unconscious and bleeding."

Camilla searched through the small forest to find the injured party, but she couldn't see past the people heading in that direction. Lady Burwell came running away from the trees in the opposite direction toward the house. When she spotted Camilla, she waved and ran her way.

"Oh, my dear Mrs. Worthington. Something terrible has happened."

Camilla's heart dropped. Lady Burwell didn't have to say another word. The woman's terrified eyes and pale face bespoke of some horror that had befallen Malcolm.

The older woman grasped Camilla's hands. "Your husband fell from his horse and was knocked unconscious. We think his leg is broken, too."

A wave of dizziness washed over Camilla as fear clutched her chest. Breathing deeply, she quickly reined in her emotions and prepared herself for the worst. "How bad is he?"

"It's too soon to tell. My husband's physician just arrived, so we shall know momentarily."

Forcing herself to stay resolute, she squared her shoulders. "Take me to him."

Two horses were brought around for her and Lady Burwell. With the pounding of the horse's hooves toward Malcolm, she prayed he would be all right. Fear numbed her mind, and anxiety propelled her limbs into motion as she guided the animal, knowing she needed to get to him quickly.

When she reached the crowd surrounding him, her hopes plummeted. The expressions on the bystanders' faces were grim. Her heart wrenched. She couldn't lose Malcolm now.

She jumped from her horse and elbowed her way through the crowd until reaching his location. His face was deathly pale. A pool of blood circled his head, and a red spot dampened his shoulder. She gasped and covered her mouth.

A physician knelt beside Malcolm, listening to his chest. She waited for his answer, praying to hear a positive word. Her numb body wouldn't let her breathe.

The physician straightened and released a heavy sigh. He nodded to her and smiled. "His heartbeat is strong. That is a good sign."

Tears stung her eyes. *Thank you, gracious Lord.* The man gently rolled Malcolm over to examine his head wound. The doctor retrieved bandages from his bag and wrapped Malcolm's head.

A knot formed in her throat as she studied him. He seemed so helpless, so still. How could she handle this? Memories of her father's death crashed in around her. The thought of losing Malcolm, too, caused her body to tremble. Although the physician had given her words of encouragement, it didn't stop the doubts that plagued her mind.

Malcolm had to live. She couldn't imagine life without him.

When the physician finished bandaging Malcolm's head, he moved down to his twisted leg. He fastened two long sticks to immobilize the break, and her stomach lurched.

"I don't believe the break is too serious. I'm certain it will heal quickly," the doctor said.

She nodded, still afraid to say anything without losing what little was in her stomach.

Behind her, the crunching of wheels on rocky soil announced the wagon's approach, and the crowd parted to let it through. The physician and four other men gently lifted Malcolm into the bed of the wagon. The conveyance began its journey to the manor. She stared after them in a mindless state of panic. When somebody beside her took hold of her upper arm, she turned.

Brandon Kennedy stood closer than she wanted. "Would you like me to escort you back, my dear Mrs. Worthington?"

Irritation rolled in her stomach. "No. I can manage by myself."

He stepped closer. "What kind of gentleman would I be if I let you return alone?"

"Thank you for your kind offer," she replied in a bitter tone, yanking herself away from his grip, "but I would like to return with Lady Burwell." Without waiting for his reply, she lifted her skirts and hurried to catch up with her hostess, who waited by the horses.

"Mrs. Worthington?" Brandon called behind her. She ignored him, but the insistent man wouldn't leave her alone. He grasped her arm again. "Mrs. Worthington, a moment, please."

Straightening, she slowed her pace, letting the unrelenting man walk beside her. "I really cannot imagine what we have to discuss, Mr. Kennedy."

"I just want to make certain you are all right."

"I will be just fine the moment I find out my husband is conscious."

"Camilla." His voice lowered several notches. "You are talking to me, remember? You don't have to pretend now. I know you are not worried about your husband."

She stopped and narrowed her eyes at him. "Then you are sorely mistaken, once again."

He grumbled softly. "I think this episode was not an accident."

"What are you saying?"

"I think somebody tried to hurt him." He glanced around the area and stepped closer.

"Then we should inform Colonel Burwell at once."

"No," he said quickly. "I don't think we should, especially if you were behind this."

"Me?" She gasped. "Why would you say such a thing?"

"Not long ago, you were in my arms making plans to kill him, or have you forgotten?"

In stunned disbelief, she grabbed the folds of her skirt to keep her nervous hands occupied. Blinking, she fought the dizziness attempting to consume her vision. *Kat wanted Malcolm dead?* "I wasn't even in the fox hunt. How could I have made him fall from his saddle?"

"I heard rifle shots just before he fell."

She breathed deeply, her chest burning with anger. "I, sir, don't have a rifle. I had just left my room when I heard of the accident."

"Then if it wasn't you, maybe somebody is after him to get to you."

"Mr. Kennedy." She tilted her head to study him. "Why would anybody want to hurt my husband?"

"I don't know, unless—" He paused and looked around once again. "Unless it is because you backstabbed them in one of your deceitful bargains. I know from personal experience how well you make plans you don't intend to keep. Perhaps there are other men you have upset lately?"

"That is ludicrous." She folded her arms and blinked away frustrated tears. "What I think, Mr. Kennedy, is that your pride has been injured due to my rejection, and you are creating tales to upset me. Either that"—she lowered her voice slightly—"or you are the one who fired shots at my husband and are trying to point the finger at me." She lifted her chin a notch higher. "In any case, I believe I will have Colonel Burwell look into this incident, since I cannot believe a word that comes from your mouth."

"I wouldn't do that if I were you."

"You are not me, Mr. Kennedy," she snapped.

Anger and fear pushed her forward in haste, and she practically ran to her horse.

Why had Kat taken up with a man like Kennedy? Camilla's sister must have been insane for certain. Perhaps the good Lord took Kat from this world before she could cause any more harm to those around her.

When Camilla arrived at the Burwells' manor, she flew up two flights of stairs to her room and stopped abruptly. The colonel paced outside her bedchamber door, his brow creased. Her heart hammered against her ribs.

"Colonel? What is wrong?"

He tried to smile, but there was a slight quiver on his lips. "Mrs. Worthington, the physician doesn't want anybody in the room until he's finished examining your husband."

She twined her fingers together in worry. "Has my husband regained consciousness?"

"Not yet." He laid his hand on her shoulder. "But all will be made right, soon. You must be patient."

"Thank you."

"I'm not certain exactly what happened out there, but I shall look into the matter."

She struggled not to cry. "I think you should talk to Mr. Kennedy. He heard rifle shots just seconds before my husband fell from the horse."

Colonel Burwell scowled. "Are you jesting?"

"I wouldn't jest about a matter so serious. Mr. Kennedy implied someone might have shot at my husband."

"Then I shall certainly look into it."

"Thank you."

The bedroom door opened, and Camilla rushed forward, meeting the physician just inside the room. "How is he?"

"He is resting. A horse stomped on his right shin, and amazing as it sounds, there was only a small break. I placed a brace on his leg to help him heal faster. His head wound is not serious, although he did lose a lot of blood. However, I was surprised to see a bullet had grazed his shoulder." He frowned and shook his head. "I imagine plenty of bed rest and proper nourishment will cure that." He turned to the colonel. "I suggest Mr. Worthington not be moved for at least a week—just as a precaution, you understand."

"Quite right." The colonel nodded. "Mr. and Mrs. Worthington can stay here for as long as necessary."

"May I see him?" Camilla asked the physician.

"Yes, but allow him to rest."

"Thank you." She hurried past the two men and into their room, closing the door behind her.

Malcolm lay on the bed stripped of his clothes, his only covering the sheet and blanket. His right leg protruded from under the sheets, braced and precisely wrapped. Clean bandages now covered his head and shoulder. The color of his skin almost matched the white strips of cloth.

Her tense muscles demanded rest, and she plunked down

into the sitting chair next to the bed. "Oh, Malcolm," she sighed. "What has my sister gotten you into?"

She didn't expect an answer, but wished she could think of a solution. What if she, or her sister, had committed some offense to upset another man, like Brandon had suggested? And what if the gunshot had been intentional after all? Staying here another week would be dangerous for them both.

MALCOLM KEPT HIS gaze on his wife as the physician finished examining him. Camilla had remained by his side every minute, tending to his needs and comfort. Even through all of this, he didn't dare believe she had become the wife he had always wanted. He couldn't have his heart broken again.

When he regained consciousness, his head had throbbed and his leg ached just as painfully, but she had done everything possible to alleviate his discomfort, which was so different from the woman he had married.

After leaving their room this morning, he couldn't help but wonder if the very loving woman who had been in his arms was really the Kat he'd married. So, was she really his wife... or was she the sister?

Lately, she had said things that didn't ring true in his presence. He first had doubts when overhearing her conversation about politics with the other ladies yesterday. Then, last night, she said a few things that didn't make sense. He wouldn't have thought anything about it if her face hadn't turned ashen when he gazed at her in surprise during those times.

His doubt had escalated after they kissed so passionately before the fox hunt. The way she kissed him let him know this was inexperienced. Could the woman thawing his cold, hardened heart actually be his wife's *sister*? He didn't know if Kat had a twin, but it would make sense, because the woman who had returned from Preston was not the one he'd married.

The physician finally pulled away and closed his medical bag, then turned to Camilla. "Your husband is one fortunate man. His injuries could have been much worse."

"Thank you for checking him over." She smiled.

"Just remember what I told you earlier about keeping him still."

"I will follow your instructions."

"You have a caring wife, Mr. Worthington." The physician chuckled as he looked at Malcolm. "Appreciate it while you can."

Malcolm grinned, but he didn't answer.

Camilla showed the physician out and then returned. "Can I fetch you anything, Malcolm?"

He reached up and brushed his hand over the back of his head, then winced. "Perhaps a glass of brandy to dull the pain."

She rushed to the supply of liquor Lady Burwell had brought up earlier and, after pouring an ample draught, carried the glass back to him. He struggled to sit. She braced her arm behind him to help, and he breathed in her sweet fragrance. Oh, why did he have to be injured now?

"Thank you, my dear." He took the brandy and gulped it down. He fought back the burning sensation scalding his throat as he handed her the glass.

"I wonder how this could have happened?" she asked.

He frowned. "I have my suspicions."

"So, you believe it's not an accident?"

"I believe someone shot at me."

She sat on the edge of the bed next to his good leg. "I hate to say this, but I think Mr. Kennedy was behind it."

He studied her pretty face, studied wide green eyes still too innocent to be real. He nodded, and then winced as he moved his hand to his head. "He is at the top of my list."

"After they put you in the wagon, Mr. Kennedy stopped me. Some of his suggestions led me to believe he knew more than he let on about your accident. He is trying to put the blame somewhere else, though."

"Yes, I'm certain he is." He covered her trembling hand with his own. "Mr. Kennedy isn't a very good sport when it comes to losing, is he?"

"Losing?"

"I think if I were in his situation, I would be very upset over losing a woman to her very own husband." Her cheeks darkened with a blush, and he stroked her cheek. "He has lost you, has he not?"

"Mr. Kennedy never had me."

"Indeed? Several months ago, it appeared that way to me."

"Please, Malcolm, do not think of the past." She squeezed his hand, and her moist eyes pleaded with him to believe her words. "Just concentrate on the future. That woman no longer exists."

Strange, but she had been saying that phrase since her return from visiting her sister. He wondered if this could be another slip-up. "Camilla? What made you change your mind about me? What happened with your sister to make you come to care for me and my children?"

The sweet smile stayed on her rosebud mouth. "I realized how precious life is, and how I had been throwing mine away. Just like my father, my sister was never happy with her life, and I want to make mine better." Her blush grew darker. "I want to be happy. I want to feel love."

"Do you realize you have never really told me about your family?" He relaxed back against the many pillows stacked behind him, still keeping her hand within his. "In fact, I don't think you mentioned your sister much."

Unlike yesterday, her expression remained unreadable, no signs of panic. "What is there to tell?" she whispered, then cleared her throat. "My mother died when my sister and I were very young, and Father never remarried. His hands were full raising two daughters, though. We lived in a small country home. My father had a prominent business as a merchant for most of my life, but as the disease ate away at his mind, he spent his money unwisely. After he arranged for an earl to marry my sister, my father's condition grew worse."

"How bad was your father's illness when I met him?"

"His mind was pretty much gone, but I don't think my sister or I wanted to believe it."

"How did you feel when I asked for your hand in marriage?"

"I was shocked, to say the least, but only because we didn't know each other, and nor did you know my father very well. I went along with it to please him, since I wasn't used to disobeying him."

Malcolm found that strange, because after they married, she couldn't *stop* disobeying him. Once again, there was a hole in her story. "Tell me about your sister."

Her expression didn't waver. "What would you like to know?"

"What is her name?"

She hesitated again. "Katherine," she said in a whisper.

Shock vibrated through him. "Katherine?" He lifted his brows. "Is Kat her nickname?"

"Yes."

"The first time I called you Kat, you threw a temper. If you recall, I was comparing you to a wild animal. You weren't the pussycat I had thought you were. After that, I called you Kat just to see you react."

"I know."

"Why did you not tell me?"

She shrugged. "Perhaps because I was so upset."

"What is Katherine like? Is she like you?"

Camilla laughed and gave a shake of her head. "Kat is nothing like me. We are as different as morning and night."

With his free hand, he toyed with the curl of hair by her ear. Pain sliced through him from his shoulder, but he tried to ignore it. He enjoyed touching her and didn't want anything to stop him. "Is she as pretty as you?"

Her smile widened. "People say we look alike."

His heart picked up rhythm. "What do you think?"

She stared at him for a few seconds before leaning over and kissing his cheek. "I think you need to get some rest. I don't want the physician scolding me for not taking proper care of you."

She attempted to withdraw, so he grasped her upper arm, halting her. "Don't leave. I have enjoyed carrying on a pleasant conversation with you."

"As have I, but the physician said you need to rest."

"I will rest, but before you go, I would like a kiss."

Her eyes smoldered. "Well, all right, but it can only be a small kiss."

"Why only a small kiss? What if I want more?"

She giggled. "You have lost a lot of blood, my dear husband, and you are as weak as a babe."

"I bet I can prove you wrong." He waggled his eyebrows.

"Malcolm…"

He pulled her against his chest, and she gasped. Touching his muscular chest changed his mood completely, making the moment more intimate. A surge of warming tremors shot through him, and he yearned for more. "Kiss me like you did yesterday morning," he whispered.

"No, Malcolm. Not yet. You must regain your strength."

"Then just give me a sample of what I can expect when I'm feeling better."

He met her mouth in a soft kiss. She pecked lightly on his lips at first, but he tightened his hold and deepened the kiss. Heat burned through him, getting hotter by the second. Her sweet kiss ignited flames clear down to his toes. Abruptly she broke away, leaving him gasping for more.

"You are a tease, my darling wife." Taking her hand, he lifted it to his mouth and kissed. "Do you have any idea what you do to me?"

Her eyes darkened. "I'm truly sorry," she whispered.

"Oh, no, my sweet. Never be sorry for making me happy." He pulled her closer again and kissed her, but once again, she withdrew.

"That is not why I'm sorry." She stroked his chin. "I'm sorry," she continued, "because I have to stop this before it goes any farther." She laughed and quickly jumped off the bed.

"Oh, so cruel." He groaned in mock torture. "You shall pay for that one."

"Later, my dear." She moved toward the door. "Now rest." She walked out of the room.

He relaxed and turned his thoughts to his previous questions. Although he had no solid proof, he actually believed Camilla was the other sister. She'd mentioned she and her sister were very different, and since she had come back from Preston, his wife had done a complete turnaround. Now he was almost convinced the woman he was falling in love with wasn't his wife. Instead of upsetting him, he relished the idea, and anticipated the moment when he learned the truth.

Chapter Thirteen

C AMILLA COULDN'T ENDURE the lazy afternoon by herself, and nor could she chance seeing Malcolm so soon. His alluring gaze was too powerful, and lately, she didn't want to fight it. Never having felt this way with Fredrick, she now wanted to experience the greater joy of being a wife. Being a *real* wife. Which meant she had to find the courage to tell Malcolm the truth.

She had spent an hour walking through Lady Burwell's flower gardens, but Camilla needed to return and check on Malcolm. When she stepped across the patio, her attention snapped to Lady Burwell, who sat sipping tea by herself. Camilla wasn't in the mood to visit her, but she smiled in greeting and approached.

"Good afternoon, Lady Burwell."

The older woman nodded, placing her teacup on the table in front of her. "How is your husband faring?"

"I believe he is getting stronger by the day. In fact, if the physician will permit, I think Mr. Worthington will be able to travel by tomorrow or the day after."

"How wonderful." Lady Burwell motioned to the chair next to her. "Would you like to join me?"

Reluctantly, Camilla sat, but refused the tea Lady Burwell tried to pour her.

"You know, Mrs. Worthington," Lady Burwell began as she

picked up her cup, "I'll confess my first impressions of you were wrong. You are nothing like I thought."

Camilla crinkled her brow. "What do you mean?"

"Well, like everyone else, I had heard rumors about you before actually meeting you, so I had formed my own opinion. Now that we have spent time together, I must admit how wrong I was. The gossip circles have judged you unfairly."

"Thank you." Camilla paused. "May I inquire to what they are saying?"

A red tint colored the hostess's face as she lowered her gaze. "Well, I'm certain you have some idea."

"Does it have to do with my brazen behavior with other men?"

Lady Burwell met Camilla's stare and widened her eyes. "Yes."

"Did you hear how incredibly selfish and underhanded I was?"

Lady Burwell nodded.

"And how I treated my husband and stepchildren with disdain?"

"Yes, to all."

Camilla toyed with the lace cuff of her long sleeve. "I'm happy to say the gossip circles are wrong. I'm not that woman."

"I know. I have seen firsthand how loving you are toward Mr. Worthington's children, and especially how attentive you are to your husband." Lady Burwell chuckled. "In fact, I must say you are a better woman than most of the ladies I'm friends with."

Camilla smiled. "I thank you for telling me that."

Lady Burwell reached over and patted Camilla's hand. "And I think your husband is very fortunate to be married to such a caring woman."

"I hope he sees me in that same light."

Lady Burwell laughed. "Oh, I think he does. I have noticed the way he looks at you, and there is a great amount of love in his expression."

Camilla's heart quickened. "You believe he truly loves me?"

"Indeed, as I can see your love for him."

Lowering her gaze to her sleeve again, Camilla confessed, "I have never felt this way toward any man. I feel dizzy around him, yet in his arms, I'm safe and protected."

"Does he know?"

Camilla lifted her attention to Lady Burwell. "I have never told him."

"What is stopping you?"

Camilla tried to hide her smile, but her lips stretched of their own accord. Lady Burwell would absolutely die if she knew what stopped her. "I'll certainly ponder your words." She stood. "But I must get back to my husband."

She turned and entered the house. The truth about her identity had to come out. Now.

MALCOLM SAT BY the open window and smiled. Since the patio was underneath the bedroom window, he had heard the conversation between Lady Burwell and his wife.

As he closed the window, his heart beat with unprecedented life, opening a new future for him. A future he couldn't wait to pursue. Camilla *loved* him.

Whether or not she admitted her love, he planned on telling her his feelings tonight. He still doubted she was the woman he exchanged marriage vows with, and that thought made him happier than he expected. If the woman wasn't his wife, that meant she hadn't been intimate with other men.

Just the thought of making her his wife in the bedroom sent his heart soaring. He wanted to have children with her, to grow old together, and love her for eternity. But... what if he was wrong?

The sudden change of his thoughts wiped away his energetic

smile. If, instead, she were really the woman he exchanged vows with, could he still love her?

When Camilla walked into the bedroom and closed the door, he tore his gaze from the curtains and focused on her. Her smile radiated, stirring a heat deep inside him. She was too beautiful to be the woman he married. He prayed he was right about her identity.

"Good afternoon, Malcolm. How do you feel?"

He ran his gaze over her attire, and his heart softened. The daffodil dress made her brown hair stand out. He wanted to stroke the curl by her ear so badly his finger itched. Before he went utterly mad, he needed to bring her closer. "I have never felt better."

"I suggested to Lady Burwell she have their physician check you over again, because I think you are strong enough to go home."

"As do I."

"I know the children miss you, as I'm certain you miss them."

"What about you? Do you miss the children?"

Her smile widened. "I'm completely lost without them."

Her words warmed his heart. "Come sit by me." He motioned to the empty chair next to him. "I would like to have a serious discussion with you."

She nodded and moved past him, but before she sat, he grabbed her wrist and pulled her beside him. He slipped his arms around her waist and brushed his mouth across her lips. Lifting his head, he gazed into her mesmerizing eyes, now laced with desire.

"Why did you do that?" she asked.

"Because I felt like it. I haven't seen you since last night, and I have missed you."

"And I have missed you."

"Then kiss me and show me."

Without hesitation, she bent her head and met his waiting lips. He turned her and sat her on his lap while he kissed her passionately. Her fingers delved through his hair, and he loved her gentle strokes.

Grudgingly, he broke the kiss. They needed to talk. Now was the perfect time to express his feelings, and it couldn't be delayed a moment longer. Keeping her on his lap, he relaxed in the heavily cushioned chair. She looked at him with a smile of satisfaction gracing her lovely mouth.

"I have wanted to do that all morning," he said.

"Me too."

"Then why didn't you come to see me sooner?"

"One of us needs to stay strong, Malcolm."

"And, as always, it has to be you," he said.

"If I let you have your way, your leg would never heal."

"Probably not, but I would be one very happy man."

She laughed and cuddled closer. Wrapping his other hand around her, he held her in place. He liked this sitting arrangement too much.

"What do you want to talk about?" she asked.

He stared into her hypnotic gaze. "Our future."

"What about our future?"

"I would like you to share it with me."

Her smile broadened. "Indeed?"

"Yes."

"But why?"

"Because I have fallen in love with you," he confessed.

A gasp escaped her throat, and liquid gathered in her eyes. "Are you certain?"

"Very certain."

A tear slid down her cheek before she buried her face into his neck. "I have fallen in love with you, as well." Her voice broke.

He kissed the side of her face. "And is the idea so terrible it brings tears to your eyes?"

She hiccupped a laugh. "I'm just so happy you share the same feelings."

"How could I not fall in love with you? You are my world

now, and you have taken over my heart."

"Oh, Malcolm… I do love you, but—"

"There are no buts. Not this time."

He kissed her again, enjoying the way her mouth melded with his. She wrapped her arms around his neck, pulling him closer. Anxious to finally make her his wife, he moved his hands to the long row of pearl buttons holding her dress together, eager to be rid of the garment, but just as he plucked at a button, someone knocked on the door.

She jumped off him and quickly adjusted her dress. Silently he cursed. He could kill whoever it was that had decided to interrupt their intimate moment.

Camilla hurried to the door and opened it. Colonel Burwell and one of his servants stood on the other side. Grim expressions marred their faces.

"I hope you will forgive our unannounced timing, but I have discovered some vital information and knew I had to share it with you."

Camilla nodded and motioned for them to enter. She moved behind them as they walked closer to Malcolm.

He met Colonel Burwell's stare. "What is it you have to tell me?"

The colonel shifted from one foot to the other, his gaze moving around the room too quickly. "The day of your accident, your wife suggested someone had been shooting at you."

"Indeed, they had," Malcolm snapped.

"Well, I asked my servants and the other guests, and nobody saw anything out of the ordinary that morning. However, just today, my gardener"—he motioned to the man standing next to him—"found an abandoned rifle in the same area where you fell from your horse."

Camilla gasped and rushed to Malcolm's side. He took her shaky hand in his and gave it a gentle squeeze, trying to reassure her.

"As I searched the area," the colonel continued, "I noticed

footprints in the dirt. What captured my attention about these markings was that they were not large like a man's, but smaller, like a young boy's." He sighed heavily. "I'm led to believe some lad must have been target shooting and missed."

Anger throbbed in Malcolm's head. *Target shooting, my eye!* Yet what other conclusion could Colonel Burwell come to?

"Is it not a misfortune that the lad left his rifle there? I would think he would take it with him." Malcolm nodded. "Nonetheless, I appreciate your assistance in this matter. And thank you for letting me know what you have found."

The colonel smiled, moving his gaze to Malcolm's injured leg. "I have heard you are doing better."

"That, I am, sir. In fact, your physician mentioned I may be able to leave tomorrow."

"That is splendid. I'm happy to know you have recovered quickly. However, know that you may stay as long as you wish in order for your leg to heal."

"Thank you, Colonel Burwell. Your hospitality has been appreciated, I assure you."

Camilla remained standing by his side until the colonel and the gardener left and closed the door. He tugged on her arm and brought her back to his lap, where he cuddled her close.

"Oh, Malcolm." She buried her head in his neck. "I fear for your safety."

He kissed the side of her face, deeply breathing in her flowery scent. "Why, my love?"

She pulled away and met his stare. "Because you know as well as I that the incident was no accident at all."

He nodded. "I know."

"Why would Colonel Burwell think a lad was target shooting? Why would anyone do that so near the fox hunt?"

He cupped her face and smiled. "My dear, you worry overmuch. Please do not fret any longer. With you by my side, nothing will happen."

"Promise?"

"Your love will be my shield, I assure you." He ended with a kiss, praying in his heart that within time he would believe his own words.

Chapter Fourteen

Happiness and gaiety filled Malcolm's home upon their return. The children ran into their father's arms and greeted him with kisses, and then turned and rained the same affection on Camilla. Her chest expanded with happiness.

For the rest of the day, she stayed by Malcolm's side as he sat on the couch and played with the children. He touched her often with gentle caresses. Was this all a wonderful, beautiful dream?

But all dreams had to end. When she first decided to play her sister's role, she was out to prove him guilty of unlawful actions. Yet now that she loved him, she didn't want anything to happen to him. Whoever had tried to kill him was still out there. Her hopes of living happily ever after with Malcolm and his children faded quickly, and she couldn't stand the suffocation tightening her chest.

The day's end drew near, and she wondered if he would invite her to share his bed. They hadn't made love yet, at which she was relieved, but she still enjoyed holding him while she fell asleep.

In the parlor, Malcolm finished his nightly reading of bedtime stories to James and Lizzy, and Camilla joined the trio on the sofa. The more time she spent with his family, the softer her heart grew toward them. This was now *her* family, and nothing and nobody would take it away from her… except her own lies or someone killing him.

No matter what, she needed to tell him the truth. Never again did she want lies to come between them.

Jane stepped into the room to collect the children. James and Lizzy gave Camilla kisses and hugs before leaving with their nanny to retire for the night. Once the children were gone, Malcolm wrapped Camilla in his arms. She cuddled against him, loving the perfect way they fit together.

"Today was wonderful." She stroked his wide chest. "Was it not?"

"Wonderful is certainly the correct word. I don't think I have had a better day." He lifted her chin, so she looked into his eyes. "And I want tonight to be just as special."

She smiled, her heart beating an irregular rhythm. "That thought crossed my mind, as well."

"And what, pray tell, were you thinking?"

"I think I quite enjoy being held by you, but—"

"No buts." A low rumble started in his chest from his laugh, and he touched his finger to her nose. "Would you think it improper of me if I suggested retiring to our room now?"

"*Our* room? Have you forgotten in this house we have separate chambers?"

"I want you in my bed from this day forth."

Excitement flowed through her, and she wanted the same thing. It was right, she convinced herself... After all, according to the certificate, they were already married. "I do like the sound of that."

He leaned down and covered her mouth with his. The kiss was brief, yet blissfully pleasing. That would never change as long as she loved him with all her heart. She pulled away and stood, reaching out her hands for him to take. Behind her, footsteps rushed into the room, causing her and Malcolm to swing their heads toward the intruder.

Broderick doffed his hat and nodded to her, then turned his attention to Malcolm. "Forgive me for this rude intrusion, but I must speak with you."

Malcolm struggled to stand, and when he did, he leaned against Camilla. "Can it not wait until tomorrow?"

Broderick twisted his hat against his stomach. "It cannot."

Camilla looked into Malcolm's eyes and smiled. "Don't be too long. I'll be waiting for you." She winked then pulled away. She walked past Malcolm's friend and nodded. "Good evening, Broderick. Please try not to keep Mr. Worthington on his leg too long. I fear the swelling will return."

"Yes, Mrs. Worthington."

She stepped out of the parlor and pulled the double doors closed behind her. The seriousness on Broderick's face worried her. Would Malcolm trust her enough to share what he learned tonight?

"WHAT DO YOU mean they suspect me?" Malcolm pushed his fingers through his hair in irritation.

"One of my friends works for the magistrate, and he overheard the magistrate and two other men talking." Broderick paced the floor. "He overheard them saying that you were the one who broke into Mr. Clarkston's office."

"That's utterly ridiculous," Malcolm snapped. "We were together at the tavern that evening. I have you for my alibi."

"There's more." Broderick stopped in front of him. "Brandon Kennedy mentioned to the magistrate that your wife had talked about killing you a few months ago."

Malcolm's blood turned to ice and his gut twisted. This couldn't be happening. Camilla would never...

His thoughts stopped quickly. *Camilla* wouldn't have done it, but *Kat* would. He still needed proof, but he felt deep in his heart that Camilla was not the wicked woman he had married.

"Camilla didn't try to shoot me." Malcolm's voice softened.

"She was in our room and still in bed when I left for the fox hunt. She was seen leaving the house after I was shot."

Broderick released a gust of air from his mouth. "That's good. However, we still need to try to clear your name before something worse happens."

"No." Malcolm's leg throbbed, so he hobbled to the couch and fell upon it, and then lifted his leg up on the stool. "I need to find the person responsible for doing this to me. That is the only way to stop this."

"I think Kennedy is behind it."

Malcolm nodded at his friend.

"Ever since your wife turned away Kennedy's attentions," Broderick said, "more things have been happening to you."

"I know, but I would rather have my marriage this way than the way it was before."

Broderick gave him a small smile. "I still cannot believe it. When you told me earlier today, I was in complete shock. Who would have guessed Kat—"

"No, Broderick. Her name is Camilla."

Broderick shifted his stance. "My apologies. I didn't mean—"

"I know. It was a shock to all of us." Malcolm chuckled. "Imagine my surprise when I admitted I was in love with her."

"Unfortunately, we don't know if it is your wife or the sister in the asylum. In a way, I wish she were still the old Kat. Then Kennedy would be occupied, and we would have a better chance of catching him trying to sabotage you."

Malcolm scratched his chin. "There has got to be another way."

"I'll talk to my friend who works for the magistrate and see what else he knows."

"Good thinking, Broderick." As his marriage was finally going the way he had always dreamed about, now more than ever, he needed to bring a stop to the person trying to ruin him. If they tried to shoot him again, the bullet just may hit his heart and kill him.

"Were you able to snoop through Colonel Burwell's study?" Broderick asked.

"No. My broken leg ruined my plans."

"That is all right. We'll find who has been stealing your drawings."

"We had better. I grow weary of this game." Malcolm struggled to stand. Broderick hurried to help, but Malcolm motioned him away. "We will have to wait until morning to figure out a plan. Hopefully, my leg will feel better, because I have many errands to run."

"Is there anything you would like me to do?"

"If I do, I shall let you know in the morning." Putting all his weight on the cane, he walked toward the door. "Now if you will excuse me, my wife is upstairs in my bed. And I'm not foolish enough to keep her waiting any longer."

Broderick laughed and clapped Malcolm on the shoulder as he passed. "I'm happy to see you have found someone to love."

Malcolm threw him a grin. "You aren't the only one happy." He winked.

It took him a while longer than he wanted, but he finally made it up the stairs to his room. He walked in and stopped. Only a single candle was lit, illuminating his wife on his bed.

Asleep.

He chuckled and ran his fingers through his hair. It looked as though tonight wouldn't be when he made love to her. Then again, Broderick had given him a lot to think about. Perhaps he needed to do some serious contemplating before taking the plunge with Camilla.

He didn't know what this woman had done to him, but whatever it was, he liked it. He also couldn't let her distract him from his fight for justice. He only hoped she would support him and still want to remain by his side.

But a nagging thought in the back of his mind told him something wasn't right. Why had more things started happening to him since his wife returned from caring for her sister? His heart wouldn't allow him to believe the worst. He must trust that she wasn't part of any of this.

Broderick Turner,

Watch Brandon Kennedy closely tonight. I have it on good authority that Mr. Kennedy is going to meet Captain Wilkes in secret to sell him some drawings. I fear your friend, Malcolm Worthington, will be blamed for something, and I want it stopped.

Your Friend, Always

Malcolm scowled as he glanced at the missive in his hand. "Who wrote this?"

"I wish I knew," Broderick grumbled. "It was left for my friend who works for the magistrate. He said a lovely woman with red hair gave it to him."

Malcolm snapped his attention toward his friend. "Do you know a woman with red hair?"

Broderick frowned. "I know a few, but none of them would be considered *lovely.*"

Malcolm pushed away from his drawing board in the office and leaned on his cane as he limped to the window. "The question is, how well do we trust this source?"

"Indeed, that's an excellent question. I think I may have an answer." Broderick moved beside him. "The missive asks me to watch Kennedy closely. So, as long as I can do it without being seen, I might be able to tell if this unknown person is trying to help us or not."

"I don't know, Broderick." Pursing his lips, Malcolm started out the window into the busy street. He was thankful Kennedy and Crowley hadn't arrived at work yet this morning. It gave him more time to think. "What woman would want to help us?"

"I was also pondering this since I received this note." Broderick tapped his finger on the windowpane. "You mentioned your wife was worried about you. Do you suppose it's Camilla who wrote this?"

"Impossible!" Malcolm moved back to his drawing board and stared at the blank page. Camilla wouldn't do this without telling him, would she? He couldn't allow her to do that. If she were caught by one of the soldiers...

He shook off the frightening chill running down his back. He wouldn't let that happen.

"Broderick? Gather all the information you can. And yes, if possible, I want you to spy on Kennedy tonight." He swung his gaze toward his friend. "I wish I wasn't a gimp, or I could assist."

"I can do it." Broderick stepped toward him. "I won't get caught."

"I pray we will be able to catch Kennedy and Wilkes in the act. I would love nothing more than to see those two men sent to the gaol."

"I agree wholeheartedly. The pompous captain thinks he can control everything. He acts like he runs Dorchester. I don't know who gave him that assignment, but whoever it was needs to retract it."

The office door opened as Brandon Kennedy entered. Both Malcolm and Broderick quickly ended their conversation. A gust of wind blew in a few leaves under Kennedy's feet as he nearly skipped toward his office. He seemed chipper today as he shrugged off his overcoat.

"Good morning, Kennedy," Malcolm greeted him.

Brandon turned and nodded. "Malcolm. Mr. Turner." He whistled as he walked to the rack and hung up his coat. "A fine morning, is it not?"

Malcolm threw Broderick a wary glance. "Yes, it is, Kennedy. You look rather cheerful today."

Brandon walked back to his desk, his grin widening with each step. "The fact is, I am extremely happy, and so will you be when I tell you the good news."

"Good news?" Malcolm limped away from the window.

"Indeed. I heard that Lord Arlington is in the market for someone to build him a gr and manor in Dorchester." Brandon chuckled. "That man is worth a lot of money, and I'm certain he'll pay a good price."

"That is good news." Malcolm nodded. "When will you meet with him?"

"I have sent him a letter in hopes of setting up an appointment to meet with him next week." Brandon leaned back in his chair and threw a skeptical glare at Malcolm. "I'm hoping your streak of bad luck has ended, because if you draw up the plans, I don't want them getting lost somehow."

Malcolm fisted his hands under his desk. Working with this man made him want to throttle him constantly. "I assure you, my streak of bad luck has ended." At least, he hoped.

"That's good to know." Brandon turned back to his desk and started writing on a blank page.

Malcolm gritted his teeth, trying his hardest not to show the elation filling him. Brandon didn't know—and hopefully, would never find out—but Malcolm already had an appointment scheduled with Lord Arlington. In three days, in fact. Malcolm would get that account before Brandon, and hopefully, this would be the last he had to work with Kennedy and Crawley.

The tower clock by the courthouse chimed the tenth morning hour. Broderick stood and cupped Malcolm's shoulder. The movement slightly relieved his tension.

"Well," Broderick said, "that is my signal to get to work. I need to run errands for my boss's wife. If I'm not back shortly, she will dismiss me."

Malcolm gave him a nod. "Let me know if she gets tough on you. I have a personal relationship with that mean Mrs. Worthington." He winked.

Broderick laughed as he left the office. Malcolm hoped his humor would cover the panic over the past few minutes.

"Worthington? I see your leg is healing nicely."

Malcolm glanced at Brandon. "Yes, thanks to my wife's loving care."

The other man chuckled as he picked up some contracts and shuffled through them. "I never thought I would hear you say that about Kat."

"I would have to agree with you."

Brandon threw him a look over his shoulder. "I suppose you have forgiven her for her unfaithfulness since you exchanged vows?"

Malcolm clenched his jaw and fought the urge to use his fists to vent his frustration. He stuffed his hands in his pockets. "Brandon, indeed. This is no kind of talk for two gentlemen."

Brandon shrugged. "I thought to make conversation."

"And I'm uncomfortable speaking about this, if you don't mind."

"I fully understand." Brandon's grin turned mocking. "I, too, would be quite embarrassed if I had a wife like yours."

Exhaling deeply, Malcolm turned away from Brandon and looked at the papers scattered on his desk. Several drawings needed to be finished by the end of the week, and he really didn't have the patience to talk nonsense with his partner. He'd rather punch the man in the nose and cause him excruciating pain.

"But I have to add how impressed I am that Kat changed her ways," Brandon added.

Malcolm tightened his grip on his drawing pen. The quill snapped in two. "Would you cease this ridiculous discussion?"

"I'm only trying to point out—"

"Enough!" Malcolm pushed away from the desk, knocking over his chair in the process. He glared at Brandon. "If you'll excuse me, I have errands to run."

He stuffed his drawings in a satchel before throwing his long, dark brown cape over his shoulders. He hobbled out of the office, not going fast enough. The wind hit his face, and he squinted through the flying debris of dirt and leaves as he crossed the street. A crowd of soldiers gathered outside the nearest tavern, raising their cups in a toast. Their boisterous laughter gnawed on Malcolm's nerves.

Down the street toward one of the several inns in town, a familiar figure caught his eye. Blinking against the blasting wind, he noticed a woman walk in front of Captain Wilkes as they entered the building. The back of her green cloak looked familiar, and he rubbed his eyes to focus better. By the time he looked up again, the couple had disappeared.

His heart hammered against his ribs and the palms of his hands sweated. The woman with Captain Wilkes wasn't whom he had thought. Camilla wasn't like Kat. Although he still didn't know for certain who she really was, the woman he loved wouldn't dally with other men. Camilla loved him as much as he loved her.

Didn't she?

Hurrying into the bank, he calmed his fears, telling himself he hadn't seen Camilla with Captain Wilkes. That must be his insecurities playing games with his mind, and he blamed Kennedy for making him doubt himself.

He turned, greeted the bank clerk, and requested a large sum of money to be withdrawn from his account. It was time he purchased a *real* wedding ring for his wife—the woman he never thought he could love so much. He wouldn't put off giving her this gift any longer.

He signed his name, and with the money in an envelope safely tucked into his vest pocket, he turned to leave. Before he reached the door, it opened, and an older man wearing a top hat and dark brown cape entered. *Lord Arlington?* Malcolm's breath caught in his throat due to the surprise. He hadn't heard the lord would be in town this soon.

Doubts quickly filled his head. Did Kennedy know, and would he try to persuade Lord Arlington to sign a contract with him and Crawley? Malcolm must stop it.

Lord Arlington brushed the leaves from his overcoat and looked up at Malcolm. His eyes widened and his grayish-brown eyebrows lifted.

"Good day, my lord." Malcolm smiled. "'Tis a pleasure to see you on this foul morning."

"The weather doesn't cater to our needs, that's for certain."

Malcolm took a step closer to the other man. "I'm surprised to see you in Dorchester. Have your plans changed since we last spoke?"

"Only a little." Lord Arlington rested on his walking stick.

"If you don't mind"—Malcolm lowered his voice, praying that those who worked in the bank wouldn't run to Kennedy with the information they would overhear now—"we could meet sooner to discuss the plans for your manor."

Lord Arlington nodded. "I'm actually free this evening."

"Then so am I."

"I'm staying at the Lion's Paw Inn." He motioned toward the street. "Would you like to meet me at nine o'clock this evening?"

"I'll be there at nine sharp." Malcolm's heartbeat quickened with excitement.

He hurried out of the building as he tried to create an excuse to tell Camilla for why he had to leave for a meeting this evening. He still hadn't told her the truth—that he was secretly trying to find patrons so as to build his own clientele. He didn't want to get her too hopeful, just in case his scheme failed, and he had to remain working for an imbecile like Brandon Kennedy.

Chapter Fifteen

C AMILLA STEPPED OUTSIDE onto the back porch, and the wind blew against her face. The children were in the nursery. This afternoon, she needed time for herself, yet the more she thought about her problems, the more worried she became.

With a heavy ache in her chest, she walked toward the stable. The maid, Beth, had informed Camilla of the conversation one of the servants had eavesdropped on while at the bank. Mr. Worthington was meeting someone tonight at nine o'clock to secure a deal. All the servant knew was that the men spoke in hushed tones.

Anxiety hammered through Camilla. Would Malcolm tell her about this meeting? Was this the illegal action Kat had mentioned before she died? She prayed Malcolm would trust her enough to tell her the truth.

Doubts filled her mind, and she groaned. Although she loved him with all her heart, she didn't think he fully trusted her. Although she had a hard time understanding why Malcolm did this, it was in his character to protect his heart. But her love for him was just as strong. She wanted him, his children, and the wonderful life she had experienced so far.

Stopping inside the stable, she glanced at her favorite horse, Thunder. The dark brown gelding neighed, bobbing his head in greeting. She smiled and walked to him, picking an apple out of the bucket by the door.

The animal acted more than happy to get the food, and as he munched noisily, she stroked his mane. She had always enjoyed being with horses, but right now, worry for Malcolm overrode all else.

From bits and pieces she had overheard him and Broderick discussing from time to time, she worried that Malcolm was trying to find the person who was stealing his work. She wouldn't blame him if he was, but what if whatever he planned would get him arrested? She couldn't bear the heartache of seeing him put in jail.

The sound of scraping wood echoed through the stable. She stopped. Listened. But didn't hear it again. "Is anyone there?"

Thunder neighed and shuffled his feet. She stepped away from him, further into the stable, and listened. Her skin prickled with fear, unease running down her spine—a feeling somebody watched her.

"Is anyone here?"

Still no sound.

Shaking her head, she turned back to Thunder. Why had she experienced a cold chill as if someone watched her every move? She chuckled and stroked the horse's mane. Must be her imagination.

"Good day, Mrs. Worthington."

She jumped and turned toward Hyrum, one of the stable boys, as he walked through the wide-open doors. Seeing a familiar face, she sighed. "How are you faring today, Hyrum?"

"Just fine, Mrs. Worthington." He picked up a brush and carried it over to her. "Thought you might like this."

She smiled, taking the brush from him. "Thank you. You seem to know what I want before I can speak it."

He grinned ear to ear, nearly displaying all of his teeth. "Did you need me to have your horse ready tonight?"

She scrunched her forehead. "Why would I want that?"

He stepped closer then peeked over his shoulder as he looked around the stable. Why did he look so secretive?

"Just in case you want to follow your husband, like you usually do when spying on him."

Camilla's breath caught in her throat. "Spy on my husband, Hyrum?" She turned to brush Thunder's mane.

"Well, you haven't done it for a while, and I thought that's why you were here in the stable."

She tightened her hand around the brush in mid-stroke. *Spy on my husband.* Her heartbeat accelerated. Yes, she *could* spy on her husband.

"And what else will you help me with?"

"Just like always, I'll have the servant's clothes in the empty stall for you to change into."

She smiled. "You have done well, Hyrum. Remind me how much I owe you."

Red stained his cheeks before he ducked his head and kicked the dirt with his foot. "Mrs. Worthington, you don't owe me anything. I like helping you all I can, and I especially like it when you teach me about working in the stables. I'm learning more and more every day."

A heavy sigh escaped her. "Well, Hyrum, you helped me, and I will help you."

"I know."

"Hyrum, will you have my horse ready tonight for me?"

He grinned. "Aye, Mrs. Worthington."

Hyrum turned and walked out of the stable, his head held high, as if he'd won the game.

She smiled. The idea of sneaking off to spy on her husband tonight sent her heart beating fiercely against her ribs.

TREES CANOPIED THE darkened sky and hid the moon, making the path harder to follow. The cool wind howled around Camilla, blowing leaves and dust in her face. With one hand she gripped the reins. With the other she pulled the hooded, dark brown cloak tighter around her head. The cool night's breeze slipped through the man's clothing she wore.

She still couldn't believe she had been reduced to doing what Kat had done—spying on Malcolm.

After supper, her husband had told her he had to finish the drawings for Colonel Burwell because he needed to give them to the man by tomorrow. Did her husband realize she knew he was lying? It crushed her that he didn't still trust her, but she couldn't blame him, since she was lying to him as well.

She had feigned sleep until she heard him leave the house. Instead of following him immediately, she waited a few minutes, then left. She scrambled out of bed and ran to the stable to dress in the servant's clothes Hyrum had left for her, mounted Thunder, and hurried on her way.

She had been trailing Malcolm at a distance for a while now, and it seemed as if he had just disappeared. Light fog had settled in the dark night. In the silence, a dog barked. Other dogs joined, and the sound grew louder as each second passed. She shivered and rubbed her arms.

When the moon broke through the fog and shone through branches, she reined in the horse and surveyed the surroundings. According to the instructions the servant gave her, the Lion's Paw Inn was around here somewhere.

She nudged the horse with her heels, urging him forward. Just a little farther down the road, she was certain the inn would come into view. If not, she would return home. After all, spying was something new for her, and she was certain she didn't know what she was doing.

After riding another mile—or, at least, it seemed that far—nothing was in sight. Discouraged, she tugged on the reins, turning the horse around. Through a group of trees, the fog had lifted enough for her to spot a building with lamps in the windows. Her heart pounded. Could this be the place?

She urged the horse forward into a gentle gait and breathed a sigh of relief when she saw Malcolm's horse standing at the side of the structure. She exhaled deeply. Comfort surrounded her at knowing he was near.

Climbing vines cloaked one side of the inn. She dismounted and tied Thunder to a tree before creeping closer to one of the windows. Inside, there were several tables and chairs, and a few patrons resting for a drink and some food. In the corner, she spotted Malcolm and an older man. Near their table was a window that was cracked open.

She smiled. Fate must be trying to help her.

Camilla took careful steps around the side of the building until she came to the window. She looked both ways, wanting to be certain nobody spotted her and thought she was up to no good. For certain, they would tell her to leave, and Malcolm might notice her.

On tiptoes, she leaned her ear closer to the window and, at the same time, kept a sharp eye out for anyone who might wander outside and see her. At first, she wasn't sure what Malcolm was talking about. Listening closer, she struggled to zero in on their conversation.

It sounded as though Malcolm was describing a manor that was very large and luxurious. Even a fancy stable. She frowned. Why would he discuss that? Was he planning on moving? Yet the longer she listened, the more she realized that Malcolm was describing something he would build for the other man.

She hitched a breath. Why weren't Mr. Kennedy and Mr. Crowley involved in this meeting? They were all partners. But Malcolm sounded as though he would take on this project alone.

Confusion swept over her, and she pulled away from the window. Slowly she moved toward Thunder. It would make sense that her husband didn't want to work with his business partners, since he suspected them of being involved in the missing drawings. So, perhaps Malcolm was trying to start his own business.

The worry resting on her shoulders lifted. That wasn't a bad idea. Malcolm's talent would enable him to become wealthy on his own. So then why did he want to keep it a secret from her?

She mounted her horse and guided the animal down the path toward home. Thoughts scrambled through her head, of ways she could confess that she had followed him. But perhaps the way wasn't to tell him, but to show him that she approved of his decision. Now, she needed to figure out the perfect way to do that.

She urged the horse forward, anxious about getting home to formulate a plan. As she neared town, familiar buildings took shape through the fog. She led her horse away from the main street, not wanting to be spotted by anyone who knew Malcolm.

Suddenly, prickles rose on her skin, and her stomach twisted in fear. She slowed her horse. Peering through the shadows, she felt as though someone was watching her.

She swallowed hard and pulled her cloak tighter around her neck. A shadow moved from behind a tree, and she caught her breath. A small animal darted in her path, and she yanked on the reins to stop the horse. Her heartbeat hammered out of control, but she breathed slower, trying to calm her fear. *It's only a cat.*

But another danger lurked out there in the night shadows. It was as if a pair of eyes burned right through to her soul. She shivered. Urging her horse faster, she turned a corner. A single rider came out from the shadows and blocked her path. She tried steering Thunder around the intruder, but the large, dark figure reached out and captured her reins, not allowing her to pass. She wanted to scream but didn't want to draw undue attention, especially if her husband was doing traitorous activities tonight.

Tears stung her eyes. She smacked the stranger's hands, but he managed to slow her horse. He scooped her off her mount and placed her on his lap. It was then she recognized the red coat of a soldier underneath his dark brown cape. She gasped. *Captain Wilkes.* His deep laughter echoed through the night as he tightened his arms.

"My dear Mrs. Worthington. What an honor it is to run into you this late in the evening."

She found her voice. "Release me." She pulled at his hands around her waist, but his hold was unbreakable.

"But it is I, the man who holds your heart. No need to fear, my dear."

Alcohol-soaked breath blew across her face. She grimaced, and her stomach knotted, threatening nausea. "Indeed, I know who you are, which is why I'm afraid."

He cupped her chin. She slapped at his hand, but it didn't budge.

He nuzzled his face against her neck. "But, my dear, you have not been to see me in quite some time, and I grow weary of your games."

"Unhand me, or I will... I will..."

"You will what? Scream?" His laughter rang through the night. Off in the distance, dogs barked. "Are you playing the reluctant maid with me again?"

Her heart lodged in her throat, making it painfully hard to breathe. How could she get out of this mess? Malcolm wasn't around to save her this time, and because she was perched on the soldier's lap while his disgusting clutches held her prisoner, she had no choice but to comply. Camilla must become her sister—the very same woman this drunken fool believed her to be.

She forced her body to relax against his, and within seconds, his grip eased. He kissed her neck, just underneath her ear. She cringed.

"I have missed you," he mumbled.

"I have been rather busy." Her voice shook, but she kept it husky, playing his game until he could release her enough for her to escape.

"I want you to come home with me."

She gritted her teeth to keep from openly displaying her disgust and losing the contents of her stomach. "Tonight is out of the question."

"Why? You are wearing the same clothes and you are headed in the same direction as when you previously visited me. What is different about tonight?"

Camilla scrambled to think of what to say. "Uh, well... I'm being followed."

His body stiffened, and his head snapped up as he scanned the area. "Followed? By whom?"

"I don't know. Perhaps my husband or one of his servants."

He looked around them once more. "Then we must get you inside somewhere quick."

"No." Panic threatened to engulf her sanity. "I must return home."

He kissed her neck again. "I can protect you, my dear. I'm not afraid of your husband or his servants."

How could she answer that one? *Think harder, Camilla.* Suddenly, she recalled his words when she met him out of the town not too long ago. She cleared her throat. "But my main purpose is to gain my husband's trust so I have information to report to you. Is it not?"

He sighed, and his foul breath blew into her face. "Quite right, my dear."

She forced herself to smile as she studied his shadowed face. Hopefully, he was too drunk to remember this in the morning. With a shaky hand and a great deal of effort, she reached out and touched his face tenderly. "I'm closer to gaining my husband's trust. Once I accomplish that, I'm certain I will have more information for you."

"I'll put him away in prison, I assure you. Then we can be together the way we planned." He relaxed and she sighed, but a deeper fear gripped her heart. Would the soldiers find incriminating evidence to arrest Malcolm? Obviously, someone was setting him up. She must do all she could to stop it.

From up the road, the clip-clop of horses' hooves echoed in the silence, though the fog shrouded the oncoming rider. She must get off Captain Wilkes's lap before being spotted. News like this would destroy Malcolm, especially now. "Please, let me down," she whispered.

"One last kiss, my dear." He leaned forward, lips puckered.

There was no other choice. She would give him one, and hopefully, do it quick enough that she could escape his hold.

Chapter Sixteen

T HE MEETING HAD gone very well. Lord Arlington was excited about Malcolm's plans and had agreed to think it over and give an answer in two days. Excitement pounded in Malcolm's heart, and he knew he was on his way to starting his own business. Yet through the excitement, guilt ate away at his gut. He would have to confess to Camilla, and he prayed for her understanding and forgiveness.

Shadows played with his vision while he traveled home, especially when he spotted a couple atop a horse in a lovers' embrace. He narrowed his eyes, not believing what he saw. His heart dropped, shattering as it hit the ground. What was Camilla doing with Captain Wilkes?

He tightened his grip on the reins, and his jaw hardened. They kept their conversation low, but it was the way the captain's arms wrapped around her in a possessive manner that made pain, cold as steel, slice through Malcolm's heart. Then she leaned over and bestowed a light kiss on his lips.

Malcolm neared, and she quickly broke away from the soldier, swinging her head toward him. The moonlight peeked through the trees, lighting her wide eyes. Although the pain in his heart caused his chest to tighten, he still held his head high as he rode toward the couple.

She pushed away from the soldier and dropped to the ground.

Wringing her hands against her stomach, she hurried to him. "Malcolm," she cried softly.

"Hold your tongue, woman." He swallowed the bile rising to his throat. "We will not air our quarrel in front of others." He gestured to her horse. "Mount and follow me home."

She inhaled sharply, and her hand flew to her mouth. Tears swam in her eyes, but it didn't matter. He closed off all feelings but anger.

Captain Wilkes didn't speak, but his self-assured grin said enough. The arrogant man lifted his chin and rode away. When Kat grabbed the reins, her hands shook and there was a slight quiver to her chin. Good. Let her worry about the consequences.

Malcolm kicked the horse's belly and let out a yell, urging the animal into a run. Wind blew against his face. Each mile closer to home made his chest tighter, threatening to suffocate him. He couldn't understand why she had done this. She had charmed him into loving her, and he fell fast for her antics. This was the same Kat he had married, not someone from his dreams.

Upon reaching his estate, he pulled his steed to a stop and jumped off, throwing the reins to Hyrum. "Mrs. Worthington is not far behind. Assist her."

He strode to the house, not looking back to see exactly where his wife was. Entering the hall, he limped, and the heavy footsteps echoed on the floor. The clamor he made as he awkwardly hurried up the stairs brought most of the servants out of the rooms in haste. Once inside his room, he slammed the door behind him.

He yanked off his cape and flung it to the floor. Anger guided his hands as he removed his waistcoat, not caring that buttons flew in all directions. He sat on the edge of the bed and pulled off his boots.

His breath came fast, as if he had run for miles. He stood and paced with a limp across the floor, raking his fingers through his hair. Unanswered questions swam in his head. Why had he been so gullible?

When his door swung open, he stopped and faced the intruder. His wife stood still, silhouetted by the moon shining through the window. She wore a servant's dark brown blouse and breeches, but her cloak was missing. She held a single candle that gave enough light to see her tear-streaked face. Her bottom lip quivered. Her hand shook, making the flame flicker.

"Malcolm," she whispered, a sob tearing from her throat. "It's not what it looked like."

He threw back his head and released a bitter laugh. Once he contained his mirth, he sneered, "If you remember correctly, that is the very phrase you used the first time I caught you in another man's arms."

She stepped inside the room and closed the door behind her. After setting the candle on the nearby table, she walked toward him. "I'm not that woman."

"Indeed? It certainly appeared that way a little while ago."

She stopped in front of him, crossing her arms over her bosom. Her brows were drawn, her lips pursed. Deep lines of anger marked her forehead.

"And looks can be deceiving," she said.

"Yes, you have definitely proven that theory."

"Malcolm, will you allow me to explain?"

"Explain what, my dear?" He shrugged. "There is nothing to explain when I can see perfectly with my own eyes."

"What you saw was a woman pretending—"

"Yes, just like you have clearly pretended with me."

She huffed. "Will you stop interrupting so I can explain?"

He sighed and folded his arms.

"As I was saying, you saw a woman pretending... pretending to be her sister to protect the man she loves more than life itself." More tears ran down her face.

He scratched the throb booming in his forehead. "Pretending to be her sister? What are you talking about?"

She took a deep, shaky breath, wringing her hands against her stomach. "I'm not the woman who stood beside you at your wedding. I am her sister, Camilla."

He chuckled, although humor was still not the emotion running amok through him. "The woman I married was named Camilla, my dear. Or have you forgotten?"

"I'm the twin sister of the woman you thought you married." She licked her lips. "In my father's confused state of mind, he absently arranged for you to marry his good, obedient daughter, Camilla, forgetting I wasn't living at home but a widow in mourning. The rebellious and not-so-innocent daughter, Katherine, stood in my place as a proxy when we were supposed to marry. Kat was living a lie, Malcolm. She wasn't your wife. I am."

Past the ache spreading through his body, his mind pieced together what she was saying. He had wondered if the woman who returned from Preston not too long ago was the sister. Apparently, he had been correct after all.

She wiped at the tears streaking her cheeks. "Malcolm, you *know* I'm different from the woman you thought you married. You have told me that several times. Even your children know. Would the woman you married have loved your children as much as I? Could the woman you married have been able to make you fall in love with her?"

Good heavens, she made sense. But... No. It was impossible to believe.

Yet he did want to believe her. He wanted to know he had fallen in love with a different woman than the one who betrayed his trust a mere month after exchanging vows. "You are telling me we are really married?"

"Yes. When I saw the marriage certificate in the Bible with *my* name on it, I was confused. I found a priest and asked him if proxy marriages were legal. He said they were. Kat knew my name was on the marriage certificate, but she went ahead and married you, knowing full well what she was doing."

"What about that kiss I just witnessed between you and Captain Wilkes?"

She sniffed. "I was protecting you."

"Protecting me?" He skeptically lifted a brow. "From what, pray?"

"From Captain Wilkes. He caught me coming back from your secret meeting, and I had to do something to distract him."

Malcolm's heart lodged in his throat again, and he caught his breath. "Secret meeting?"

"The secret meeting you had at the Lion's Paw Inn."

He scowled. "How do you know about that?"

"I followed you."

"Why did you follow me?"

"Because my husband didn't trust me enough to confide his whereabouts this evening."

He swallowed hard. "And the captain knew about the meeting?"

"No. At least, he didn't say he did. Because of the way I'm dressed, he thought I was out trying to find him. Apparently, Kat had been meeting him secretly for some time before she went to the insane asylum in Preston. I couldn't let him think differently and suspect there was more to my midnight tryst. I explained I was on my way home, and I was being followed. He would not let me go." More tears streamed from her eyes. "The only way I could get him to release me was to give him a kiss." She sniffed and wiped her eyes. "I'm truly sorry you had to witness that, but I was acting. Nothing more." Her shoulders drooped and she placed her trembling hand on his chest. "You are the man I love—the man I will love until I die. Me, not the woman who deceived you on your wedding day. I'm not my sister. I would never hurt you like she did."

Tears stung his eyes and he held back a sob of relief. She seemed truthful. Dare he hope? During their stay at the Burwells', he had wanted her to be a different woman—the woman of his dreams. Could this be real? She was correct—the woman he'd exchanged vows with had never shed a tear when he caught her with other men. His children would have never loved that woman.

"Who is in the asylum?" he asked.

"Kat, the woman you thought you married, *was* in the asylum."

"What do you mean?"

"She died before I traveled here." Her voice broke. "Malcolm, I planned on coming here to beg for your help. I did not have the funds to pay for Kat's stay at the asylum, nor her burial. Since you were her husband, I thought it was only right you pay for it." She took a deep breath. "But when everyone mistook me for my sister, that was when I decided to play along. Then when I saw my name on the marriage certificate, I knew what had really happened."

She stared at him with huge, watery eyes. He said nothing, trying to absorb her confession. The pain on her face told him what he needed to know.

"Malcolm, if you don't believe my story or my true identity, I can take you to London and have you meet my aunts and uncles. They know the difference between me and my twin. They can tell you I'm Camilla Hardy, who married an earl. Even my servant, Timothy, knows the truth."

Malcolm continued to stare at her in silence. He couldn't react. The shock was still too real. Camilla covered her face with her hands and sobbed. Her whole body shook. Seeing her like this tore at his heart. Camilla definitely wasn't her sister. The woman he married never would plead for forgiveness. The woman he married never had any kind of feelings.

His heart soared with relief. But he had been so quick to judge, and now the woman he loved was in pain because of him.

He gathered her in his arms and pressed her face against his chest. He squeezed his eyes closed and breathed in her flowery scent. He had been a fool. Then again, he hadn't known the truth. Now he did, and he would make up for his horrid treatment.

"Oh, Camilla, forgive me." His voice broke as he held her tight. He buried his face in her hair, his eyes filling with tears that slid down his cheeks. "I love you so much. I'm so grateful you aren't Kat. I want you and none other."

"You shall always have me," she muttered into his shirt.

Her warm breath brushed his skin, stirring awareness inside him once again. "Will you forgive me?"

He kissed the side of her face, and she turned and met his mouth with her lips. Holding her head, he devoured her mouth, hoping his love would show with every touch. She clutched his shirt, pressing against him. He ravished her mouth, then trailed his lips over her tear-streaked face and down her neck.

He pulled away and gazed deep into her eyes. "Are you truly my wife? Are we indeed married?"

She nodded. "My name is on the marriage certificate. And as I said, the priest confirmed my belief that proxy marriages are legal."

"Please, Camilla, let me love you the only way a husband can. Now."

She held him closer. Love burst in his chest, and hope for a new beginning was finally within grasp.

"Yes, my darling husband. Make me your wife."

Tenderly, he lifted her in his arms and carried her to the bed, not caring about the twinge of pain in his leg any longer. Taking great care, he placed her on the mattress. Tears still glistened in her eyes, but it was the love shining on her face that made his heart swell with happiness.

Before joining her on the bed, he shrugged out of his shirt and cravat. Her gaze moved slowly over his chest. Never had a woman looked at him with such longing anticipation dancing in her eyes.

He crawled next to her and cupped her face. "I love you, Camilla. I don't ever want to stop telling you that."

"I don't ever want you to stop saying it."

He pressed his mouth against hers for a kiss, situating them on the bed a little more comfortably. He moved one arm behind her back and wrapped the other around her waist, bringing her up against his body.

The kiss was slow and meaningful. She participated fully, running her hand over his chest before moving it up his neck. Her touch sent heat surging throughout his body. This was not surprising, since he had always enjoyed the way she touched him so adoringly.

Breaking the kiss, he moved his mouth to her earlobe, suckling it gently. He shifted his hand to the top button on her shirt. Strange, but he'd never had to undress a woman wearing men's clothes before. Yet he wasn't repulsed. Instead, excitement grew inside of him—these clothes would come off a lot quicker.

He flicked open the first button, and then the second. As he trailed kisses down her neck, she tilted her head back to give him better access. Once the third button came apart, he had more room to slip his hand inside.

A low crooning came from her throat. He lifted his head to see the effect it had on her. Her eyes flickered open, greener than he had ever seen them before. Her skin was so soft, so silky—he couldn't stop from wanting to feel *all* of her.

She'd once mentioned being married, but her husband had died. Although this wasn't the time to ask about him, Malcolm wondered if she had loved that man. Yet if she had, she wouldn't have loved Malcolm so quickly.

Without knowing anything about this other man, Malcolm vowed to make his wife blissfully—and passionately—happy tonight... and every night for the rest of their lives.

Chapter Seventeen

B RANDON KENNEDY STALKED across the office floor, his hands bunched into fists at his side. He kicked his chair from under the desk, and it toppled and landed on the floor. Yanking off his overcoat, he cursed. He tossed it toward the coat rack but missed the mark, and it slid to the ground. He exploded with another set of curses as he marched over, picked it up, and hung it on a hook.

Malcolm leaned back in his chair, holding back the grin that threatened to sneak across his mouth. He was dying to know what had his partner in a dither. When the grin threatened to make its debut, Malcolm quickly rubbed his hand over his mouth, trying to wipe off his smirk. Now was not the time to gloat.

"What ails you, Kennedy?"

The man spun around, his eyes dark with fury. "You recall my telling you about Lord Arlington yesterday, and how his estate would bring us a lot of money?"

Malcolm's heart stilled. "Yes."

"It appears that someone else has beaten me to it." Kennedy slammed his fist on the wall.

"Are you certain?" Malcolm tried to lift his voice in irritation, playing the part of someone who was upset over this news.

"Most certain." Kennedy moved behind his desk and dropped into his chair. "I had heard the man was in town, so this morning I looked for him. When I finally was able to speak with him, he told me he decided to go with someone else."

"No," Malcolm said, rising to his feet. "He didn't even give you a chance to tell him about our business?"

"He didn't give me even one minute of his time." Growling, Kennedy pushed his fingers through his hair. "I wish I knew who could have gotten to him first. Mr. Clarkston really isn't that astute. I don't see him sneaking behind our backs to try to win Arlington's contract."

"I agree. That isn't Clarkston's personality at all." Malcolm moved to another table and retrieved a drawing, bringing it back to his desk.

Silence lasted for thirty minutes before Kennedy growled and pushed away from his desk. He stormed over to the window, leaning his shoulder against the side. The man's mouth pulled tight.

Malcolm wanted to laugh over his partner's misfortune. He prayed that within a few months, he would have enough clients on his own that he could start up his own business again. Malcolm felt he was getting closer to proving Kennedy and Wilkes were the ones stealing the drawings. When Broderick had followed Kennedy last night, as the woman's note instructed, he did witness the two men bent over a table at one of the taverns down the street, discussing something very secretive while sharing a bottle of whiskey. Malcolm suspected that keeping an eye on Kennedy would soon prove fruitful. Within time, he would be able to turn his proof over to the constable and have Kennedy and Wilkes arrested.

A rumble of laughter from his partner snapped him to awareness, and Malcolm turned to see what Kennedy found so amusing. The man wore a knowing grin, and his arms were folded across his shaking chest as he chuckled.

"What is so humorous?" Malcolm asked.

"Oh, just what is going on down the street."

"And what is it?"

Kennedy glanced his way and scratched his chin. "It seems

your wife has become bored with her latest interest and has gone back to spending time with Captain Wilkes."

Malcolm stiffened. But then he recalled what had happened before when he jumped to conclusions, and he relaxed. Kat was dead. Camilla was his wife now, and she loved and only him.

Last night's lovemaking was so wonderful, it had been hard for him to leave her this morning. Never had he felt so complete as he had last night, before, during, and after their night of passion. Without a doubt, Camilla would always be faithful to him.

Malcolm pushed himself away from his desk and stood. Taking deliberate, slow steps, he made his way to the window. As Kennedy had stated, Camilla stood in front of a shop with a basket hooked over her elbow, chatting with Captain Wilkes.

A stab of pain tore through Malcolm's heart. When his wife laughed, the invisible knife in his chest twisted. He breathed slowly, calming his heart. Camilla needed to act this way. They must not make the captain suspicious, especially now.

Malcolm forced a laugh. "It doesn't appear she has gone back to Captain Wilkes. It looks like she is having a friendly conversation."

"If you keep telling yourself that, perhaps you will believe it."

Malcolm fisted his hands, feeling the urge to punch his business partner in the face. "I must say, Kennedy, the green monster of jealousy has taken hold of you again." He shook his head. "You must learn to control that beast before it ruins your life."

Malcolm walked back to his desk. Seeing Camilla with Captain Wilkes was difficult, but it needed to be done. If only he could find a way to keep the doubt from twisting his gut every time he saw her with another man. After all, she was portraying her sister. Yet why hadn't she done so until lately? She had never acted like Kat until after they returned from the Burwells' estate.

In frustration, he raked his fingers through his hair, wishing he wasn't so suspicious. He had no right. She loved him, and he loved her. That should be the end of the subject.

So why wasn't it?

"MAY WE CALL you Mother?"

Camilla gasped at James's question. Her heart quickened, and tears stung her eyes. Slowing the horse they had been riding, she smiled down at his upturned face. Amazing how fast she became emotional lately, but James's sudden request had caught her by surprise.

"Of course you may call me Mother."

"You won't get upset?"

"Why should I get upset?" She stroked her gloved fingers across his cheek. "I love you and Lizzy as though you were my own children."

He beamed. "Lizzy is going to be happy when I tell her. She said last night how much she wanted you to be our mother."

Camilla's heart melted, bringing with it a feeling of motherhood she'd never thought she would experience. "Then let us hurry home so we can tell her."

She reined the horse around and urged the animal into a gallop. A smile stretched across her face, and as each minute passed, her heart pounded quicker. Finally, she would have the family she had always wanted.

In the distance, the figure of a cloaked woman darted behind a tree. Camilla slowed the horse, studying what she had just witnessed. There wasn't another horse in sight, and this would have been a long walk for someone traveling by foot.

She neared the tree, but didn't see anything out of the ordinary.

Camilla shook her head. Perhaps her eyes played tricks on her today. Putting it aside, she kicked the horse into a gallop and continued on her way. When they approached the house, Hyrum ran out of the stable to take the reins.

"Did you have a nice ride, Mrs. Worthington?"

"Yes, thank you, Hyrum. James and I had a pleasant morning."

"Somebody came to see you while ye were gone."

She helped James off the horse. "Who was it?"

"Don't know, Mrs. Worthington. Just a lady."

"Did she leave her card?"

"No. Said she would return at a later time."

She shrugged. "I suppose it was not very important, then."

"Aye, I suppose."

She dismounted and took hold of James's hand. They started out walking, but the closer they came to the house, the more their steps quickened, until they were running. Laughing, they nearly slammed into the door.

James hurried inside the house first, but before Camilla could enter, a cold chill ran down her spine, causing her to pause. She shivered and hugged her waist. Glancing over her shoulder, she studied the yard and the stable. It bothered her that she would have these feelings lately, like someone watched her.

Rubbing her arms, she stepped into the house, putting the feeling behind her. Certainly, it was utter nonsense. She let out a small laugh, remembering her father had become skittish just before...

She froze. *Father's disease.* He had been acting strange, thinking somebody watched him, also. Her heart sank. It wasn't possible. She couldn't have the same disease. Yet Kat had it, so why not her?

Camilla shook her head. She must not think in such a way. If, by chance, she had the same illness as her father and sister, she would have known before now.

"Mother, hurry. Lizzy is waiting." James tugged on her dress.

Taking a deep breath, she smiled. "Coming, my dear."

With unsteady hands, she smoothed out her bodice and skirt before following James upstairs into the nursery. Lizzy and Jane were playing together, and when the little girl spotted Camilla, she ran to her and threw her arms around Camilla's legs.

She laughed and picked the girl up, hugging her tight. "You have certainly made my day, Lizzy."

James jumped up and down in excitement. "Lizzy, Milla says we may call her Mother."

The little girl's smile stretched across her face, making it glow. "We may?"

"Yes, my dear." Camilla stroked the girl's hair. "You may call me Mother."

Lizzy laughed and buried her face in Camilla's neck. James joined in and hugged her legs. Across from them, Jane stood and clasped her hands to her chest as tears swam in her eyes. Camilla's own eyes filled with moisture from the happy occasion.

Yet fear carved a hole deep in her conscience. Was there a chance she would someday become like her father and Kat? If so, her dream of a loving family would soon end.

CAMILLA DECIDED TO surprise her husband at work, so she had Horace pack a picnic basket. The weather this afternoon would be wonderful for sharing a meal under a tree, sitting on a blanket.

She took the buggy into town and stopped in front of Malcolm's office. As she dismounted, she glanced up and down the street, hoping she didn't run into Captain Wilkes again. She was sick of portraying her sister just to protect Malcolm. And although she would do anything to keep her husband safe, she wanted to avoid the captain as much as possible.

She left the picnic basket in the vehicle and walked into the office. The chiming of the bell announced her. Mr. Kennedy jumped to his feet and rushed to greet her.

"What a pleasant surprise, Mrs. Worthington." He took her hand and placed a kiss on her knuckles.

She allowed his attention but kept a close eye on him to make sure he didn't get out of line. "Good afternoon, Mr. Kennedy. I have come to see my husband. Is he about?"

"No. He stepped out of the office for a few minutes. Would you care to sit and wait?"

"Do you know how long he will be gone?"

"He has been gone for a good thirty minutes now. I'm certain he will return momentarily."

Inwardly, she cringed. She really didn't want to sit in the same room with Mr. Kennedy, especially alone. But what other choice did she have?

"I suppose I can wait, but only for a moment."

He pulled out a chair for her, and she sat. "What brings you to our office on this fine afternoon?"

"I thought to surprise my husband with a meal for lunch. The day is too lovely to be indoors."

He smiled and nodded. "I'm certain Malcolm will be surprised. He has been moping about the office, acting as if something weighs heavily on his mind."

She arched a brow. "Indeed? I wonder what it is."

"I had hoped you could shed some light on the problem. Whatever it is makes him quite irritable."

"I wish I knew."

"I'm certain you can work your charm on him and pull him out of this mood."

Strange, but Brandon acted differently, especially since they were alone. She'd hoped he would finally give up on the idea of their being together. "I shall certainly try."

She stood and walked to the window. The busy street bustled with people hurrying from one shop to another. Through the crowd, she searched for Malcolm, hoping he would come quickly.

Behind her, Brandon's footsteps echoed on the hardwood floor as he neared. His image reflected off the glass. She tightened her fingers around the basket. Heaven help her, because if he made one improper move, she would punch him in the face.

"Mrs. Worthington, I—I want to apologize for my behavior

of late."

She held her breath, surprised he would even say such a thing. She remained silent, wondering what else would come out of his mouth.

"Your beauty and charm have enchanted me, and when you stopped coming to see me, the wound left a deeper hole in my heart than I was prepared for."

She swallowed hard and continued to look outside. "Mr. Kennedy, you must believe I'm in love with my husband. I'm a completely different person than the woman you knew."

"That is what Malcolm says, too. Will you forgive me?" His voice was laced with sincerity.

She moved away from the window to put distance between them. "I will forgive you, Mr. Kennedy, as long as you make no more overtures toward me."

"As you wish."

"I think you are a nice man, and I cannot help wondering if your wife even knows this. Have you shown *her* your passionate side?"

His forehead creased. "My wife and I are but strangers."

"An arranged marriage, I presume?"

"Yes."

She tilted her head. "But the question remains, do you love her?"

He shrugged. "We have had only one child in our five years of marriage. I fear love has not even entered our home."

"Would you like it to?"

"I never thought about it."

"Mr. Kennedy, your wife has been extremely forgiving of your actions. From the little time I have gotten to know her, she seems a knowledgeable woman."

He chuckled and shook his head. "Kat, you know me well enough to know what kind of woman I enjoy."

"Please don't call me Kat, Mr. Kennedy."

"My apologies."

"But you were saying…?"

He walked away from the window to his desk and sat on the edge. "You should know I have always enjoyed having a woman of remarkable beauty on my arm."

"Would you like your wife to be this woman?"

"It's impossible."

"Nothing is impossible."

He arched an eyebrow. "And how can we change it?"

She dared to step closer. "Let me give you a little hint about women. Just like a rose, they don't blossom unless given sunlight."

"What are you saying? You wish me to keep her outside in the sunshine?"

She nearly laughed. Could he really be that ignorant? "No, Mr. Kennedy. You need to compliment her and make her feel pretty. If you really want her to come out of her shell, you will have to help her along."

The corner of his mouth tugged up in a grin. "You're an amazing woman. I cannot believe you're trying to assist me in winning over my wife."

"Encourage her, Mr. Kennedy, or she has no other reason to blossom. But you will also have to do some serious groveling for your past mistakes. If she loves you, she will forgive you, just as Malcolm has forgiven me."

His brown eyes twinkled. He grasped her hand and squeezed. "Thank you for such astute advice."

The bell from the door chimed, and Camilla jumped away from Brandon, but not before Malcolm's gaze rested upon her. Her heart plummeted, yet there was no reason to feel guilty. She had done nothing wrong, but would Malcolm believe that? From the scowl on his face, she feared the worst. He glared at her with accusing eyes. *Not again.*

Brandon moved past her toward Malcolm. "Worthington, you have returned just in time. Your wife has a surprise for you."

Malcolm's brow lifted when he looked at her, but a frown still marred his handsome face. "Indeed?"

Her stomach churned violently, and she clasped her hands against her middle to calm the waves of nausea. She didn't speak for fear her voice would crack.

"Malcolm," Brandon continued, "I must tell you what an incredible wife you have."

Wrong comment to make, Mr. Kennedy.

"Do I?" Malcolm asked.

"Indeed. She was just now giving me advice on how to woo my wife."

Malcolm's lips quirked into an unexpected grin. "Woo your wife?"

Camilla laughed uneasily and walked toward her husband. "Yes, Malcolm. Mr. Kennedy knows who holds my heart." She stopped in front of him and touched his cheek. "I tried to tell him how to win over his wife properly."

Malcolm chuckled and shook his head. "This is, indeed, a surprise."

"That is not my surprise for you, however." She linked her arm with his. "I'm stealing you away this afternoon for a picnic—if you approve, of course."

"But of course. How could I turn down such a charming woman?"

Her heart hammered with each step out to the buggy. Malcolm took her arm, assisting her up, and then climbed inside to sit beside her. He gripped the reins and urged the team forward.

Seeing the distrust in his eyes made her heart ache. Although he smiled, it didn't make his eyes sparkle. She slipped her arm around his and cuddled next to him, laying her head on his shoulder. "Should I scold you now or later?"

His head snapped toward her. "Scold me, my dear?"

"Do you think I'm blind? I saw the look of suspicion on your face when you entered the office."

He remained silent.

"Malcolm, how many times must I defend myself? I'm not

Kat. I love you completely and would never do anything to hurt you."

His body relaxed. "I'm but a normal man, my love." He chuckled. "A man who succumbs to jealousy quite easily, I might add. Please, be patient with me. Both my first wife and Kat found me repulsive, so forgive me if I can't trust my own feelings."

Camilla reached up and cupped his chin, and he glanced at her. "Why would another man turn my head when you are the most handsome, the most loving person I have ever met?" She trailed her fingers across his bottom lip. "I don't want any other man because I have you."

He laughed and turned his attention back to the road. "Sometimes I don't think I deserve your love."

"You do, and I'll not give it to anyone else."

"You truly are a forgiving woman."

She squeezed his arm. "I know you have had a lot on your mind. Mr. Kennedy has even noticed how irritable you are."

He sighed heavily and slumped his shoulders. "Broderick followed Kennedy last night, and he met with Captain Wilkes. They were discussing something in secret."

"Was this before or after he accosted me?"

"Before."

"Oh." She nodded. "Did Broderick discover what they were discussing?"

"Unfortunately, no. But curiously, Broderick had been given a note from an unknown woman who alerted him to the secret meeting."

"And you don't know who this woman is?"

Malcolm's gaze stayed on her a little longer this time before he returned his attention to the road. "No. We have no clue."

Her heart twisted. Why did she have a feeling he was still keeping secrets from her? She longed for the time he would trust her completely.

He stopped the wagon near a patch of wildflowers. Although the sweet scent of spring wafted through the air, she didn't take the time to enjoy it. Malcolm's problems weighed heavy on her mind. Sometimes she wanted to take him by the shoulders and shake him senseless, then kiss him to distraction. But none of these methods would force him to trust her.

He turned to climb down, but she grabbed his arm to stop him.

"Malcolm?"

He gazed into her eyes and smiled. "Yes, my love?"

"What is truly bothering you? What have I done to lose your trust?"

His eyes widened, and she detected panic. This wasn't good at all.

Chapter Eighteen

MALCOLM SMILED AND took Camilla's hand, helping her out of the buggy. Shadows of doubt filled her eyes, making his chest ache with sorrow. He had been an imbecile, plain and simple. But he didn't want to doubt her, and he didn't want her to mistrust him. Bringing her hand up to his mouth, he kissed her knuckles. "My love, I trust you with my life."

"Then prove it. Tell me what bothers you so."

He hooked her arm over his and grabbed the quilt. She picked up the basket of food and walked next to him to the grassy field. After laying out the quilt on the ground, he sat.

She placed the basket of food in the middle and knelt in front of it.

"Camilla, forgive me for not speaking my worries sooner." He paused, assisting her with preparing the food.

"Will you tell me now?"

"The night you were spying on me and I caught you with Wilkes, I had been meeting with a prospective client. You see, before I married your sister, I had my own business. Your sister didn't think I made enough money, and so she arranged for me to become one of Mr. Kennedy's partners. But I wasn't happy. I knew he and Kat were having an affair. Of course, I wasn't in love with Kat, but I hated how that man gloated every time he was around. I hated his telling me what I could and couldn't do. I realized I wanted to go back in business for myself. Of course, it doesn't help that I think he has something to do with stealing my drawings."

He took a deep breath, took her hands in his, and continued. "One of the secrets I've been hiding is that I'm secretly gaining my clients back, but I'm in constant fear that Kennedy will find out and break our partnership before I'm ready. I don't want to leave my family desolate because I can't make enough money."

"Oh, no, Malcolm." She shook her head and kissed his knuckles. "We shall be fine. If you're not happy with Kennedy, I will support you in leaving the partnership. If we run low on funds, I was a seamstress before I married Lord Hardy—"

"I wouldn't dream of asking you to do that again." Malcolm caressed her cheek. "But before I can leave him, I need to repair my reputation. I want to prove that Kennedy and Wilkes are behind this. Of course"—he frowned—"I'll have to find out *why* Kennedy is doing this to his partner when it's clear that my downfall will hurt his name, as well."

She nodded. "Indeed, it would. Are you certain he is behind it?"

Closing his eyes, he shook his head. "I wish I could be certain, but I'm not. I thought Colonel Burwell was involved, and I had wanted to snoop through his study during our stay, but because I broke my leg, that stopped my plans."

"Oh, my dear husband." She leaned over and kissed his mouth briefly. "I wish I could assist you in some way."

He clutched her shoulders, trying to keep her close to him. Whenever she was near, doubt had no room in his heart.

He gazed into her troubled green eyes. "My dear, it's as I told you before—I don't know how dangerous this is. I would rather know you and my children are protected, so please don't try to help me." He stroked his thumb across her bottom lip. "Promise me now that you will do as I say."

She placed a kiss on the tip of his thumb. "Of course, my wonderful husband. You know all I want is to make you happy."

He sighed, and relief flooded through him like a broken dam. It pleased him to hear her confession. He wouldn't ask her if she was the unknown woman who had that letter delivered to Broderick. Malcolm's heart told him she wouldn't have done such a thing.

"Now we have that out of the way," he said, "tell me what you and the children have done today."

Her face lit up, and that familiar twinkle came back in her eyes. His heart melted with love the longer he stared at her, and he thanked the Lord once again for his good fortune in finding her.

The time passed much too fast, and soon the meal was over, and he needed to return to work. But before he ruined this perfect setting, and the mood, he reached into his pocket and withdrew a small box.

"Camilla, I have a surprise for you. I thought about presenting this to you at home with the children, but I feel I must give it to you now."

She wiped her mouth with the linen napkin. When she spotted the box, her eyes widened, and her face pinkened. "What is it, Malcolm?"

"I want to give you a token of my love for you and our marriage." Reaching over, he took her left hand and brought it to his lips for a kiss.

"But Malcolm, I missed our first marriage. And I want to marry you in a church, and actually be present this time."

He chuckled. "And we shall. Soon."

"With the children in attendance?"

"Of course. Anything you would like."

He opened the small box and withdrew a diamond ring. She gasped. "Oh, Malcolm."

He slipped the band over her finger then kissed it. "I hope you will wear it always."

"Yes, of course." She laughed and cried at the same time.

He cupped her face and drew her near, sealing their promise

with a kiss. She flung her arms around his neck and pressed herself against him, causing him to lose his balance and fall backward. They laughed together, but, thankfully, their mouths didn't part.

Although the position was most intimate, he didn't care. Especially since the position of her lying on him was very comfortable and brought back memories of their night of pleasure. He moved his hands down her back to her hips and pressed her against him.

A deep cooing sound rattled through her throat, and her body relaxed completely. He groaned in delight... and agony. He wanted to repeat what they had done last night—however, they were where anyone could walk by and see them. What a scandal that would make. He really didn't care about himself, but now that Camilla was making others respect her, he couldn't ruin it now.

The horses neighed and brought him more alert. Grumbling in defeat, he broke away and smiled. "As much as I would enjoy doing nothing for the rest of the day but making love to you, I think we are in the wrong location for that."

"Quite right." She giggled and sat up, smoothing her dress around her legs.

"Do you know how much I love you?"

She lowered her lashes and gazed at his mouth. "Hopefully as much as I love you."

He silently counted the minutes before he would be in her arms again. This woman would prove the death of him, but he would enjoy every moment.

THE DOOR TO the office opened, banging against the wall with a resounding crack. Malcolm jumped in his chair and spun toward the noise. Broderick rushed inside, his face flushed as he wheezed to catch his breath. He glanced toward Brandon's empty desk before hurrying over to Malcolm's side.

"Broderick, what ails you this afternoon? You look like you have been running for miles."

His friend placed his hand over his chest, nodding. "It seems I have." He chuckled. "But when I received the letter, I couldn't wait to show you." He handed over a folded piece of paper. "Read it."

Malcolm opened the missive and glanced at the contents. "What? I don't believe this."

"Imagine how I feel right now." Broderick wiped his sweaty brow.

Malcolm scanned the contents of the letter, slower this time.

Broderick Turner,

I have personally seen one of the stolen drawings in Captain Wilkes's hunter's cottage. Meet me tonight at midnight in front of his cottage. I have enclosed the directions. I shall help you obtain the proof that will clear your employer, Mr. Worthington, of the rumors circling town. I indeed want to finally meet you, Broderick. I have admired you from afar.

Affectionately, EC

Malcolm raised his gaze toward his friend and frowned. "Why would this mysterious woman want to meet with you and not me as well?"

His friend's smile stretched. "I assume it's because I have been diligently asking questions about her, and because of what she wrote." He waggled his eyebrows and pointed to the letter. "Apparently, she has become enamored with me—proving, of course, she is not your wife."

Malcolm threw back his head and laughed. Once his mirth was contained, he said, "No, my good friend, this woman is not my wife. I spoke with Camilla earlier this afternoon, and she is not this mystery woman."

"Then let us hope the main reason this woman wants to help us is because she wants to get to know me better."

"Indeed, that must be the reason." Malcolm glanced at the letter again. "So, tonight at midnight? I wonder why so late."

"Secrecy, of course."

Unease gathered in Malcolm's stomach. "Broderick? Would you like me to come along? Just in case you need help. I'll hide in the bushes outside."

"What could go awry when two strangers meet for the first time as they work together to clear your name?"

"I don't know, Broderick. I have an unsettling feeling. The whole affair smells of a trap."

"Cease your worrying." Broderick slugged Malcolm's shoulder. "I'm a grown man and can take care of myself. Besides, I'm very cautious, and I shall be suspicious of her when we meet."

Malcolm chuckled over the irrationality of it all. "You are correct, my dear friend." He handed back the letter. "Then I wish you good fortune. Be certain to let this woman know she will be rewarded for her kind, generous help."

"Of course. That will be the first issue we discuss."

Malcolm arched an eyebrow. "I'm certain it won't be the *first*." He pushed away from his desk and stood. "Shall we return home?"

Broderick led the way to the buggy with a bounce in his step. Malcolm grinned. He prayed the meeting would be to his friend's satisfaction, and especially for the love interest Broderick was desperately trying to find.

CAMILLA MADE HER way down the stairs to the dining room the next morning. Angry voices rose from the study. Malcolm's voice boomed louder than the others, sounding panicked.

Curious, she hurried toward the room. Malcolm and five of

his servants clustered inside his study. The door stood ajar, so she peeked inside. All the men held the same worried expressions of drawn brows and sorrowful eyes. Malcolm's hands were balled at his sides.

He stalked to the liquor tray and poured a glass of bourbon—something he rarely did. He tipped it to his lips and gulped as if it was water. She had never seen him drink like that before.

Raking his fingers through his hair, he spun toward the group of men. "I don't care about the soldiers," he shouted. "Broderick has been arrested, and it shouldn't have happened. I will do *anything* to get him out. We just need a plan, and quickly."

Camilla gasped. Broderick in jail? *No.* Her heart sank. Malcolm would certainly get himself arrested if he tried to break out Broderick. Chills of fear ran down her spine. She couldn't let Malcolm give his life for his friend.

"What if we hired an attorney?" one of the servants asked.

Malcolm growled and slammed his fist into the wall. "No. That will take too long, and knowing Wilkes, he will only prolong the procedure."

"What about a distraction?" another man asked. "We can draw the soldiers away from the cell while somebody sneaks in and sets him free."

Malcolm inhaled, and his nostrils flared with anger. "What kind of distraction?"

The man's worried expression relaxed, and he smiled. "Oh, I know a few harlots who wouldn't mind helping out."

"I can see the possibility in that, but how do we break Broderick out?" Malcolm asked. "Someone needs to be inside the jail, and Captain Wilkes isn't allowing Broderick to have any visitors." He grumbled loudly. "I had a feeling the letter from that woman was a trap. Why didn't I go with him?"

"Master," Timothy said in a comforting voice. "Ye cannot blame yourself. It was Broderick's decision."

"Aye, but I should have done something." Malcolm filled his glass with bourbon again and drank it down.

All heads lowered while silence filled the air.

Suddenly, an idea sprang to Camilla's mind. She could help. But fear of the unknown washed through her. Malcolm might not agree, but she would convince him that this was the only way.

With a shaky hand, she pushed open the door and stepped inside. Malcolm's gaze snapped toward her.

"Malcolm, might I have a word in private with you?" His brows drew together, and she feared he would turn her down. "Please, it's important."

He ran his fingers through his hair and nodded. "Excuse me. I will not be but a moment."

She grasped his hand and pulled him into the parlor, closing the doors behind her. She met his gaze and cupped his face. His eyes didn't hold the familiar sparkle, and her heart wrenched. "Malcolm, I overheard your plans to break Broderick out of jail, and I have an idea."

He smiled, but not fully as he wrapped his arms around her. "My love, I appreciate your willingness to help, but I'll not allow you to be put in danger. I love you too much."

"Then do you know someone else who has been intimate with Captain Wilkes lately? Because I don't think he will trust anybody but Kat."

"Whatever is in that pretty little head of yours, the answer is no."

"Will you just listen before you give an answer?"

A nerve in his cheek jumped, but he nodded.

"Kat could make that man behave in ways he would not normally do. She had some kind of hold over him, and I think if I play my sister, I might be able to help break Broderick out of jail."

"What is your plan?"

She exhaled slowly. "I'm thinking about getting him drunk."

His eyes widened. "And how will you manage that?"

"I can arrange to meet with him at the jail—alone—then get him intoxicated. Because of the man he is, I don't believe he will turn down a secret rendezvous."

"You are correct. Go on."

"After he passes out, I can help you and the others inside. I will get the keys from Captain Wilkes, and we can sneak Broderick out."

"My dear Camilla, I don't want you putting yourself in harm's way."

"I trust you will protect me when I need it." She stroked his cheek. "I know you will be watching me from afar, so I'll be protected."

"You're right. I will."

"If you allow me to help you with this, I will be able to get the keys so we can sneak him out."

Malcolm's lips twitched into a grin. "Or Broderick can walk out on his own."

Confused, she wrinkled her forehead. "What do you mean?"

"Think about it. Broderick and the captain are the same height, the same build. They even have the same raven-black hair. After the captain passes out, you can unlock Broderick's cell, and he will steal Captain Wilkes's uniform and walk out with you on his arm." Malcolm shrugged. "The other soldiers will not think any different."

She laughed and hugged him. "I have faith this will work."

He kissed her on the mouth. "So do I."

Chapter Nineteen

CAMILLA TOOK A deep breath and steadied her shaky limbs. *Pretend you are Kat.* It shouldn't be that hard. After all, she had started to portray her sister when she first arrived in Dorchester. But this time was different.

To play the part of her sister, she donned one of Kat's immodest dresses. And heaven help her, she *would* flirt like she had never done before. The plan must work. Both Broderick and Malcolm's lives were at stake.

Lifting her chin, she squared her shoulders and walked across the street toward the jail. Wilkes stood outside with four other soldiers. When he spotted her, he moved away from the men and strode toward her, his smile stretching more with each step. She swallowed the lump of fear in her throat and breathed slowly.

"Good day, my dear Mrs. Worthington." Captain Wilkes stopped in front of her and picked up her hand, running his lips over her wrist. When he met her gaze, his eyes darkened.

I am Kat, Camilla reminded herself, and smiled. "Good day to you, you handsome devil."

He grinned and took a step closer to her. "Have you missed me, my sweet?"

"Always." She batted her eyelashes and gave him a pout. "And I cannot go another day without you."

He waggled his eyebrows. "How do you suggest we solve

that problem?"

She glanced around to see if they were out of the others' earshot. Thankfully, they were, but she lowered her voice nonetheless. "I will meet you tonight, in the jail."

"In the jail? But why?"

"Shh." She placed her fingers over his mouth. "We must not be heard." She grinned. "I have never been there, and… well, I have many wild ideas of what we can accomplish together in such a wicked place." She nearly gagged on the words, and she prayed she didn't have to touch him too much tonight. She wasn't that good of a performer.

His chest shook with silent laughter. Bringing her hand back up to his mouth, he kissed her knuckles again. She shuddered inwardly.

"But you must know there is a prisoner who will see us," he said.

"Let him watch." She chuckled. "He might learn a thing or two."

The captain's eyes turned dark. "Are you certain?"

"Very."

"What time should we meet?"

"Late." While pretending to think about this, she pursed her lips. "How about midnight?"

"You are a naughty woman, but I love your idea."

"And we must celebrate, so bring lots of spirits."

"Oh, I will. I have been celebrating the capture of Broderick Turner for quite a while, so I foresee no problem."

"Good. Then I expect to see you tonight. Alone. And make certain to bring plenty of rope."

"Rope?" he asked with a laugh.

She nodded. "I want to try something new." Giving him a wink, she turned and walked away.

His husky laugh vibrated the air around her, sending chills down her spine. Was she strong enough to go through with this? She had to be. There was no other way.

Keeping her back firm, she crossed the street and walked into the nearest store before releasing her pent-up breath. She gathered the cloak tighter around her neck, so as not to show anyone else her immodest gown. She glanced out the window. Thank goodness Captain Wilkes had returned to his men.

And thank heavens Malcolm had kept up his end of the plan. He'd made arrangements with Mr. Percy, who usually sold his homemade liquor to the soldiers, to make certain this batch was extra potent for tonight. The good man had delivered the bottles earlier this afternoon, and from what she could see, the soldiers were already starting their night of pleasure.

From behind her, a man cleared his throat. She spun around to see one of the servants who had been at the house this morning. She was grateful that Malcolm had kept his word and kept all eyes on her to make sure she was safe.

He smiled and nodded. "Good day, Mrs. Worthington. Are you enjoying this fine weather?"

"But of course, Mr. Tolland." She smiled. "How is your wife?"

"She is doing well."

"Is she still suffering from headaches?"

"Only occasionally now."

"Give her my regards."

"Will do, Mrs. Worthington." He nodded before leaving the shop.

She hurried out of the store and to her buggy. There was much to do before tonight's entertainment, and she had to make certain every detail had been thought out. She couldn't afford to make any mistakes. She also wanted Malcolm's strong arms around her to feel the security in his embrace.

She smiled. With his love, nothing could go awry. Nothing at all.

CAMILLA BLEW ON her cold hands. Her nerves jittered out of control, making her body shake from more than just the cool night breeze. She slowed her horse, leading him toward the back of the jail. Voices from the soldiers out front of the building echoed through the night.

She reassured herself everything would turn out as planned. She had nothing to fear. Malcolm would make certain of that.

After dismounting, she tiptoed to the back window and peeked inside. Captain Wilkes sat in a chair, leaning his elbow on the table as he twirled a stick between his fingers. It appeared as if he were the only person inside.

Forcing her legs to move, she hurried around to the front. One soldier sat in front of the door, slumped against the building, asleep. The other soldiers were far enough away that she could slip through without being caught.

She held her breath and inched closer. Her hand touched the doorknob, and she pushed. The hinges squeaked, and thankfully, the men didn't turn to look.

Once inside, she closed the door. Captain Wilkes jumped from his chair, grinning. She scanned the surroundings and breathed a sigh of relief. He had indeed followed her instructions. From the corner cell of the room, Broderick rose from the cot and moved to the bars, his eyes widening.

She focused on the captain. A half-empty bottle of spirits sat on the table. She smiled. "Good evening, my darling man," she whispered.

"Take off your cloak."

As she unhooked the outerwear, she tried to steady her hands. The garment fell to the floor. The captain's quick intake of breath told her that he approved of her choice of dress. It had taken three servants to alter one of Kat's old gowns to make it more alluring, more scandalous than before.

Wilkes's mouth hung agape. From the corner cell, Broderick groaned, resting his head against the bars. Her heart wrenched for this man and what he must be thinking of her.

"Woman, you are beautiful." Wilkes's gaze was riveted to her. "Come here."

She swallowed hard and took her first step toward him, and with each step, her heart hammered faster. By the time she stood in front of him, her chest heaved so hard from fear that she thought she would lose the contents of her stomach. When he reached out, she held her breath, willing herself to remain strong. He grasped a lock of hair and caressed it, then let his fingers slide down the strands.

"You are very lovely tonight, my dear."

She forced a laugh. "Thank you." She let an uneasy breath out. "But I think I need a drink. Are you going to share that bottle or hoard it all night?"

He dropped his hand from her hair and grabbed the bottle instead, bringing it up to his lips. He gulped back a good amount before handing it over to her. She took it, brought it to her mouth, and tipped it back. She pretended to swallow, but kept her lips firmly pressed together so nothing would enter her mouth. She hoped the captain couldn't tell the difference with the room's dim lighting.

She glanced at Broderick, who frowned and shook his head. "Why are you doing this? I thought you loved Malcolm."

Pain gripped her heart, and she wanted to tell him the truth. But now was not the time. He would understand soon.

"Shut up, Turner," the captain snapped. "Just watch and learn."

After placing the bottle on the table, she stepped closer to Wilkes. "Are you ready for what I have planned?"

He nodded. As he reached for her, he swayed. She prayed he would lose consciousness soon.

Her wish was granted, because just as he gave her a lazy grin, he crumpled to the floor.

She let out a deep sigh. "Oh, thank the Lord." She looked back at Broderick. "Do you honestly think I would betray Malcolm? I love him completely."

Broderick nodded and smiled. "Thank you, Camilla."

She knelt beside the captain and grabbed the set of keys from off his belt then threw them to Broderick. "While you find the right key to get out, I shall remove his clothes. You will need to dress in them so we can walk out of the jail together. The other soldiers won't realize you are their prisoner that way."

"I can certainly do that." He jiggled each key in the lock, but nothing was opening the cell. He growled. "I cannot find the right key."

Behind Camilla, a shrill laugh echoed through the room. Chills of fear shot through her. She spun around just as the figure of a cloaked woman walked out from the shadows.

"Sadly, you will never find the right key." The other woman held up the brass object in her hand. "Sorry, but your rescue plan just failed, Camilla. There is nothing you can do to save Malcolm's friend."

Camilla gasped, and her cold, shaky hands flew to her mouth. *That voice. It sounds like… But it can't be.*

"Who are you?"

The woman's shriek of laughter made Camilla's stomach churn. *Dear Lord, no!*

She drew closer and yanked Camilla to her feet. "Who am I? I'm the woman in charge now, and I'm the one who will destroy yours and Mr. Worthington's dreams." She raised the bottle Wilkes had been drinking and slashed it through the air and down on Camilla's head.

Pain pierced her skull, and her world turned dark brown.

MALCOLM SAT FORWARD and focused out the carriage window, waiting for his wife and Broderick to exit the jail. The silvery full moon gave him plenty of light to keep a close eye on the soldiers from down the street, and thankfully, most of them had passed out minutes ago. Any time now, Camilla and his friend would leave the jail. There was no room for their plans to go awry.

Then why did his gut clench as if something had gone seriously wrong? He wiped the moisture from his palms against his legs. His heart hammered, and all he heard was the pounding in his head. What if Camilla screamed and he couldn't hear?

Growling, he slid off the seat, pushed open the door, and jumped out of the carriage. The driver's head snapped his way, and he leaned forward as if ready to spring into action. Malcolm held up his hand and stopped him. "No need to fear, Timothy. I'm merely a little anxious."

Timothy nodded. "I'm nervous meself."

"Have you heard anything?"

The older man shook his head. "Not a sound, sir."

Malcolm released a frustrated breath and raked his fingers through his hair. "Do you think everything is all right?"

"Aye, sir. If I know the mistress, she'll get the task done."

"Yes, but I still cannot help but worry about her." Malcolm flexed his hands as he paced the length of the carriage. He looked toward the jail every chance he could. What was taking them so long?

A shadow drew his attention. He stopped and narrowed his eyes at the movement by the door. When the figure of a cloaked woman hurried outside, he sighed and relaxed his hands. But where was Broderick? Something terrible must have happened.

He hurried inside the carriage and waited for his wife to join him. When the door opened, he took her hand and helped her in.

"Where is Broderick?"

She sat across from him and lowered her hood. Her eyes were wide as she shook her head. "Everything proceeded as planned." She wrung her hands against her stomach. "Captain Wilkes became intoxicated and passed out." She sniffled. The moon's glare through the window showed tears in her eyes. "But we couldn't find the key to Broderick's cell. When one of the other soldiers came in, I knew there was nothing more I could do." She shrugged. "I hurried and left before they suspected my true purpose of being there."

Malcolm balled his hands and hit the seat. It wasn't Camilla's fault, yet the plan should have worked. "Did the soldier say anything?"

"Thankfully, Captain Wilkes was mostly undressed, so I pretended to act intoxicated also. The soldier didn't have to ask what was going on. He knew." She moved next to him on the seat and touched his hand. "But now what will we do?"

His chest tightening, he raked his fingers through his hair. Time was running out. The magistrate had scheduled Broderick's trial for two days hence. Malcolm was certain Wilkes would see Broderick hanged just for trespassing.

"I will think of something, my love." He caressed her cheek. "I appreciate your willingness to help. You have been very supportive, and I love you for it."

"I wish I could do more."

He took her in his arms. She rested her head against his chest, and he closed his eyes, breathing in her scent. But she didn't smell the same. Of course, alcohol overpowered any other smell about her, but there was also something different. Yet he couldn't pinpoint what it was.

Silence stretched through the carriage during the ride home. He racked his brain for ideas, but every one of them had a flaw. Whatever they did to break Broderick out of jail, they would have to cover their tracks. Malcolm truly couldn't afford to get arrested. Not when he had his wife and children to think about.

Camilla's silence bothered him. It wasn't her fault the plan hadn't worked. No doubt she blamed herself. He would have to ease her worries. But how could he do that when he feared for his friend's life?

Timothy pulled the vehicle to a stop in front of the house. Camilla moved to leave, but Malcolm grasped her arm. She swung her head and looked at him.

"My darling, it's not your fault. Please don't blame yourself for tonight's mishap. I shall find a way to release Broderick, I promise."

"I know you will."

Timothy opened the door and helped Camilla down. Malcolm climbed out behind her.

"Thank you, Timothy."

The older servant's wide eyes followed Camilla. Unease pricked up Malcolm's spine. Why was he looking at her that way?

"Timothy? Is something amiss?"

The man blinked and shook his head. "No, Mr. Worthington. Nothing. It is just that... Well, Mrs. Worthington seems out of sorts this evening."

"That she is. Rest assured, I will take care of the problem."

Timothy nodded, and then turned and climbed back to the top of the carriage.

Malcolm hurried inside. Camilla stood next to Beth as she shrugged out of her cloak. The maid bobbed once before turning and leaving the room. He ran his gaze over the very provocative dress his wife had altered for tonight's purpose. Although sensual, she looked too much like Kat at this moment. That bothered him.

She turned and caught his stare. A smile stretched across her face, and she hooked her hand around his elbow and pressed against his arm. "Shall we retire for bed?"

"Yes." He kissed her forehead. "Why don't you go on ahead? I shall be up momentarily. There is too much on my mind right now to sleep."

She giggled. "Who said anything about sleep?"

"No, my dear. Not tonight. I need to think of a way to release Broderick."

She huffed and folded her arms across her bosom. He narrowed his eyes as a slight throb began in his forehead. Why was she acting in this manner? She should be as upset as he right now, so why did she act like nothing had gone wrong this evening?

He stroked her cheek. "I promise not to stay up too late."

"I shall wait for you." She closed the space between them and linked her arms around his neck. "I will need you to keep me warm tonight." She stood on her toes and placed her mouth over his. The kiss wasn't the same as when he had kissed her before. Perhaps it was because Mr. Percy's homemade brew stained her lips.

He broke the kiss and pulled back. Through her half-closed eyes, he detected a glaze. "Camilla, I thought you were not going to drink with the captain tonight."

She shrugged. "I had to act my part. Captain Wilkes wouldn't believe me any other way."

He nodded and kissed her forehead. "Go to bed and sleep it off, my love. Have Beth help you to bed." He chuckled. "I fear you will have a headache in the morning."

She pouted and turned away, stomping up the stairs.

Strange behavior for certain, but then, he'd never seen Camilla intoxicated before.

Chapter Twenty

C AMILLA FORCED HER eyes open, ignoring the pain slicing through her skull. The room tilted. Nausea spun in her stomach, and she clenched her jaw to keep from disgracing herself. She tried to roll over, but her feet wouldn't move. Even her hands were bound together. Confusion made her head throb harder.

A dirty floor came into view, followed by cobwebs and hay. She squinted against the morning light pouring through the dust-streaked window beside her. She moved her hands, but the ropes burned her wrists. Her mouth tasted of dirty cotton because of the cloth resting between her teeth. She ran her tongue across the material, and then gagged again. What was going on?

Deep laughter lanced through her head. Like a spear, the rough sound pierced the already painful tissue. She peered toward the sound. In the corner of the barn, leaning up against the wall, Captain Wilkes stood wearing a cocky grin.

"Ah, my dear, you are finally awake."

She scowled. The imbecile. Of course she was awake.

He pulled away from the wall and sauntered toward her holding a bottle of whiskey. "Thought you might like a drink to dull the pain in your head. Your sister whacked you pretty good last night."

Although Camilla would rather not drink alcohol, she needed

something to moisten her dry throat—and an excuse for him to take this vile rag out of her mouth. She nodded.

He knelt beside her and loosened the gag. Once it had been removed, she opened her mouth, stretching her achy jaw.

"Here." He held the bottle to her lips. "Just take a little sip."

She studied his eyes, evil as the devil himself. The liquor touched her tongue, and then burned her throat. She jerked away, making the whiskey dribble down her jaw to her neck. She coughed, but the scalding pain in her throat increased.

He threw his head back and laughed. "It would appear you have not formed a liking for spirits."

She glared at him. "My throat was dry, you dolt."

"So, last night you were just pretending?" he asked.

She bit her lips together, not wanting to even waste her breath on him.

"You know," he continued, "if not for your sister, I would have never known the difference." He touched her hair and rubbed a lock between his finger and thumb. He grinned. "I really cannot tell the two of you apart."

Her stomach lurched again, and this time she prayed something would come up and dump on him. Her prayers went unanswered. She cleared her throat. "Where is Kat?"

"She will be here momentarily. I'm certain she is as thrilled to visit with you as you are to visit with her."

"Not likely," Camilla muttered.

He laughed again and stood. "I have no idea what your sister has planned for you, but let me give you a bit of information. Your lover will die, as will his friend Broderick."

She narrowed her eyes. "My lover? Are you referring to my husband?"

"Mr. Worthington is not your husband. He is married to your sister."

"You are wrong. Malcolm Worthington married Camilla Connelly, and my birth certificate states the name of Camilla. I refuse to believe my father has lied to me all these years."

The smirk remained on Wilkes's face as he shook his head. "Your sister did mention how sick in the head you are. Now I can see why she would say such a thing."

Camilla's heart sank. The pain from her head moved to her chest, making it hard to breathe. Kat was the sick one, not her.

Tears stung her eyes, but she blinked them away. She wouldn't give Captain Wilkes the satisfaction of seeing her this way.

Thundering hooves neared the stable and made her heart spring to life again. *Please let it be Malcolm.*

Wilkes grabbed his pistol and ran to the window. His shoulders relaxed and he sighed. "Your sister is finally here." He tucked the pistol back in his belt before hurrying out to meet Kat.

Through the opened doors of the stable, Camilla spied her sister dismounting. Kat ran to her lover, throwing her arms around him. Their mouths met in a hungry, slobbery kiss. Camilla squeezed her eyes to cut off their hideous display.

Kat's shrill laughter made Camilla snap her eyes open. The woman stalking toward her wasn't the pathetically ill wastrel she had talked to in the asylum, although malice still lingered in Kat's eyes. Camilla's heart sank further.

Kat crouched to her level and snickered. "My dear, foolish sister. You fell right into my trap."

"Why are you doing this?" Camilla whispered. "Why did you lie to me about being sick, and then fake your own death?"

Kat shrugged. "Because I wanted everything to go my way. Malcolm is a rich man, but I didn't want him to be my husband. When I saw the chance to marry, I took it, but with the intent of making a better life for myself." She glanced over her shoulder at Wilkes. "And now, the captain has offered me that better life."

"By pretending to die?"

"Of course. I couldn't have pulled any of this off otherwise."

"But Kat, eventually the truth will come out."

"Not if I can help it."

"What about those people who love you? What about me,

your own sister?"

Kat laughed eerily, sending ripples of fear up Camilla's spine.

"Oh, my poor, pathetic sister. You still have your head in the clouds." She leaned in closer. "When are you going to start thinking about yourself?" She pushed her finger into Camilla's chest. "No one is going to get you where you want to be in life. You cannot rely on anybody but you."

"I don't think the way you do, Kat. The reason I came here in the first place was for *you*," Camilla explained. "I planned to avenge your death and get your husband to pay your hospital and funeral debts." A sob tore from her throat. "You are the only family I have."

Kat frowned and cupped the side of Camilla's face. "Not to worry. I will take care of you."

Camilla scrunched her forehead. "You will?"

"Yes. The asylum for the mentally insane in Preston is still looking for you."

Fear pierced through Camilla like ice. Kat was actually going to commit her own twin.

MALCOLM SQUINTED AGAINST the sunlight pouring upon his face through the window. Every muscle in his body screamed in pain—even his eyelids ached. An intense throbbing began in his skull. He jerked his head up from his desk and sat straight. Cursing, he rubbed his eyes as he tried to remember what had caused him to sleep in his study instead of going upstairs to join his wife in their bed. He stretched his stiff neck and rolled his achy shoulders.

The pitter-patter of small feet echoed outside his study mere seconds before the door flung open. James, still wearing his nightshirt, came running toward him. Malcolm stood and stepped toward his son.

"Papa," James sobbed, his eyes puffy and red. "Mama is gone."

Malcolm blinked to clear his tired vision. Kneeling, he took hold of his son's shaky hands. "James, what are you talking about?"

The boy's bottom lip quivered, and his eyes filled with tears. "Mama is gone."

Malcolm patted his son's tousled hair. "Perhaps Mama just went riding this morning."

"No, she is gone."

A deeper pounding vibrated through Malcolm's head, and he squeezed his eyes closed. "I'm certain she will return momentarily."

"No, because that mean lady will not let her."

He didn't know if his headache grew worse from stress or his son's words. He looked at his son. "What mean lady?"

"The lady me and Lizzy don't like."

Malcolm rubbed his forehead. Where was Jane? He couldn't take any more of this, and she would certainly set things right with his children.

He inhaled, hoping to clear his head. "Son, we can discuss this later today. Right now, I have to get cleaned up and meet some men. Broderick is still in jail, and we need to help him." He patted James's cheek. "Do you understand?"

His son's mouth drooped as tears fell down his face. "But Papa, that mean lady—"

"*James.*" Malcolm's tone turned harsh. "We will talk about this later." He stood, urging his son ahead of him. "Now run along and get dressed. Camilla is probably out riding, so have Jane help you."

The boy's chin trembled as he shook his head, turned, and fled from the room.

Malcolm's heart wrenched, which certainly didn't make his stressful headache any better, but he couldn't concentrate on his son's problem right now. Freeing Broderick was of the utmost importance, and he needed a clear head in order to think.

He hurried out of the study and up the stairs to his bedroom. He rushed through his morning ritual of readying for the day, and within an hour, he exited his room feeling more refreshed. Yet his heart still hurt for his friend.

On the way down the stairs, he passed Beth.

"Mornin', Mr. Worthington."

"Good morning. Have you seen my wife?"

She nodded. "Mrs. Worthington left the 'ouse early to go ridin'."

"Thank you."

He continued down the stairs and into the dining room. Breakfast had been prepared and set out on the table. James and Lizzy looked up at him when he entered, both wearing drawn expressions, both having red eyes that swam with tears.

"Why do you look so glum?" Malcolm asked.

Lizzy sniffed and swiped the back of her hand under her nose. "Mama is gone."

He rolled his eyes skyward. "Lizzy, she will return, I promise. She is just out riding."

"No," James shouted, slamming his hands on the table.

Malcolm jumped and scowled at his son's eruption. "James, you will explain this outburst."

Squaring his shoulders, the boy pushed away from the table and stood. "Papa, you have to believe us. Mama is gone."

Malcolm growled and ran his fingers through his hair. He strode around the table and grabbed his son's arm. "I have heard enough. If you continue with this, you will spend the rest of the day in your room."

"Papa." Lizzy sobbed as she rushed to him and grabbed his free hand. Big, soulful eyes pleaded with him. "James isn't lying. Mama is gone."

He studied his children, saw their little hearts breaking over what must be a misunderstanding. They had never acted in such a manner before.

He knelt and wrapped his arms around them. "Please don't cry. I'm certain she will return—"

"No, Papa." Lizzy's blonde ringlets bounced as she shook her head. "Mama is gone. But that mean lady you married is back."

A different pain sneaked into his chest. All the air in his lungs left in a rush. With a deep, calming breath, he gathered his wits. "What do you mean, the woman I married?"

James wiped his eyes and swallowed. "Mama—the lady who loves us—is gone. The mean lady you married is here instead."

Confusion swam in his head. The idea was impossible. Camilla's sister was dead. "Kat's back?"

Both children nodded, their eyes wide with fright.

"How do you know?" Malcolm asked.

"She yelled at us this morning." James hiccupped a sob. "She called me and Lizzy mean names again. Our mama loves us and would not do that. We tried to find her, but she is gone."

Malcolm's blood turned to ice, chilling every inch of his body. Kat was still alive... and had returned? What had that woman done with Camilla? He knew Kat had never been in her right mind, but if she were still alive, would she cause her sister harm?

He leaned over and kissed James's head, then Lizzy's. "No need to fear. I shall find her."

"Promise?" James asked.

"Yes." He stood. "I will also get rid of that mean woman."

Smiles crossed his children's puffy faces, and his heart melted, yet it still felt heavy from Camilla's loss. Panic surged through him, more powerful than it had when he heard of Broderick's arrest.

The first place he looked for Kat was at the stable, but she hadn't returned from her ride. Impatient, he stormed back inside the house, waiting for her return.

In the next hour, he gathered his trusted servants and instructed them to search everywhere for his wife. Malcolm even bribed them with an incentive for getting a bonus.

He paced the parlor, each step increasing his anger. He fisted his hands at his sides, eager to take his frustration out on somebody. Anybody. Kat hadn't returned, and it had been three hours since the children told him about the switch. When did it happen? And why hadn't he detected it?

He stopped at the window, looking toward the stable. The switch must have happened last night at the jail. When she'd climbed into the carriage and kissed him, it felt different. And her attitude once they walked inside the house was off, too.

Strange how his children would know the difference between the two women. They never once mentioned they knew Camilla was a different woman, and even if they didn't fully understand now, they knew enough to warn him.

Off in the distance, a rider approached. He gritted his teeth and scowled. It was Kat. Even from here, he recognized the haughty tilt of her chin, the straight edge to her back, as she slowed the horse to a stop. She jumped down, and the holier-than-thou way she tossed the reins to Hyrum confirmed his suspicions.

Kat had indeed returned. But not for long, if he had his way.

Exhaling the contained anger in one gust, he ran his fingers through his hair. The echo of her boots outside the front hall had him hurrying to the parlor door to catch her as she passed. The clinging red riding habit was not the one Camilla usually wore, but the one Kat had liked to taunt him with. The first time she had purchased it, he compared her to a fancy-dressed strumpet. Holding her head high, she told him it fit her true nature.

But he mustn't let Kat know he suspected. Not yet.

"There you are, my dear." He stepped out of the parlor and into her path.

Her sudden stop caught her off balance, and she reached out to grasp his shoulders. When she righted herself, she yanked her hands away as if she had been burned. The smile she gave him looked forced. Kat's eyes had never twinkled like her sister's.

"Oh, you startled me." She chuckled. "What are you about this afternoon?"

He stepped closer, closing the space between them as he slid his arms around her waist. She stiffened, just as he knew she would. "I missed holding you last night. I thought we could rectify that situation."

The laugh she forced out grated on his nerves, and all he wanted to do was shake her senseless and demand she tell him where Camilla was. But he wouldn't get aggressive. Not yet.

"But... but... right now?" she stammered.

"Yes."

"Um, what about the children?"

"They are with Jane."

Her gaze darted around the hall. "But what about Broderick?" Her focus returned to his eyes. "I thought you were going to devise a plan to rescue him."

"Others are working on that at this very moment. Right now, I need to hold my wife, since I missed doing so last night." He leaned in and buried his face in her neck. Another man's scent clung to her skin, and his stomach lurched. Lifting his head before vomiting, he growled and hoped it didn't emphasize his anger. He swept her in his arms. "Come, my love, for I cannot wait another moment."

Panic slashed across her face, making her eyes wide, her face pale. But he tightened his hold and rushed up the stairs to their room. After entering, he kicked the door closed then dumped her on the bed. Taking his time, he yanked off his over-jacket and waistcoat. She scooted back toward the headboard.

She placed her hands over her bosom as if to protect herself. The shining gold ring he had given Camilla glimmered as the sun's rays hit it. *That's not Kat's ring!* Anger tore through him once again, but he tried to maintain his composure.

"Please, think of the hour of the day," she said.

He laughed. "It didn't bother you the other afternoon."

"Yes, but... but... I don't feel well today."

He stopped unfastening his shirt. "Indeed? You looked fine just a moment ago in the hall."

She placed her hand to her belly. "I don't know what ails me, but it's churning my stomach."

He knew exactly how she felt. He knelt on the bed and stroked her face. She withdrew into the pillows. He found it odd that he couldn't tell the difference between Kat and Camilla before, but he could now. His real wife was more beautiful inside and out. "Do you think you are in the family way?"

She grimaced. "Of course not."

He leaned over her and wrapped a lock of hair around his finger. "Then perhaps we should do something to fix that."

She splayed her hands across his chest and pushed. "Malcolm, no."

He grasped a handful of hair and yanked, putting his weight on top of her. She cried out.

"I thought I told you once never to call me Malcolm." He scowled. "I would rather a hussy not be so personal with my name, *Katherine*."

She gasped, and the color faded from her cheeks.

"Yes, I know who you are." He narrowed his eyes. "And you have exactly two minutes to tell me where you are keeping my *true* wife, Camilla."

Her expression changed, and laughter filled her eyes as her lips curled into an evil grin. "And if I don't?"

He tightened his hold on her hair. "I'll not be held responsible for what I shall do."

Tilting back her head, she laughed, and the high-pitched sound raked over his nerves. "You know I shall never give you that pleasure."

"Why didn't you die as you led Camilla to believe? Who did you charm to get released from the hospital?"

"I charmed no one. The physician Camilla spoke with that evening was a friend of mine. It was all part of my plan."

"What plan?"

"To send my sister here to play me so I could sneak behind your back and watch you closely. It was rather entertaining finding ways to steal your work and give them to Henry Wilkes."

"What does Captain Wilkes want with them?"

She laughed again, her voice turning even more evil. "He is one of Mr. Clarkston's spies. The man wants to see what kind of ships you'll be making for the navy so that he can make better ones."

Malcolm growled. He wondered if Clarkston was behind all of this. "Why is Wilkes involved?"

"Because he is the man who can arrest you and take the credit, which will make him a colonel soon."

Confusion consumed his mind, yet he had always known Kat was greedy. She could have the world served to her on a silver platter and it still wouldn't be enough. "You won't win this time, Kat."

"I already have. Plans are in place, and you and my foolish sister are falling into the trap, just as I wanted." She arched a haughty eyebrow. "And Broderick fell just as easily. Indeed, I *am* the victor."

"What does Broderick have to do with this?"

"It's called revenge. I don't take kindly to men who turn away my advances." She shrugged. "So, I charmed him one last time as a different woman."

"You were the woman he met?"

She laughed again. "Correct."

Events in the past few months flitted through his head. Suddenly, everything made sense. He scowled. "And were you perhaps the one who tried to kill me on Colonel Burwell's fox hunt?"

"Unfortunately, that part of my plan didn't work." She rolled her eyes. "I was never a good shot with a rifle."

He tightened his grip on her arms. "Where is Camilla?"

The evil grin on her face stretched wider, and she shrugged.

He shook her once. "Men are searching the city to find Camilla. I have instructed them to shoot whoever stands in their way. I would prefer not to kill anyone right now, but what if one of your lovers takes a bullet? Is it worth your silence?"

"Sorry, my dear Mr. Worthington, but I shall not tell you a word."

He had never hit a woman before, but Kat made his hands itch to do so now. He moved off her but kept hold of her wrist.

"Come here." He yanked her out of the bed and over to a chair. "Timothy?" he called.

The servant hurried into the room, holding ropes. "Do ye need these now, sir?"

It surprised him that Timothy was so perceptive. "How did you know?"

"I knew last night when I brought ye 'ome from the jail. I just was afraid to tell ye."

Malcolm nodded. "Remind me to give you a raise." He motioned to the ropes. "Will you help me tie her up?"

"Certainly, Mr. Worthington."

Kat squirmed and kicked at the servant. "You traitor! You should be taking orders from me, not him."

"I serve Mr. Worthington, Miss Katherine."

Malcolm tied her hands, and then held her struggling legs while Timothy wrapped the ropes and knotted them. Malcolm turned to his dresser and pulled out a pair of Camilla's stockings. "I think we shall have to stuff these in her mouth to keep her quiet." He grinned and stalked toward her.

Her eyes widened. "Don't you dare!"

"Those will be the last words I hear from you." He wrapped the stocking around her head, stuffing part of it into her mouth. Once done, he pulled Camilla's ring from her finger before stepping to his closet and retrieving his pistol and saber. He glanced over his shoulder at the servant. "Come, Timothy. My wife is in danger, and we need to find her."

Chapter Twenty-One

C AMILLA'S BODY SCREAMED in pain. Her skull had long since stopped throbbing, but being in one position for a lengthy amount of time stiffened every muscle in her body. When Captain Wilkes wasn't looking, she tugged both her arms and legs, trying to free herself from the ropes. But to no avail. After several hours, she slumped in the corner in exhaustion.

She leaned her head against the wall. Where was Malcolm? Kat must have stepped back into her role as Mrs. Worthington, which meant nobody would be the wiser. She blinked back the tears threatening to streak down her face. Crying wouldn't assist Malcolm in rescuing her, so why waste her energy?

Captain Wilkes had stepped outside the barn, and relief flooded through her, if only for a moment. He had wanted to touch her improperly, but Kat's jealousy overrode her revenge. She'd instructed him not to lay a finger on Camilla.

Her stomach knotted and she bent over. What had happened to her sister to make the woman so evil? Kat had always been the twin who could wrap their father around her finger. She had always received everything she asked for. Even Camilla had given in to her sister's spoiled antics. But Kat had always wanted more. Much more—this time at the cost of her own sister.

Captain Wilkes sauntered back inside, smirking. The sun was making its descent, forming shadows. He picked up the lantern and lit it.

"You had me fooled, you know. I honestly thought you were Kat all this time." He knelt beside her and lifted a lock of hair, pressing it to his nose, inhaling deeply. "Although, I must admit, you smell so much better than your sister."

"I hope my sister doesn't hear you say that. You know how she gets when she is angry."

He sighed and let her hair fall from his fingers. "Yes. She can be such a devil."

"Captain Wilkes? Tell me, do you believe me to be insane?"

He sat back, running his gaze over her face and neck. "If you are, you certainly don't play the part."

"What about my sister? Do you think she is ill?"

"No. But you are completely different. She is wild; you are tame." He stroked her cheek. "I almost wish you *were* like Kat."

"If I were, Malcolm wouldn't have fallen in love with me."

He laughed and stood. "He is a fool. But then, I have known this all along."

"What are your plans for Malcolm when he comes to rescue me?"

His chest shook with silent laughter. "You think he will come?"

"I know he will."

"What a faithful, devoted woman you are."

"What have you planned, captain?"

He stepped over to the window and peered out. "Well, if Mr. Worthington does come, I shall just have to arrest him for trying to break a prisoner out of jail. Kat planned this months ago. You see, with both Turner and Worthington in jail, there will be an accident and both men will die. Kat will become the wealthy widow, and I will earn my promotion to colonel and become wealthier myself. With Kat by my side, there isn't anything we cannot conquer."

"Don't be too sure of yourself. You are underestimating my husband. He is a brilliant man."

He turned and faced her, crossing his arms over his chest. "Do you think me dimwitted? Kat and I have a foolproof plan."

She squirmed, hoping again to loosen the ropes, but they didn't budge. She sighed in desperation. "All I can say is that evil men like yourself always come out the losers."

He laughed, stepped away from the window, and headed in her direction. The dark look in his eyes sent chills over her body. Should she remind him of Kat's warning? The lowering sun threw shadows on his face. He appeared meaner, yet more determined. She swallowed hard.

"I have had enough talk for now." He knelt beside her and ran his knuckles along her cheek. "I'm bored, and you are the only person who can remedy that matter."

She pulled back but couldn't get away from his touch. "Please, captain. My sister will be very upset."

"Your sister doesn't need to know."

She narrowed her eyes. "I will tell her."

"I will rebut your story."

His hand moved down her neck, and he stroked the skin at the base of her throat. She wanted to spit in his face but resisted. He would certainly strike her.

She struggled once more with the ropes at her wrists, but they were still too strong, making it impossible to free her hands. "Get away from me," she yelled.

"Never. I have come to care for you a great deal."

Following her first instincts, she spat in his face. He pulled back, eyes wide, jaw slack. He scowled and backhanded her across the face. She cried out. Her skin stung from his blow. He raised his hand again, and she cringed, preparing for the next strike.

WHEN MALCOLM RODE closer to the deserted barn, he wondered

if his friend had been correct by telling Malcolm that he'd seen a soldier bring a woman here that resembled his wife. But when he heard his wife's scream, he said a silent prayer that his friend had been right.

Malcolm rushed into the barn—and then stopped. In the corner, Captain Wilkes's red uniform caught his attention, as well as the squirming woman he held.

A burst of anger shot through Malcolm, and he itched to grab the sword at his side. Instead, he ran toward the soldier and seized the man by his coat. Malcolm found the strength to pick him up and fling him against the wall.

His wife's eyes widened, then she squealed his name. He knelt beside her and took her in his arms. "Are you all right?"

She sobbed into his chest, and his heart shattered. He wished he had arrived sooner. It tore him apart knowing he hadn't stopped another man from harming her. What kind of husband did that make him?

"Shh…" he soothed, stroking her hair. "Captain Wilkes won't touch you again."

A yell ripped through the air, and he snapped his head toward the soldier. Wilkes's foot connected with Malcolm's chest and knocked him away. Pain shot through his body, and he inhaled sharply, clutching his chest. The captain raised his foot to strike him again, but Malcolm rolled in the opposite direction. He jumped up and faced his opponent.

Hunched over, arms outstretched, the other man circled him.

"I don't want to kill you this way," the captain said. "We have other plans for you."

"Sorry to disappoint, but it won't happen." Malcolm narrowed his eyes. "Because I plan on killing you right now."

Wilkes laughed and shook his head. "What a brave man you pretend to be, but I know many men who are cowards just like you. Killing you will be rewarding."

"And it will be rewarding to rid Dorchester of greedy buggers like yourself."

Wilkes lunged at him and tightened his hands around Malcolm's throat. He struggled to take in air, but he couldn't. His head pounded, and his lungs burned. The pressure in his throat began to numb his mind.

He pulled at Wilkes's hands, but they were immovable. Using his foot, Malcolm lashed out, hitting his opponent's knee. The man cried out and fell to the ground. Malcolm jumped on him and squeezed the man's neck, giving him a taste of his own medicine.

The captain choked, gasping for air. Malcolm tightened his grip. The soldier struggled, rolling them both over. But Malcolm still held the man's throat. Wilkes rolled once more, and Malcolm's foot struck an object. Breaking glass from the lantern flew through the air. In a whoosh, flames ignited the hay.

He glanced over his shoulder. Fire danced too close, and the heat touched his skin. Smoke curled around him, stinging his nose. He coughed. The flames licked at him and threatened to jump on his clothes.

Camilla screamed. "Malcolm, hurry."

He cursed and bounded away from the fire, releasing Wilkes. The captain stood and reached for his saber. Malcolm unsheathed his own sword from its scabbard, bringing it up just in time to stop his opponent's lunge.

The man parried with such skill that Malcolm felt at a disadvantage. Yet it didn't matter. Outrage and justice backed him. He fought for his wife, which gave him the needed strength to counterattack.

"I'm going to kill you, you blackguard," Wilkes said. "You have humiliated me for the last time." He was breathless and sweating, his lips curled in an evil grin. "This will be the day I cut out your heart."

"I'll deny you the chance." Malcolm moved swiftly away from the other man's weapon. His own breath came labored, more from anger than weakness.

Around the room, they parried. Malcolm lunged, and Wilkes

jumped away. Fire roared behind the captain, and he scrambled away, stumbling over a burning board.

"You're growing weak, captain." Malcolm snickered.

"Nonsense."

The captain thrust his sword forward, slicing Malcolm's arm. A spot of blood quickly dampened his shoulder. He ignored the pain. The movement stilled the other man for a brief moment, and Malcolm lunged and stuck the tip of his saber into Wilkes's chest. Immediately crimson liquid stained the soldier's white shirt front as he fell to his knees, the weapon in his hand clinking to the ground beside him.

Malcolm stepped over and kicked the steel across the floor. Wide eyes stared up at him, and color abandoned Wilkes's stunned face.

"Are you... going to let... me die... slowly?" he rasped.

For all the anger surging through Malcolm, he sensed the fright in the captain. He couldn't bring himself to be anything less than merciful, even to his enemy.

"Malcolm!"

His wife's terrified plea brought his attention to her. Flames had spread through the barn, nearing her. He hurried over and knelt beside her. He fumbled with the ropes at her wrist.

The burning wood cracked. The roof creaked, and he glanced toward the captain. The man lay on his back, wide-eyed as he stared at the roof. Within seconds, it caved in on top of him.

Malcolm grabbed Camilla, turning away from the burning man. He picked her up and rushed out of the barn.

He gazed into the tearful eyes of his wife. Using his thumb, he wiped away the liquid from her cheeks. "I feared I had lost you."

"And I feared you wouldn't find me."

"I would move heaven and earth to find you." He kissed her forehead.

"Malcolm, your shoulder."

"It's only a scratch. I will live." He reached behind her and tugged at the ropes on her wrists. They loosened. "There." Relief flooded through him.

She shook off the binds and reached for the ties at her ankles. Through the crackling of the burning wood, another blast resounded through the night. A pistol exploded nearby. Pain pierced his injured arm, and he cried out, falling onto Camilla.

She screamed.

He grabbed his wound and spun around. Kat walked away from a tree, pointing the still-smoking weapon his way. Her brown hair framed her head in an untamable silhouette.

"Katherine, no," Camilla cried.

Malcolm winced as the pain made his arm useless. "How did you get free?"

Kat laughed, and the eerie lift of her voice drifted through the air like a whistle. "You forgot about my maid, Beth."

He tightened his hand around his bloody arm. "She'll not be working for me much longer."

She shook her head. "Once again, I must prove you wrong. She will continue to be my maid. After all, the Widow Worthington will need all the support she can get when her husband dies."

Camilla sobbed beside him. He blocked her with his body, keeping himself in front of Kat's pistol.

"Kat?" His wife sniffed. "Why are you doing this?"

"Because I don't want to be *his* wife."

"But you're not. I'm his wife." A sob made Camilla's voice tight.

Kat shrugged. "I will be once you are out of the way, and I step back into my role as Mrs. Worthington. Besides, I need his wealth in my fight for power."

Malcolm scowled. "What are you planning to do with Camilla?"

A smile slowly crossed her face. "Don't you mean Kat, my poor, insane sister? I will send her back to the asylum from where she escaped, of course."

"You have no heart, Kat." He glowered.

She shrugged. "Yes, in a sense." She neared, still pointing the weapon at him.

"You'll have to reload if you plan to shoot me again." He dropped his focus to the pistol.

She shook her head, and then brought around her other arm from behind her, displaying a saber. "Not if I kill you another way."

Kat lifted the rod of sharp steel. Her eyes blazed dark and evil as she tightened her hands on the handle. Narrowing her gaze, she focused on him.

Without a doubt, she would kill him. He brought up his arm to block her attack.

CAMILLA SCREAMED AND pressed her body firmly to her husband, closing her eyes. She said a silent prayer that his life would be spared.

Off in the distance, a man's shout rent the air, and seconds later, another pistol fired. And then something thumped heavily on the ground.

Camilla snapped her head up. No longer was Kat standing over them holding a pistol. Instead, she lay on the ground as blood covered her chest.

Malcolm's gasp alerted Camilla to someone walking their way... holding a smoking pistol. Broderick frowned, and his gaze stayed on Kat's lifeless body.

Camilla scrambled to stand, pushing Malcolm away. She ran and fell to her sister's side. With a shaky hand, she touched Kat's cold, colorless face. Her lips were turning blue.

"Oh, Katherine," Camilla sobbed. She took her sister's hand, lifted it to her cheek, and kissed the palm. Kat's chest gradually stopped moving.

Camilla's heart ached with sorrow, and as she sobbed, her

cries echoed in the night. Malcolm knelt beside her and slipped his arm around her shoulders. Across from her, Broderick knelt next to Kat's body.

He placed the weapon on the ground. Tears glistened in his eyes. "Please forgive me, Camilla, but I couldn't have your sister killing my friend."

Her breaths were ragged as she calmed her cries. "There is nothing to forgive. You did what needed to be done." She glanced down at Kat and tenderly touched her cheek. "My sister is well now." Her voice cracked with emotion. "No longer will she be able to hurt people."

Malcolm grasped his friend's shoulder. "How did you escape?"

Broderick wiped his wet eyes. "The soldiers were searching for Captain Wilkes and left me unattended. Jane, Timothy, and the children found the keys and rescued me." He shook his head. "Can you believe the soldiers didn't take the keys?"

"The children?" both Camilla and Malcolm gasped at the same time.

"They are safe," Broderick reassured them. "Absolutely no one noticed them."

Men's shouts rose from a distance. Camilla hitched a breath and looked toward the trees where the voices came. "The fire." She turned to Malcolm. "We need to get Broderick out of here."

Her husband's attention dropped to Kat. "What should we do with her? If the soldiers see her, they will think she is you."

Camilla jumped up and glanced toward the burning barn. There was only one course of action. Her heart wrenched. This was no way for her sister to end her life on earth, no matter how evil Kat was. But the fact remained that there could not be two Camilla Worthingtons. And Kat was already dead.

"We must place her body inside the barn."

Malcolm touched her shoulder. "Are you certain?"

Her throat tightened with a sob, and she nodded. While Malcolm and Broderick rose to their feet and lifted Kat's body,

Camilla picked up the saber and turned to follow.

"Stay back," Malcolm instructed her. "Don't get too close to the flames."

She held her breath, her hand to her mouth as she witnessed her sister's body thrown in the fire. Squeezing her eyes closed, she said a prayer for her sister. But it had to be done. She only hoped the good Lord would forgive her.

Malcolm and Broderick ran back to her. Her husband grasped her arm. "We must hurry and get out of here."

"Let us head toward the docks," Broderick said. "Timothy informed me that a boat will set sail at any moment. There is no other way. I must leave Dorchester forever."

Voices coming from the wooded area grew closer. She clutched Malcolm's arm as he led them away from danger. She ran, and her limbs throbbed with each step. Malcolm wrapped his arm around her waist and held her tightly to his side. Burning streaks of pain shot up her legs, reminding her she hadn't run like this in ages. But they were running for their lives. For Broderick's life.

She stepped on the hem of her dress and stumbled. Malcolm grasped her with both hands.

"Malcolm, my legs—they aren't strong enough. You go on without me."

"I'll never leave your side again." He lifted her in his arms and winced, his right shoulder sagging.

"Put me down. You cannot carry me."

Broderick stepped to them. His breaths came fast. "We are close enough to the docks. I shall go by myself."

"No." Malcolm grasped his friend's hand.

"All will be well now." Broderick stepped closer and wrapped his arms around Malcolm. The two men embraced, and then drew apart. Broderick leaned in and kissed Camilla's cheek. He smiled. "Make him happy."

Tears collected in her eyes once again. She nodded. "I intend to."

"I love you… both of you. Now hurry. Return home before you are caught. Please, be safe." Broderick lifted a hand in farewell, then turned and ran down the hill toward the water.

Camilla tightened her arms around her husband's waist. "Will we ever see him again?" She looked up at the wonderful, brave man beside her.

"Yes. After all of this dies down, I will find my good friend."

"I shall miss him."

"As will I." He leaned down and kissed her forehead. "But Broderick is not safe here. The soldiers will be looking for him because of his escape, and now they might suspect him of killing Captain Wilkes."

"What if they do not? What if they suspect you?"

"There is no proof."

She touched his chest and pleaded with her eyes. "But what if they do?"

"Only Captain Wilkes had reason to see me dead, and of course, that was because of your sister."

Camilla leaned her head against him. The tender look in his soft gaze made her heart melt. "You are my life, Mr. Worthington, and I want to be right by your side forever."

He tightened his arms around her. "You are my life, also, and I live for you and my children."

Tears of joy stung her eyes, and she buried her face in his chest. Her love for this man grew, making her heart swell.

"Malcolm, do you know how happy you have made me?"

He withdrew only inches, gazing down into her eyes. His smile stretched across his face. "And you have completed my life, and the lives of my children. What more could I ask for?"

She chuckled and traced her finger across his bottom lip. "How about another child?"

With a growl, he pulled her to him and kissed her lips for only a moment before he led her toward the safety of their house. "How soon can we get started?"

Epilogue

CAMILLA NODDED TO Lady Burwell as they stood inside the ballroom. The other woman lifted a glass of wine to her lips and sipped. Due to her pregnancy, Camilla didn't want to drink any wine. Although she had just discovered she was pregnant a week ago, she didn't want to harm the child in any way.

The past six weeks had seemed a dream. A wonderful dream where only Malcolm and their children resided. After Broderick's rescue, she and Malcolm remained on their best behavior so as not to draw suspicion. It must have worked, because everyone treated them like royalty after that. They had even gone to the Burwells' on a few occasions for dinner parties. After all, the name Malcolm Worthington was popular in the community since he had broken away from his partners and started doing business on his own. It also helped that he'd found the evidence against Mr. Clarkston for stealing the drawings, which got the man arrested.

Camilla glanced around the crowded room and smiled. The women now treated her as their equal instead of the loathsome creature who had attended the Burwells' weekend party not long ago. Camilla had impressed them all. Mainly her own husband.

And speaking of Malcolm…

She spotted him with a group of men. The smile he wore was fixed upon his face as if he struggled to keep it there. The poor man still had to endure the foolish talk about politics he had loathed.

Malcolm lifted his gaze to hers. Even from across the room, his eyes sparkled with love. He motioned his head toward the side doors, and she nodded.

"Excuse me, Lady Burwell," Camilla said, cutting the older woman off in mid-sentence, "but I need to step outside for a moment. The heat in the room is smothering me, and I feel I might have the vapors."

Lady Burwell gasped and touched Camilla's arm. "Oh dear. Will you need help?"

"No need to fear. My kind husband will attend me."

The other women in the circle nodded and smiled. Camilla tried to walk with calm reserve, but her heartbeat pounded a fast rhythm, and she quickened her step. She narrowed her eyes and looked through the shadows. A few couples stood along the white picket fence near the shrubbery, but none had ventured further into the yard, since it wasn't lit properly.

Then she saw him. The moonlight outlined his masculine shoulders and the curves of his face as he peeked around a section of shrubbery. She grinned and casually strolled toward him. As she neared, he reached out and grabbed her waist, quickly pulling her inside a darkened cove.

"I missed you, my love."

She sighed and wrapped her arms around his neck, kissing his waiting lips. She met his demanding kiss with an urgency of her own, until he pulled away and smiled down at her.

"Why, you scandalous devil." She chuckled. "If we are caught, our names will be ruined."

"No. The men will be jealous, and the ladies will wish they were here with a man, too."

She playfully slapped his shoulder. "You are just horrible."

He tilted his head. "I'm quite certain I can change your mind, love."

"And exactly how do you propose to do that, my dear husband?"

"Marry me. Tomorrow."

She blinked and her mouth hung open. "Wh—what? Marry you? But we are already married."

"I was told of a minister a couple hours away who will marry us. Since our first marriage was done without the woman I love being present, I want us to be married again before our baby is born." He rubbed her belly not yet large with child. "God led you to me, Camilla, and God will continue to bless us in our life."

"Indeed, He has."

"Will you marry me in a church so that God will be with us always?"

If she hadn't loved this man before, she definitely loved him now. Her heart burst and tears gathered in her eyes.

"Oh, Malcolm." Her voice broke. She swiped her hand across his cheek before weaving her fingers through his hair. "You continue to surprise me at every turn. There is no way I can say no to you."

"Good. Because I will have plenty of surprises throughout our marriage. I cannot stop loving you, my beautiful woman."

He kissed her lips again, and she clung to him, answering back with all the emotion built inside her. It was hard to believe, but she'd found happiness. Finally.

She need not pretend any longer. In Malcolm's arms was where she wanted to be.

The End

Other published stories by Marie Higgins

www.authormariehiggins.com/books

Join my newsletter and start your reading collection

www.authormariehiggins.com/newsletter

About the Author

Marie Higgins is an award-winning, best-selling author of clean romance novels that melt your heart and have you falling in love over and over again. Since 2010, she's published over 100 heartwarming, on-the-edge-of-your-seat romances. She has broadened her readership by writing mystery/suspense, humor, time travel, and paranormal, along with her love for historical romances. Her readers have dubbed her "Queen of Tease" because of all her twists and unexpected endings.

Website – www.authormariehiggins.com
Facebook – facebook.com/marie.higgins.7543
TikTok – tiktok.com/@author.mariehiggins
Instagram – instagram.com/author.mariehiggins
Bookbub – bookbub.com/authors/marie-higgins